BLUE HALO SERIES BOOK FOUR

NYSSA KATHRYN

An NW Partners Book
Cover by L.J. Anderson at Mayhem Cover Creations
Developmentally and Copy Edited by Kelli Collins
Line Edited by Jessica Snyder
Proofread by Marla Esposito, Jen Katemi and Amanda Cuff

❀ Created with Vellum

Some pasts are harder to escape than others.

When Carina Murphy is accused of a crime she didn't commit, a fresh start in a new town is her only option. Unfortunately, Cradle Mountain may not be the safe haven she'd thought. The son of her new patient may be tall, dark and handsome...but he also knows all about her past.

Keeping her job should be the hardest part. Keeping her heart safe seems to be much harder.

Former Delta Flynn Talbot was kidnapped, separated from his sick mother and irrevocably changed. His enemies now dead, he's back in his hometown with his teammates, running Blue Halo Security, and his mom is his top priority. So when it turns out her new nurse has a questionable past, Flynn's first instinct is to keep her the hell away from his mother. But Carina's adamant she's innocent. And something in her deep blue eyes makes him inclined to believe her.

When one too many ill-fated events leave Carina needing help, Flynn steps up. It isn't long before both discover there's more danger surrounding her than they thought. And Flynn will risk everything for the woman who's stumbled into his town, into his life...and into his heart.

ACKNOWLEDGMENTS

Thank you to my team on making this book the best it can be. My editorial team, Kelli, Jessica, Marla, Jen and Amanda, this book wouldn't be what it is without you.

ARC readers—you're amazing. You pick up everything that's left and you're my people.

To my readers, you always ensure the next book gets written. Thank you.

And my husband and daughter, you two give me the life and space I need to create these books. I love you. Thank you for all you do.

CHAPTER 1

"No!" Carina Murphy massaged her temple, her eyes shuttering. "I'm sorry, I just...I only started the job a week ago."

Her fingers wrapped so tightly around the phone that she was sure her knuckles were white. But, dammit, she couldn't help it. She'd already withdrawn her application at the hospital, and there were no other nursing jobs available in the small town of Cradle Mountain. If she lost this one, how would she pay for rent and food and every other usual adult expense?

Barbara sighed. "I know."

She *knew*? That was it?

Sweat beaded Carina's forehead. "There was another job I applied for when I got here, but when you hired me, I withdrew my application. If you let me go, I've got nothing."

So, she was screwed. If they fired her, she was utterly and completely screwed. And maybe homeless.

"I'm sorry, Carina, our hands are tied. It's not our choice."

She scrubbed her eyes, trying to decipher Barbara's words when they made *no freaking sense*. The older woman worked admin for the Home Care Agency, so Carina knew this wasn't her doing. But then, whose was it? "I just… I don't understand. Did I do something wrong?"

"We received a call from a family member requesting a different nurse."

Carina frowned. "A family member…" Patricia Talbot only had one living relative. Wait, that meant— "Her son. Flynn."

She went back to rubbing her head, already feeling a gigantic, the-world-hates-me headache coming on. She'd just met the man yesterday, and they talked for maybe two minutes. How could he already hate her?

What the heck had she done to piss him off?

"Yes," Barbara said, confirming what Carina already knew.

Carina scrambled to come up with a solution that didn't leave her jobless. She'd never gone down without a fight, and she didn't intend to start now.

"What if I talk to him? Convince him to let me stay? I mean, I only replaced Joy Anderson on such short notice because you had no one else in the area and needed someone immediately, right? So, won't it take you time to find another replacement now?"

She already knew the likelihood of Joy returning was slim to none. They'd been friends since college. The other woman was older and had decided to become a nurse later in life, but they'd clicked. And she'd told Carina she'd probably be staying with her sick father in Florida.

Barbara's sigh was heavy across the line. "Yeah, I'm going to have my work cut out for me getting someone down there in the next couple of days."

"Give me an hour before you start looking," Carina said quickly. "Maybe two. I swear, I'll change his mind about me. I can be very persuasive."

Desperate. She could be very desperate. And that desperation often came out as persistence.

"Maybe it's my age," she mused. "I'm a lot younger than Joy. Maybe he thinks I can't handle the job."

In actuality, she'd handled a lot worse in her ten-year career. She was totally capable of providing adequate care for his mother. No, not adequate. Better than adequate. She was damn good at her job. Something Flynn Talbot obviously needed to learn.

Another beat of silence. Carina bit her bottom lip, hoping and praying the woman took pity on her and agreed.

"Okay."

Thank Christ. Carina sagged in relief.

"But if he doesn't agree by early this afternoon, I'll need to reach out to other nurses."

"Yes. Of course." She shot a quick look at the time. It was nine in the morning. That gave her a minimum of three hours to convince the man. That was enough. It had to be.

She grabbed her keys off the kitchen counter. "Thank you, Barbara."

The second she hung up, she was running out of the house, dodging boxes left, right, and center as she went. Boxes that held a million and one things that needed unpacking but she hadn't gotten around to. Boxes that had been sitting there for a good week and a half.

That *had* been today's job. But if she wasn't successful in this chat with Flynn Talbot, she might not even need to unpack them.

Argh.

She slid behind the wheel of her car, her stomach convulsing at the thought. Quickly, she typed Blue Halo Security into her GPS before pulling onto the road. Blue Halo was where he worked, and she only knew that because Patricia hadn't stopped talking about her son. How he was a former Delta Force soldier. How he saved people. She'd also mentioned him being really fast and strong, but hell, all a person needed to do was look at the guy to know that.

He was ridiculously tall and sexy, with these crazy-wide shoulders. His intense, smoldering gaze went perfectly with his chiseled jaw. Then he'd spoken to her, and holy Christmas, she thought she'd pass out on the spot. His voice was deep and husky and basically what every woman heard in their sexiest dreams.

Carina's thoughts stayed on Flynn as she drove. She didn't live far from Blue Halo. In fact, everything seemed to be close to everything else in Cradle Mountain. Joy had raved about this small town. About the wildflowers that hedged the paths and scented the air. The coffee shop with the funny mugs and colorful walls. She'd mentioned a place called Perry's Desserts. Apparently, it had the best chocolate mousse and ice cream in Idaho.

Carina needed that. Her *soul* needed that. All of it. Especially after the hell she'd lived through in Michigan. But now, her fresh start was in jeopardy.

No. She could turn this around. She would.

What had she done wrong? One time. She'd met Flynn *one time.* And for what? Two seconds? The man had been like a big, broody tower of muscle, and he'd barely spoken to her. He'd basically just asked her name and why she was there.

Could Patricia have instigated this? Told her son she didn't like Carina?

The second the thought entered her mind, she dismissed it. The older woman had advancing Alzheimer's, but she still had good days. And on her good days, Patricia was coherent and kind and talked nonstop about Flynn and her late husband. Carina hadn't sensed a single thread of animosity or dislike.

She turned the corner, and that's when she saw them—three men. None of them were Flynn, but holy mother of God, they were all just as big, muscled, and beautiful.

Her jaw dropped open.

Patricia had told her that Flynn owned and ran the security business with seven of his friends, all of them former military. And, yeah, this definitely had to be three of them. They all had the whole bulging-biceps, tight-shirt-pulled-across-a-big-chest thing going on. Were they all Delta Force?

Just as she thought, the three guys pushed inside a building with a sign for Blue Halo Security.

She scanned the building. She hadn't researched the company. In fact, she rarely got on a computer. She never watched TV or listened to the radio. And the second everything had gone down in Michigan, she'd deleted all her social media accounts.

These days, she was more of a Chardonnay-on-the-back-porch kind of gal. It was better for her peace of mind.

The second the car was parked, she took a moment to breathe. *You can do this. You've done nothing wrong, and you're great at your job. Convince him.*

She repeated that three times in her head. Then she slid out of the car and through the door, stepping inside a small hallway and, following a sign, moving up a set of stairs. When she reached a door on the second floor labeled Blue Halo, she pushed inside, only to quickly stop.

Empty.

Well, not *completely* empty. There was a desk with a computer and a phone and all the normal reception stuff...but no actual receptionist.

Carina stepped up to the desk, scanning the small space for a bell or something. She'd just come to the conclusion that there was no bell or any other obvious way to alert someone to her presence when a guy stepped into the room. Her eyes widened, and she jumped back like she'd done something wrong, even though she hadn't.

"Hi." Sweet Jesus, had her voice just hiccupped in the middle of a single-syllable word? She cleared her throat. "Ah, my name's Carina Murphy, and I was wondering if Flynn might be here? I really need to talk to him."

The guy shot a look over his shoulder. He was one of the men she'd seen walking in from outside. With his pouty lips and bright blue eyes, he reminded her of a dark-haired Brad Pitt. A lot of women probably got lost in those eyes.

But not her. No way. She was on a mission and would not be distracted by any of these sexy, too-hot-for-their-own-good men.

When he looked back to her, he smiled, and a dimple formed on his cheek. "Sure, he's down here. I'm Tyler, by the way."

Carina almost sagged. She needed that smile. It took the edge off her jagged nerves.

She followed him down a hall, and he stopped by an open office door.

The first thing she saw was the back of a woman sitting on the edge of a desk. She had perfectly straight hair tied up in the neatest ponytail Carina had ever seen. The woman turned her head, and of course, her hair wasn't the only perfect thing. No, it matched her perfectly applied makeup and perfectly shaped brows.

Figured a man like Flynn would date a woman like that. She was probably ridiculously smart, too, with a doctorate in psychology or something.

Good. This was good. It would shut down that stupid fantasy she'd developed the second she set eyes on Flynn yesterday.

And it would definitely make her forget about that dream she'd had last night...

God, don't think about that, Carina.

Her gaze flicked behind the woman to Flynn, and she swallowed. Yep. Just as good-looking today as he'd been yesterday. And just like yesterday, his eyes did that smoldering thing when they landed on her.

"You have a visitor," Tyler said, almost sounding amused as he tapped the doorframe.

Flynn's eyes narrowed on his friend as he walked away. Then he stood, reminding Carina of just how tall he was. Huge. The man was *huge*.

"I'll chat with you later, Vic."

The woman rose, then wrapped her arms around Flynn's neck and lifted to her toes. Carina was sure the woman was going for Flynn's lips, but he turned his head to the side at the last second, and her kiss pressed to his cheek.

"I'll call you on my lunch break," she said in a voice that was entirely too husky and sexy for this time of day. Carina received a tight smile from the woman before she stepped out of the room. And then it was just her and Flynn.

Her stomach did a little flip. One hundred percent of his attention was on her, and it felt...paralyzing. Intoxicating.

She swallowed, forcing a smile to her lips before moving forward. "Hi, Mr. Talbot. It's good to see you again. I was wondering if you had a moment to chat."

He nodded toward the seat across the desk. "Take a seat, Miss Murphy."

The way her last name rolled from his lips in that deep, rumbly voice almost had her breath catching.

Keep it together, Carina. The man's hot, but he also wants you fired.

She lowered into the seat, watching as he did the same. Suddenly, her throat felt ridiculously dry. "I need to talk to you about my position as your mother's nurse."

One small nod.

Jeez, the man was going to make her say it. He knew why she was here and what she was going to ask, yet he wanted her words. Fine. She could do that.

"I'm not sure if I said something to put you off yesterday, or if I gave you the impression that I wasn't up to the job, or maybe you think I'm too young. I know I'm younger than Joy. But I assure you, I'm very experienced and my patients receive the best care."

There was a beat of silence, and she tried not to squirm as he watched her. It was hard. Damn hard. Because the man studied her like he saw entirely too much.

"I'm sorry, Miss Murphy," he finally said. "But I can't have you working for my mother."

A tense quiet followed his words. Was that it? He wasn't going to expand on that little statement?

"Can I ask why?" Could she *scream* why? Could she walk over to the sex god of a man, grab his shirt, and demand answers?

He leaned back in his seat. "Because I can't have a woman who's been investigated for stealing drugs caring for her."

Carina blinked. It was one of those slow blinks, where her mind scrambled to make sense of what had just been said. She frowned and opened her mouth but quickly closed it again. Then she shook her head.

"How exactly do you know that I've been investigated for stealing drugs?"

She knew the information wasn't on her file at the agency. In fact, after she'd won her court case, it was specifically stipulated that she be allowed to practice nursing without restriction or sanctions on her license.

A small smile touched his lips, one of those you-should-know-the-answer-to-that smirks. "We're a security company, Miss Murphy."

They were a security company—so they got to dig into all her little secrets. Even the ones that were supposed to be locked away, never to be found again.

Flynn stood, all million and one feet of him, and walked to the door. "I appreciate you coming in, but my mind's set."

Then he placed his hand on the frame, waiting.

Did he think that was it? That she'd just accept what he said, lie down, and give up? Leave without a word, and yet again be punished for a crime she didn't commit?

Hell no.

CHAPTER 2

*F*lynn watched the array of emotions flutter across Carina's expressive face. It took everything in him to focus on *that*, and not just her eyes, which were the palest blue he'd ever seen, like the sky on a spring day. To not drag his gaze down to her full lips, which were currently opening and closing in quick succession. Lips that would be far too easy to obsess about. To dream about how they'd feel pressed against his own.

Shut it down, Flynn. The woman was investigated for stealing drugs. You shouldn't be thinking about her like that.

When Carina stood, she smoothed her hands on her jeans like she was trying to compose herself. He didn't miss the slight tremble in her fingers. She was trying to act confident, but she was nervous. And hell if that didn't tug at his damn chest.

When she looked up, those pale blue eyes bore into him. "I can see how the information makes me look bad. But if you found that, I'm sure you *also* found that the allegations were dismissed. I was falsely accused. And my statement stands—your mother would have the best care with me."

Flynn watched her eyes. Listened to her voice, her breaths. She seemed to be telling the truth, but she was still a risk. And anyone with a questionable background check could not work for his mother.

"I'm sorry, Miss Murphy. I can't take that chance."

Frustration suddenly drowned out every other emotion on her face. "My name's Carina. I would love for you to use it. And why exactly can't you 'take that chance'? I did nothing wrong."

"She's my mother."

That was all he should say—all he should *need* to say. But at Carina's pleading eyes, he continued.

"I don't know you, Carina." Her name felt smooth on his tongue. "All I have to go by is a background check that tells me you have a red flag."

She took a step closer, and her scent permeated the space. It was peaches and vanilla—all sweet.

Damn, he hated that.

"Then get to know me," she said quietly. "You could even stay at the house while I care for your mom. *Please*. Give me a chance."

He'd expected the woman to turn up. He'd expected anger. Frustration, maybe. But pleading? "Why do you need this job so badly?"

"Because I went through hell in Michigan to keep my nursing license, and this is my first job since. Because Joy told me about the wildflowers and the quirky coffee mugs and the ice cream that tastes so good, you'd want to bathe in. All of that disappears without a job. And because I don't quit. I started this job, and I want to finish it."

He gave her a small smile, knowing she wouldn't like what he said next. "You're not quitting. I'm letting you go."

A puff of breath escaped her mouth, and for a second, his gaze lowered to her lips. His groin tightened, and he forced his attention back up.

She took another step forward. He thought she was leaving, but instead, she wrapped her fingers around his biceps.

That simple touch sent heat spiraling through his body and flaring in his gut.

Jesus Christ, what the hell was wrong with him? Or better question, who the hell was this woman that she could do this to him?

"Please." Her soft plea had his chest constricting. Or maybe that was her touch again. Whatever it was, he almost caved. Because really, who the hell could ever say no to this gorgeous woman? Everything about her had his senses on high alert.

He took a step back, forcing his body to turn it off. The heat. The emotion. All of it. Something he'd become good at after everything life had thrown his way.

Her hand dropped.

He almost wanted to look away and save himself from seeing the gut-wrenching disappointment that would cross her face. He didn't. "I can't."

Yeah, there it was. And for some reason, it hurt like hell.

She gave one small nod before stepping around him and leaving his office silently.

The silence was the worst part. Fuck, but he wished she'd screamed at him, made some sort of huge fuss. At least then he wouldn't feel like an asshole.

The second he heard her footsteps on the stairs, he moved through the hall, stopping at the doorway to Tyler's office. "You couldn't have called? Given me a heads-up before walking her over to my office while I was busy?"

Tyler leaned back in his seat. "Sorry, I thought you were almost done with Victoria."

"I was actually moments away from breaking up with the woman."

That had Tyler straightening. "Don't mess with me, brother. Are you serious?"

He ran a hand through his hair. "Yeah. I should have done it a while ago."

Their relationship was only ever a casual one, but the woman was starting to want more. More of his time. More overnight stays at his place. Hell, she'd even started holding his hand when they walked down the street. He didn't have a problem with PDA, he just didn't want that kind of relationship with Victoria.

Tyler nodded. "About damn time, man. She's a good enough doctor, but she's too…"

"Cold?" Flynn finished for his friend. Plenty of people had used that word to describe her. And it was true. He hadn't cared before because she wasn't cold to *him*. But now? He was starting to care.

"Yeah, cold. You need someone warm." One side of his mouth lifted. "Someone like that woman who just came in. She kind of reminded me of sunshine and flowers."

For some reason, the idea of Tyler being anything but cordial to Carina had his gut twisting. But that was ridiculous.

"She was assigned to be Mom's nurse while Mrs. Anderson attends to some family emergency in Florida." Flynn leaned his shoulder against the doorframe. "I was in the hospital after the car crash when Mrs. Anderson left, so they couldn't reach me for approval."

That damn car crash. Every time he thought about it, every muscle in his body tightened in anger. He'd been assigned protective detail to his friend's wife and daughter. A car had hit them, and while he'd been unconscious, the woman and child were taken. They were okay now, but the memory would probably always haunt him.

Tyler's smile grew. "So, you'll get to see a lot of her, then."

"No. She actually applied for the job to temporarily replace Mrs. Anderson a few months ago, when Joy took a vacation. I did a background check then, and it showed she was investigated for stealing prescription pain medication from a patient in Michigan." The smile slipped from Tyler's face. "The allegations were dismissed, but…"

"You don't know her well enough to trust her with your mother. Gotcha."

Of course Tyler got it. His entire team had relocated and started the security business here in Cradle Mountain, Idaho, specifically because Flynn needed to be with his mother. Her advancing Alzheimer's meant she needed significant in-home care. Some days she was fine. Others, she left raw meat in the microwave, got lost on her walks, and thought Flynn was his deceased father.

He pushed off the frame. "Anyway, I'm gonna follow up on a job before stopping to see Mom and letting her know what's going on."

Tyler dipped his head. "Send her my best."

"Will do."

Flynn headed back to his office, where he checked the time on his phone before opening up his laptop, ready for his Zoom call with a potential client. Having a big team of eight guys running the place meant they could offer a good array of security work, including private and corporate protection, consultation, personal security, and self-defense education.

They also did a bit of off-the-books work for the US government. Steve, their FBI liaison, contacted them whenever he had a job.

When the Zoom call came through, he clicked on to find a middle-aged bald man on the other end.

"Hi, Paul. I'm Flynn Talbot. Good to finally meet." They'd connected a bit over email before initiating the Zoom call.

Paul Simmons smiled, but the expression was strained. "Hi. Thank you for getting in touch."

"You said in your email that you feel you and your wife are being stalked by someone. Is that right?" Flynn wouldn't be surprised. The man was a high-ranking attorney for a private company. His position and income made him vulnerable to that kind of thing.

"We just moved to Idaho Falls from Chicago. I get the feeling that not everyone in the office is happy I got the promotion. Not that I thought anyone would go to this extreme to scare us away."

Flynn nodded. "Have you seen the person you suspect to be stalking you?"

The guy's eyes flared. It was quick, and Flynn almost missed it, but it answered his question before the guy spoke. "A few times. Once at my kitchen window. I have high-security gates, so he shouldn't have been able to get in. My wife also saw a guy following her when she went on her morning run. And then...I thought I saw him chasing my car. He was *fast*."

Flynn's brows tugged together. "Fast?"

Simmons swallowed, pausing for a moment before answering. "That's actually why I contacted your company. I think he's like you guys."

Flynn almost laughed, even though there was nothing funny about the situation. *No one* was like him, bar the seven members of his team, and another team in Marble Falls, Texas.

Three years ago, he'd been part of Combat Applications Group, or what civilians knew as Delta Force. Then he'd been taken. Held in a compound. Routinely drugged. Trained. And changed irrevocably. Now he was faster and stronger than he should be. He healed quickly. He could see through a pitch-black night. Hear things he shouldn't.

All of that was supposed to remain hidden from the public. But several months ago, the media found out and leaked the story. Now everyone knew.

"That's not possible," Flynn said quietly. "But we'll look into your situation, investigate your coworkers, and put a guy on you."

Paul didn't look convinced, but he didn't argue the point either. "I'd like to hire your company to provide twenty-four-hour security for both me and my wife."

Flynn dipped his head. "We can do that."

He spent the next twenty minutes asking Paul questions about his colleagues, his job and his and his wife's everyday routines, all while noting everything down. Once the call ended, he sent the notes to his team. From there, they'd come up with a schedule that worked for everyone.

Flynn didn't believe for a second that whoever was stalking this guy and his wife was like him. What he *did* believe was that fear muddied the mind. It could make you see and believe things that weren't true.

It was about eleven when he headed out of the office and down the stairs to his car. The drive to his mother's house was short—a perk of living in a small town. It was the town he'd grown up in, although just about everyone he'd known from school had moved on. Another thing about small towns. People left.

Of its own volition, his mind trickled back to Carina. He'd re-read her entire background check last night. Both parents were still alive and living in Michigan, as well as an older sister who was married with kids. She'd graduated from the University of Michigan School of Nursing and had lived there her entire life.

So why had she left? Why was she here? She'd said something about the flowers and the coffee…

God. Why did he even care?

He pulled into his mother's driveway before climbing out of the car and walking up the path. As soon as he stepped into the house, he spotted his mother by the stove.

Immediately, she cast a glance over her shoulder, smiling. "Hi, dear. For a moment, I thought you were Carina. She must be running late."

He paused before moving across the room and pressing a kiss to her cheek. "How are you doing today, Mom?"

He studied her, noticing that, although there were exhaustion lines beside her eyes, she looked clear and alert. She'd had him when she was almost forty. So she'd always been older than his friends' mothers.

"I'm okay."

She moved to pick up the kettle, but Flynn slipped his hand below hers, lifted the hot water and poured it into her mug. "I've got it. You sit down."

There was a slight shake in her hand as she patted his arm before nodding. His chest tightened at the sight. Despite being older, his mother had always been a vibrant and charismatic person. Watching Alzheimer's and old age ravage her mind and body... It gutted him.

His mother had lost him for two years to Project Arma. Now he made sure he saw her every day. He couldn't make up for the lost time, but he would sure as hell try.

He removed the tea bag before taking the cup to the table and sliding it in front of her. The second he lowered into the seat beside her, she slipped her hand over his.

"Thank you, dear." A smile slid across her lips, and her eyes brightened. "Have you met Carina yet? She's a sweetheart. I have a feeling you'll like her." Patricia moved her head closer. "She's also very beautiful."

Christ. Had his mother taken a liking to the woman already? It had only been a week.

He opened his mouth to tell her Carina wouldn't be back when his phone rang from his pocket. He never let a call go without checking to see who it was. With his work, that wasn't an option.

He glanced at the screen. Victoria.

He silenced the call before sliding it back into his pocket.

His mother's eyes narrowed. "Was that the doctor woman you've been dating?"

If there was one thing that *hadn't* changed, it was his mother's judgment of the women he dated. Open judgment. And just like with most of the others, she hadn't taken a liking to Victoria.

"Yes."

She scowled. "I don't like that woman. She's no good for you."

So everyone kept telling him.

"Do you want something to eat?" He rose, needing to distract her before she went on a rant. Because she would. When it came to Victoria, she usually did. "Lunch?" He opened the fridge, his gaze falling on the ham and cheese.

"No. I'm waiting for Carina. She's going to make me a pumpkin salad. Apparently, she does something special with the pumpkin."

Well, when the woman wanted to remember something, she definitely did.

He grabbed the ham and cheese before moving to the counter. "Carina won't be working here anymore, Mom."

There was a second of silence. Flynn almost groaned. The woman could be feisty when she wanted. But her silence... It was worse.

Finally, she spoke. "What happened? Is she okay?"

For a moment, he debated lying. But he'd never been able to lie to his mother. He could be the deadliest Delta operator in the world, and he couldn't lie to the woman who'd given him life. "I asked the agency to find a new nurse."

There was another heavy pause. His skin tingled in anticipation of what was to come. Give her a minute, and—

"Flynn Adam Talbot."

God. She was full-naming him. This was going to be worse than he'd thought. Her chair scraped against the wooden floorboards as she stood.

"Tell me right now that's not true!"

He looked up. Yep, his mother was giving him the same look she'd used when he was ten and had somersaulted off the porch and broken his elbow after explicitly being told not to.

"I had to. I did a background check and found that she—"

"Was accused of stealing prescription pain medication from a patient. Yes, she told me."

How could the woman have such a good memory on some days, while not remembering a damn thing on others?

She moved across the room. "She also told me she didn't do it. So is there another reason you fired her?"

"I can't have her working here, Mom."

"Like hell you can't!" Was it him, or had all the lines of exhaustion left her face and she suddenly looked ready to battle? "Is she caring for you or me?"

He tilted his head. "Mom—"

"Well?"

"You."

She gave a quick nod. "So it's my decision, and I want her here. Make it happen."

CHAPTER 3

*C*arina flicked through the job ads on her laptop. Nothing. Abso-freaking-lutely nothing. Nothing within driving distance, anyway. Unless she wanted a three-hour commute each way.

Nope.

Argh. *Looks like your dream of smelling flowers, eating good ice cream and getting away from Michigan is dead, Carina. Dead!*

Her parents had told her this would happen. They'd asked her to stay in Michigan. No, they'd begged her. But they weren't the ones who'd been walked out of work like a criminal. Who'd had every colleague looking at them like they were junkies, so desperate for a fix that they stole from a patient.

No. Leaving and getting a fresh start had been essential.

Yeah, great fresh start, Carina.

Plonking the laptop beside her on the couch, she stood, stretching her arms over her head. She glanced at the time on the wall clock, and barely stifled a groan. Twelve thirty. Barbara was probably already reaching out to other nurses now.

The worst part about her world turning upside down was that none of it was her fault. None. She *hadn't* stolen the drugs. But even now, after the investigation was dropped, she was still dealing with the fallout.

The world hated her, right? Maybe she'd done something wrong in a past life. Or maybe she'd accidentally run over someone's cat and was forever paying penance for it.

Whatever it was, it sucked.

Blowing out a long breath, she looked toward the window, catching the mail carrier slipping something into her mailbox. Moving outside, she opened the box and tugged out the contents. She was about to close it when another envelope shoved way in the back caught her attention. An unstamped letter.

She lifted it out and studied it. Strange. Her name was on the front, but there was no address. She flipped it over. No return address either. Interesting. Was it from a neighbor? Maybe a welcome-to-town note? That would be nice. It might even turn her bad day around a little bit.

On her way back to the house, she tore open the unstamped envelope. She'd just stepped inside when she pulled out a small piece of paper. The second her gaze swiped across the words, her body stopped, unease coiling in her belly.

Get out of Cradle Mountain. You're not welcome here.

The fine hairs on her arms stood on end. What the hell? Who had put this in her mailbox?

Nervously, she shot her gaze to the street, scanning the houses around her, before looking back down at the note. For a single heartbeat, her mind flicked to Flynn, but she quickly scrubbed that thought away. She'd only met the man yesterday, and even though she didn't know him that well, something told her he wasn't immature enough to do something like this, regardless of how he felt about her.

What about the kids next door? Two teenage boys lived there. They looked about the same age—fifteen, maybe sixteen— making her think they were fraternal twins.

Just two days ago, the boys had invited a houseful of people over and pumped the music. No one answered the door when she knocked, and she had no idea where their parents were. So Carina had done what any normal too-old-to-be-awake-at-three-a.m.-listening-to-rap adult would do. She'd called the police. She'd been receiving side-eyes and angry glares ever since.

Should she talk to the mother? She'd only caught one brief glimpse of the woman since moving in.

When a gust of wind swept inside the house, Carina pushed the door closed before moving into the bedroom, then the connected bathroom.

Maybe she'd sit on it and let it percolate. Right now, she needed to shower and wash away this horrible day of job loss and threatening notes. Bad things came in threes, right? Did that mean she could expect another little surprise before the day was over? A fire in her rental? A break-in?

God, don't give the universe ideas, Carina.

She quickly undressed and stepped into the shower. Though she tried not to let her thoughts wander back to Flynn, it was impossible. The man was one big attractive nightmare. A man who would soon be a mere memory. Just like this town.

Once she was clean, she dried off quickly before putting on a bra and panties. Now she just needed her favorite sweatpants and Big Bird sweatshirt so she could drink a bottle of Chardonnay on the porch and drown her sorrows. Not an entire bottle, but definitely a good couple of glasses before she went back to job searching.

Digging around in her closet unsuccessfully, she groaned out loud when she realized the comfy items in question must be in the last remaining unpacked box of clothes—which was stacked in the closet with a bunch of other random boxes. Why the heck had she stacked anything on such a high shelf?

Actually, she knew the answer to that. Because she'd wanted the illusion of a tidy, organized bedroom...without the trouble of actually unpacking everything.

Your laziness is coming back to bite you, woman.

Shaking her head, she slid over a full box of knickknacks she also hadn't unpacked, placing it beneath the shelf before climbing on top. Then, bit by bit, she shuffled the box in question toward her. The thing was super heavy. How the heck had she even gotten it up there in the first place? She must have taken her strong woman pills that morning. Or maybe she'd just been high on life with her new town, new job…

The box was right at the edge. One more little nudge—

She tugged too hard, and suddenly the thing tipped back and fell right on her head.

A screech slipped from her lips, and she fell to the floor right before the box crashed onto her face.

She'd barely landed when a voice boomed from the bedroom door.

"What the hell?"

As the box was lifted from her face, she rolled to her side and cradled her cheek. Bruised. Definitely bruised.

Okay, so this was the third thing to go wrong, right? Now she was done?

Warm hands touched her upper arm. "Carina, talk to me. Are you hurt?"

Oh God. Was that—

Flynn?

"Carina?"

Definitely Flynn. His deep, rumbly voice rippled down to her tummy, almost blocking out the pounding in her cheek. Almost.

She lowered one hand to her chest. Her *bare* chest…

Holy shit, she didn't have clothes on!

Carina shot up to a seated position, cringing at the jolt to her head before pulling her knees to her chest.

"Whoa, slow down!"

She ignored his words. What underwear had she put on?

Please, baby Jesus, tell her she wasn't wearing her old, high-waisted granny panties.

She shot a quick glance down, and the air rushed from her chest when she saw the matching black set. Not the sexiest she owned, but definitely not granny level.

The thumb on her arm shifted, grazing her sensitive skin, and finally she looked up. Heat rushed to her cheeks. As always, Flynn was watching her closely, but for the first time, instead of mistrust and suspicion, she saw concern.

Her gut gave another small kick.

He tilted his head to the side. "Are you okay?"

"Yes." *No.* Her life was falling apart, and the sexiest man she'd ever laid eyes on was staring at her while she was in her underwear.

He frowned, his other hand reaching up and gently grazing the bruise. The air cut off in her throat and her body warmed. And not because the touch brought on any sort of pain. The opposite.

"This needs ice," he said softly, his brows tugging together.

The gentleness in his voice, in combination with his touch, almost had her forgetting how bad her day had been thus far. It almost had her forgetting that he'd *contributed* to that bad day. Her skin burned where he touched and every little part of her wanted to lean in.

What would it taste like to kiss a man like him? He looked like a coffee and bourbon kind of guy. But there was a small whisper in her head that said maybe he'd be sweeter than he looked.

Without conscious thought, her gaze dropped to his mouth. It was so close that she could almost feel the warm exhale from his lips. When she dragged her gaze back up, her breath caught in her throat.

Fire danced in his eyes. That fire spoke of danger and heat and—did she already say danger?

"You shouldn't look at me like that," he said quietly. So quietly, it almost sounded like a warning.

The words that slipped from her lips felt strained. "Why not?"

"Because it's dangerous."

Had he read her mind?

She wasn't sure if she was tempting him, or she just had absolutely no self-control, but her gaze zipped back down to his lips.

The fingers on her arms tightened, and an actual growl rippled from his chest.

Her lips separated, tingling in anticipation.

Then he stood, his warm touch replaced by cold air. He whipped his shirt over his head and lowered to his haunches again. Before she could move, he was fitting the shirt over her head then slipping her arms through.

Suddenly, he was all she could smell. His scent surrounded her. And the heat of the material—material that had just covered his bare skin—nearly drowned her.

His hands returned to her arms, tugging her to her feet. "You sure you're okay?"

One small nod, because words were nowhere to be found. In fact, it was possible she'd forgotten the entire English language.

A warm hand pressed to her back, then he was leading her to the kitchen and helping her to a stool. He went to the freezer, found a bag of frozen peas and wrapped it in a tea towel as if he owned the place. When he returned, he held her shoulder while pressing the ice to her face. The heat from his hand was a sharp contrast to the coldness of the peas.

"What were you doing?" he asked, his gaze on the ice.

"Looking for my sweatpants and Big Bird sweatshirt." Oh good, she had words again.

"Big Bird sweatshirt?"

"My dad bought it for me on our last Disneyland trip when I was twelve. I wear it when I'm having a bad day."

His jaw clicked. Even that was sexy. She had a feeling anything this man did would be.

She swallowed. "How did you know I'd fallen?"

She'd screeched, but had she done it loud enough to be heard from the other side of the front door? Also, how the heck had he gotten in? Had she forgotten to turn the lock?

"I heard you."

Okay, maybe she *was* louder than she'd thought. "You were crazy quick. I'd barely hit the floor when you were suddenly there."

Something flickered in his eyes. Confusion maybe? "I'm fast."

Well, yeah... She got that.

"You should lock your door," he said, disapproval darkening his features.

Her face ached, but not enough to miss the twitch in his six-pack abs. Shit. She needed to *not* look at his chest. Or his arms. Could she look at his hair at least? Probably not.

"How did you know where I live?" She shook her head quickly, then cringed again, not missing the tugging of his brows. "Whoops. Big bad security man. You can find anything. Almost forgot."

"Not everything." Did the thumb at her collarbone just caress her through the shirt? "I don't know why you chose to come to Cradle Mountain. You applied to be my mother's nurse previously but moved here before being called for the *current* job, so you came without employment. I don't know why you did that, either."

"Joy decided to become a nurse later in life. We studied together and have been friends ever since. She told me a lot about when she was younger, when she spent summers here with her aunt and uncle. A few months ago, she got in touch and told me she was going on vacation, and suggested I apply to cover for her. Check the town out." Obviously, she hadn't gotten the job then. "A month ago, a job was advertised at the Cradle Mountain

Hospital. I applied and moved here, taking a chance since I knew I had a good shot at it."

"What happened with that job?"

She lifted the shoulder he wasn't touching. "The agency called me about caring for Patricia, so I withdrew my application at the hospital. They hired someone else."

Sounded like fate, right? That she'd move into a new town and a perfect job would pop up the same week. Ha. Good trick, universe.

"What are you doing here, Flynn?"

His jaw did that sexy tensing thing again. The one that made it look even more chiseled. "I want you to come back and work for my mother until Joy returns."

Her heart thumped against her ribs, but she was careful not to get too excited. Not yet. "You want me to come back and work for your mother?"

"Supervised visits."

A bit of the excitement dulled. So she *had* heard right, but there was a catch.

"My mother really likes you."

And by the look of it, he hated that. Because the man didn't trust her at all.

She took the ice pack from his hand, her fingers grazing his as she did so. Even though the ice was cold, his hand remained warm. Did the man not feel the cold?

"I'd be happy to come back and work for your mother under supervised conditions."

The last part killed her to say, but she wasn't going to turn down a perfectly good job for her pride.

He nodded, stepping back. Their physical contact broke, and her heart did a little flop.

"Great. I'll be spending most of the day with her tomorrow, so maybe you can go back on Thursday."

She gave a polite smile and nod. "Sounds great."

She hopped off the stool, ignoring the small pang to her head. Standing put her level with Flynn's chest. She quickly walked— okay, she basically ran—toward the door and had almost reached it when her phone rang from the couch.

She knew who it was likely to be. Her ex, Greg, a doctor she'd dated in Michigan. She'd broken up with him before she left, but he still called often. *Too* often.

She beelined for the couch and canceled his call before continuing to the front door. Flynn stopped in front of her as she opened it, and she could have sworn he stood closer than people normally would. Or maybe she was just delusional. Yeah, that was probably it.

His gaze flicked to the phone. "Everything okay?"

Had she looked worried by Greg's call? "Of course. Thank you for stopping by and getting the peas out for me." Her gaze flashed down to her top, and she gasped. "Your shirt! Hang on, I'll—"

He grabbed her arm before she could move. "I've got a spare in the car." Then his eyes hardened. "No more climbing on boxes. It's dangerous. Okay?"

Yet again, he touched her and her voice disappeared. So she just nodded.

She thought he'd turn to leave immediately. Instead, his gaze caught on her lips for a prolonged second.

Finally, his head bobbed, and he turned away, leaving her feeling hot, bothered, and completely unhinged.

CHAPTER 4

Flynn turned onto the street where Pizza Malloy was located. Victoria sat beside him, chattering about work. She hadn't stopped talking the entire drive. Something about misogyny keeping her from getting a promotion.

He'd tuned out about two minutes into the drive. That probably made him an asshole.

Actually, no, what made him an asshole was dating one woman while being unable to get another out of his head.

Memories of how badly he'd wanted to kiss Carina yesterday plagued him. Images of her sitting on her bedroom floor almost naked, her creamy breasts plumping out of her sexy black bra.

His hands tightened around the wheel. *Stop. Get through tonight, do what you have to do, then tackle what comes next.*

Whatever the hell that might be.

"Don't you think, babe?"

Flynn pulled into a parking spot right outside the pizza shop. "Yep."

Yeah, he was an asshole. Whatever he and Victoria were doing, it had run its course, and it was time to end it. Past time.

He climbed out, not surprised when she didn't move a muscle.

As per usual, she was waiting for him to open the door for her. That didn't use to annoy him…

The second she was out, she linked her arm through his, and they walked toward the door.

"I heard there's this fabulous new French restaurant up north," she said. "Maybe we could try that next time."

Flynn said nothing, knowing perfectly well there wouldn't be a next time. Because tonight, he was ending things. He'd intended to break up with her at lunch—*again*—but unlike yesterday, his mother hadn't been having a great day. He should have canceled this dinner, but he'd been too distracted, what with his mother and thoughts of Carina and this new security assignment.

He held the door open for her, and before even stepping foot inside, he saw familiar faces at the counter—Tyler and Logan, as well as Logan's partner, Grace.

His friends smiled, but when their gazes hit Victoria, the smiles dimmed. It was subtle—so subtle that he doubted Victoria noticed. But he did. No one was a fan of the woman, not even her patients. Probably why she didn't get that promotion.

Flynn stopped in front of them. "Hey."

"Hey," Grace said in her usual soft voice. "You guys getting takeout too?"

"We're eating here," Victoria said, her fingers tugging lightly on his arm, encouraging him toward the tables. In the couple of months they'd been dating, she'd made it no secret that she wasn't interested in getting to know his friends.

"Did you visit your mom?" Logan asked.

He nodded. "Yeah, she had a rough one. Thanks for covering me while I was out of the office. Everything okay with the Simmons case?"

"Yep. Callum and Aidan are out there now."

One less thing to worry about. "Thanks."

"You end up taking that nurse back?" Tyler asked, a hint of a smile on his lips.

Asshole.

Victoria turned to look at him. "You didn't mention your mother has a new nurse."

Because he'd barely said two words this evening. "Mrs. Anderson had a family emergency in Florida."

Victoria frowned. "I thought her family lived here in Cradle Mountain?"

"Just her aunt and uncle."

"Is the replacement nice?" Grace asked.

"I don't really know her." Damn, why was his voice so gruff?

Tyler got that look on his face, like he was going to say something that could cause shit between him and Victoria, so Flynn stepped away. "We'll see you tomorrow."

Why make tonight worse for the woman?

The waitress showed them to a table in the corner. He sat with his back to the wall so he had a view of the entire shop. He liked to watch his surroundings. Not that it was as important as it used to be. With his advanced hearing, he knew the second someone approached from behind.

"So...is she the same age as Mrs. Anderson?"

He glanced across the table. "Who?"

He knew who. But damn, he didn't want to answer that. Victoria was clearly fishing for information.

"Your mom's new nurse."

He lifted his menu, scanning it even though he knew everything on the page. "No. She's younger. Maybe mid to late twenties."

Twenty-nine. He knew her age. Her birthday. It had all been on her background check and was now ingrained in his head.

At Victoria's silence, he shot a glance up to see her lips had thinned. She was looking at her own menu, but he was almost certain she wasn't really reading.

Suddenly, she lowered it. "Wait—was that her yesterday? The woman who interrupted us in your office?"

The waitress returned to the table. "Can I get you guys something to drink?"

"Guinness, thanks." He had a feeling he'd be ordering a second soon enough.

"Chardonnay, please."

The waitress was about to walk away when Flynn stopped her. "Can we order our food as well?" The sooner they ordered, the sooner they ate, and the sooner this could be done.

"Sure."

"Oh." Victoria's mouth opened and closed a couple times before she refocused on the menu.

"I'll have the smokehouse pizza and some Parmesan fries." He handed his menu to the woman.

"You got it." She wrote the order on her pad of paper before turning to Victoria.

"I'll get the shrimp linguine. Can you make sure the cook removes all the shell from the shrimp though? I can't stand having to shell any of it myself. Oh, and make sure he doesn't overcook the pasta."

Jesus.

"Uh…okay." The waitress took her menu. Flynn was sure the woman rolled her eyes the second she turned away.

When it was just them again, Victoria looked at him. "You've had that happen, right? When they leave some shell on, and you need to scrape it off."

If he had, it wouldn't have bothered him. "Sure."

"I had the best shrimp linguine during my time in San Feliciano in Italy. Honestly, it was to die for."

As she continued to talk about the pasta, his gaze caught Tyler's. It was just him now, still standing by the entrance. His brow was raised, silently asking Flynn how it was going.

At the touch of Victoria's hand on his, he looked back across the table. "So, I was thinking. We should get away for a weekend.

Just you and me. Something quiet and romantic. I so need a break from work. What do you think?"

He scrubbed a hand over his face. He'd wanted to wait until after they'd eaten, but every second that passed made it harder. She deserved more than his partial attention.

"Vic—"

"Think about it, okay?" She squeezed his hand. "I'm just going to run to the ladies' room before our food comes." Before he could get another word in, she was on her feet and across the room.

Flynn shook his head, looking over at his friend again.

But he wasn't alone anymore.

Flynn's gut clenched at the sight of Carina. She wore tight black jeans that hugged her thighs and ass like a second skin.

Heat flared in his chest. Heat that had no business flaring.

When she threw back her head and laughed at something Tyler said, Flynn didn't think. He just acted, rising to his feet and crossing the room in under a second, for no other reason than he was completely insane. It definitely wasn't because he was jealous of his friend.

When Carina saw him, he heard her breath catch, along with a slight elevation in her heart rate.

She wet her lips with her tongue. "Hi."

Goddamn, why did her voice have to be sexy as well? "Hey."

"We were just talking about how she got that bruise on her face," Tyler said. "I thought maybe your big clumsy ass pushed her over."

Carina chuckled. "Don't worry. I told him the entire embar-rassing story."

He didn't find the story embarrassing. In fact, he had a very different take on it.

He studied the bruise, his hand twitching to reach out and graze the skin around it like he had yesterday. "How's it feeling today?"

She lifted a shoulder. "As long as I don't look in the mirror, I barely remember it's there."

Two pizzas were set on the counter, and Tyler grabbed them. When he turned back, that same grin was on his face. "Well, I'm off. Have fun, kids."

He socked Flynn on the shoulder before leaving.

When it was just the two of them, Flynn looked back at the bruise on her face. It was blue and purple. He hated that. "You've been staying away from those boxes?"

She chuckled again, and the sound hit him right in the gut. "I haven't been standing on them, if that's what you mean. You'll be happy to know that I unpacked the rest of my clothes today, so no more dangerous behavior."

"Good." The word had barely left his mouth when he heard Victoria's heels clicking against the floor. Then she was there, standing beside him, touching his elbow.

"Hi," Victoria said, her voice sounding strained.

Carina's smile slipped, only for a second. Then it was back, but this time too bright. "Hi, we kind of met yesterday. I'm Carina."

"Patricia's new nurse."

"Yes."

Those fingers on his arm tightened. "It's nice to officially meet you, Carina." She looked at Flynn. "I think our drinks are at the table."

His gaze didn't leave Carina. "I'll see you tomorrow morning."

She dipped her head. He held her gaze for another beat before moving back across the room. Once he was seated again, it took everything in him to not stare at her, still standing by the door.

Their food arrived right as Carina's did. She'd just opened the door when she stopped, giving a small glance at him over her shoulder. When their gazes clashed, her cheeks pinkened a second before she stepped out.

"Flynn! You're so distracted tonight."

He looked back at Victoria, running a hand through his hair. Such an asshole.

"Victoria, we need to break up."

Fuck!

He hadn't meant to say it like that. Not so abruptly. But to be honest, the words were so overdue, he wasn't able to hold them in any longer.

Her brows rose. "What? You're breaking up with *me?*"

The way she said "me" made it sound like no one had ever broken up with her before. "Yes. Whatever we've had going on has run its course."

"Whatever we've had going on…"

Shit, had he worded that wrong?

"We've been dating, Flynn. Dinners. Texting. Sex. That's dating."

He cringed. "Sorry, Vic, I—"

"I don't want you to be sorry. I want to know why." Suddenly, she straightened, a frown marring her forehead. "Wait. It's *her*, isn't it?"

"No."

One of her perfectly manicured brows rose. "I saw the way you looked at her. Like you were undressing her with your eyes."

God, if he could just disappear on the spot, that would be nice. "I wasn't—"

"Save it." She stood from the table, tugging her bag over her shoulder. "I'll do us both a favor and leave. For your sake, I hope this isn't a decision you come to regret."

GIRLFRIEND. The woman with the perfect hair and makeup and the expensive designer dress was his girlfriend. Of course she was. Carina had suspected the second she'd seen her in his office yesterday.

She lowered into her car before setting the pizza on the passenger seat.

That meant it was in her head, right? The way his fingers had lingered on her cheek yesterday. The heat in his eyes when he looked at her.

The moment she'd thought he was about to kiss her.

Yep. Definitely in her head. Because if a man had a girlfriend who looked like that woman, there was no way he'd be itching to kiss or touch plain-Jane Carina.

Her stomach gave a sad little squeeze, but she quickly shook it off.

Why do you care? The man doesn't even trust you enough to do your job without supervision.

Nothing was going to happen. Nothing *could* happen.

A couple of minutes later, she pulled into her driveway. She was still loving the fact that everything was so close in Cradle Mountain. She was a street away from Patricia's house, so could walk to work on the days she didn't feel like driving. And she could probably walk to the town center too, if she wanted. Key word—*if* she wanted.

She'd just stepped out of the car when she stilled. What was that? Laughing? And was it coming from the side of her house?

Quickly, she grabbed the pizza. She'd only just made it to her porch when she heard more quiet laughter. She set the pizza on her porch chair and jogged to the side of the house.

Then she saw them—the two teenage boys from next door, running toward their backyard.

Before she could follow, her gaze caught on her side windows. Her mouth dropped open.

What the...

Eggs? They smashed *eggs* against her windows?

Where the heck were their parents, and why hadn't they stopped them?

Well, she wasn't just going to accept this. She should have gone over there the second that letter arrived.

Carina marched to the neighbor's house and hit the wooden door hard with her fist. When a moment passed and no one answered, she knocked even harder. "Hello? Is anyone home?"

Well, she knew someone was home—the boys. Where were all the adults?

The door suddenly opened, and a woman stood there, cigarette in hand. She wore a leather jacket, and tattoos snaked down from under the arm, onto her hand.

Her brows rose. "What?"

For a moment, she was put off by the terse greeting but recovered quickly. "Hi. I'm Carina, your new next-door neighbor. Are the boys who live here your sons?"

"Yes."

She took a deep breath, only just keeping her anger in check. "I'm not sure if you're aware, but they egged my house tonight. And I'm pretty sure they're also responsible for a letter I received in the mail about not being welcome in this town."

The woman's brows rose higher. "Why are you telling *me*?"

Was she serious? "Because I was hoping you could talk to them. Explain why those actions are wrong?" *Maybe, I don't know, ask them to apologize and not do it again?*

She laughed. "I'm guessing you don't have kids, let alone twin teenage boys. They do what they want. You got a problem with them, deal with it yourself."

The gasp had just slipped from Carina's lips when the door slammed shut in her face.

CHAPTER 5

"The doctors can't do anything for your knees?"

Flynn's fingers tightened around the wrench at the sound of Carina's soft voice from the other room. For the hundredth time that day, he wished he'd gotten someone else from his team to supervise her.

"Dorothy, you know I've had both knees done. I'm not going through that again."

Then he was immediately reminded why he hadn't asked someone else to be here. Because it was another not-so-great day for his mother. She'd taken to calling Carina by his aunt's name—his mother's sister. She'd passed away four years ago after a late cancer detection.

"Do you need some pain medication?"

Carina hadn't corrected his mother once, so it wasn't a surprise that she didn't now.

He'd been alternating between getting some work done on his computer and doing some odd jobs around his mother's house. Right now, he was fixing the leaking tap in the kitchen. With his enhanced hearing, he'd caught every word that was said between them, of course, and Carina had been nothing but kind and nurturing.

"You know I don't like those things. Rest is a perfectly good pain remedy."

"Are you sure? You could just take half a pill."

"Dorothy, I said I'm fine."

Of course she was. Because when was Patricia Talbot *not* fine?

He'd just finished fixing the pipe when his phone rang. He rose to his feet, moving to the table and swiping it. "Callum, how's the job going?"

"That's what I'm calling about. It's still early days, but just letting you know we haven't seen anyone yet."

That was a bit surprising, considering how panicked Paul had been. "You and Aidan coming home tonight?"

"Yep, and Logan and Blake will replace us."

"And I'm on after them."

He'd intentionally asked to be put later in the shift rotation, because he was hoping he'd have figured out this whole Carina-caring-for-his-mother business by then. If he hadn't, he could always ask one of the other guys to go for him. But he hated doing that. Protective detail was part of his job, and every man deserved a break. Also, Jason and Liam were currently away on a short mission for their FBI liaison, Steve, so they were two men short right now.

"Will you be in the office tomorrow for a briefing?" Flynn asked.

"I'll be there at nine."

He gave a small nod, even though his friend couldn't see him. "Great, see you then."

He hung up, putting his phone down and hefting the wrench.

"Remind me who you're dating this week."

Flynn almost laughed at his mother's words to Carina from the bedroom. His aunt Dorothy had been a serial dater. In fact, she used to tell him and anyone else who'd listen that no man could tie her down.

"I'm not dating anyone," Carina replied. "I was dating someone for a while, but I didn't feel that *thing*."

Flynn paused halfway to the sink, his fingers tightening around the wrench. Was she just playing the role of Dorothy right now?

The idea of her dating *any* man had something inside of him twisting and squeezing. And yeah, he was aware of how fucking ridiculous that was, when he'd only met the woman days ago.

"Yes. The *thing* is important. I had that with David."

Flynn swallowed at the mention of his father. They'd lost him six years ago. It had been tough for everyone. He was the best man Flynn had ever known.

There was a small sound, like his mother was patting Carina's hand.

"I hope Flynn finds *the one* soon," his mother said softly. "He keeps dating these floozies. Women he knows there's no future with. Maybe that's why he dates them."

Okay, story time's over.

Flynn walked to the bedroom. His mother was sitting up against the pillows on the bed, and Carina sat on the side. Both women looked up.

His mother's brows rose. "David. I didn't know you were home."

He smiled. The first time she'd called him by his father's name had been like a kick in the gut. Like her mother had forgotten him. Lost him. And in return, he'd lost his mother. In the early days, he'd corrected her. But after realizing that only made her upset, he'd stopped.

"I'm just checking on how everything's going in here."

His gaze flicked to Carina, but she quickly averted her own.

Patricia blew out a long breath. "I'm fine. I just need a nap."

Carina rose from the bed, helping his mother tug the sheets down and ease between them. Then she handed her some water and a pill.

His mother sighed loudly. "Dorothy—"

"This isn't pain medication. It's to help you sleep."

His mother's eyes softened seconds before she took the pill and water.

Carina's gentle approach with his mother once more had him pausing. Everything he'd seen today made him think she was telling the truth about whatever had happened in Michigan. He knew the woman would be on her best behavior today, what with eyes on her and all. But this—the gentle way she treated his mother—it was more. Too genuine to be faked.

She took the empty glass as Flynn moved across the room and pressed a kiss to his mother's head.

When he turned to leave, he touched the small of Carina's back and led her out, closing the door after them.

"You're good with her," he said quietly as they entered the kitchen.

She glanced at him over her shoulder, a twinkle in her eye. "Surprised?"

Yes. "No."

A quiet, lyrical laugh sounded as she stopped at the sink. "Liar."

Dragging his gaze away, he grabbed his own glass from the table and joined her at the sink. He was just reaching around her to set it down when she turned and stepped right into his chest. His hands went to her hips to steady her. Both her palms pressed against his chest.

For a moment, her sweet scent—that damn peach and vanilla —filled his nose, tormenting him.

The pitter-patter of her heart speeding up touched his ears. Then her lips parted and, this time, he didn't stop his gaze from falling to her mouth. Everything in him wanted to wrap her in his arms and taste her. The need had his fingers tightening, his breath coming faster.

He was seconds from gritting his teeth and stepping back when her thumbs grazed his chest. He felt the touch like it was fire against him. It singed him. And when her tongue slipped from her mouth to wet her lips, he lost the last scrap of self-restraint and dove in.

THE MAN'S eyes pierced her. Claimed her. And his hands…they burned where they touched.

When he stared at her mouth, her breath caught. Those fingers on her waist tightened and the thumping of her heartbeat increased.

A quiet voice in her head whispered for her to look somewhere else, step away, but it was impossible. She was rooted to the spot.

Almost of their own volition, her thumbs grazed the hard ridges of his chest. Her mouth suddenly dry, she swiped her tongue across her lips. The blue of his eyes deepened to navy as a soft growl rumbled from his chest.

That was all the warning she got before his head dipped and his mouth took hers.

A small hum reverberated deep in Carina's throat as his soft lips swiped against her own. When the hands on her hips slid under the fabric of her top, grazing bare skin, she gasped. Immediately, his tongue plunged inside her mouth, touching and dancing with hers.

For some reason, she'd expected a light kiss. A soft exploration. This was the opposite. This was an explosion of heat and touch. This was everything her body craved.

She leaned into him, moaning into his mouth. He tasted of spices and mint, his musky scent everywhere, overpowering every other smell. It was intoxicating.

His hands caressed the bare skin of her back, so large they felt like they touched her everywhere. Then they lowered, grabbing her against him. A shudder rocked her spine as her core rubbed against his bulge, and she grabbed his shoulders, steadying herself. She felt small and fragile and feminine in his arms.

Her fingers eased up his neck before burrowing into his hair.

Suddenly that mouth tore from hers, sweeping across her cheek and below her ear. She tried to silence her gasp, but it sounded loud in the room.

One of his hands moved to her front, sweeping beneath her shirt. Then it crept up, inch by inch, leaving a trail of fire as it went.

Her throat closed as he reached her ribs, skirting below her bra, teasing. Her breasts ached, crying out for him to touch them, swipe his thumb against her hard peak.

He nibbled on her neck, another soft growl rising in his chest.

And that small noise was just enough to penetrate the fog. For reality to crash back down around her.

He had a *girlfriend*. A living, breathing woman he'd taken on a date only last night.

Holy Christmas, what the hell was she doing?

She grabbed his wrist seconds before he touched her breast, her fingers not long enough to wrap around it.

All movement stopped. His mouth. His hand. Even his chest seemed to pause.

With her free hand, she pushed at his big chest. "Put me down."

There was another pause—a second where she felt his gaze on her like a hot beam. She wasn't looking at him anymore though. She couldn't. There was a crease in his shirt, and she stared at it like it was the most interesting thing she'd ever seen.

Guilt slithered up her spine, souring her mouth. She'd kissed a taken man. That wasn't okay. She wasn't the kind of person who did that.

Finally, he slid her to the floor, her over-sensitive nipples brushing against his hard chest as she went.

The air whooshed out of her. Torture. All of it.

"Carina—"

"My shift has finished. I need to go."

She rushed past him, grabbing her purse off the kitchen table. She hadn't even reached the door when he was in front of her, and for the second time that day, she almost ran into him.

How the heck had he gotten there so fast?

He stepped deeper into her space. "I don't understand what just happened."

She didn't understand either. Where the heck had her sense gone? "We shouldn't have done that. It was wrong."

She tried to step around him, but his arm swung out and grazed against her stomach, his hand on her hip. "Carina—"

"Don't."

Another beat of quiet. Then his arm dropped, and the loss of touch was like a kick to the chest.

God, she was a terrible human, crushing on a man who was spoken for.

She moved quickly, almost running out of the house.

She scanned for her car before cursing under her breath. She'd walked today. Dammit. All she wanted to do was slide into her car and drive away, disappear as quickly as possible. As it was, she felt his eyes on her the entire time. As she ran down the driveway. As she hurried along the sidewalk. When her bag slipped from her shaking shoulder. He saw everything.

Then she did something she knew she shouldn't. Just like at the pizza shop, she turned her head, glancing over her shoulder.

Her foot immediately caught on the path, and she stumbled, a new wave of heat blasting through her abdomen.

Because there he was—still standing in the doorway, looking at her like she was the only thing that existed in the world.

It was a look that claimed her just as thoroughly as his kiss.

CHAPTER 6

*F*lynn's fist shot forward, hitting the bag so hard the thing flew up, barely missing the roof. The bag had just returned to him when he hit it again.

He was vaguely aware of footsteps moving down the Blue Halo hallway behind him. It was early. So early that the place was empty when he arrived. Not that he cared if his team saw him pounding away at the bag or not. He cared about getting rid of some of this pent-up frustration.

Frustration that a woman he barely knew was stealing his sleep, his self-restraint, and his goddamn sanity.

Carina consumed his thoughts, all but torturing him.

The footsteps stopped just outside the gym room. "What did that bag do to you?"

For the first time in over an hour, his fists dropped. He wished he was spent. He wished he'd been able to use every last scrap of energy he had, but it was impossible.

He turned to look at Callum. The man had his arms crossed over his chest and was leaning a shoulder against the doorframe.

"It's not the bag that did something to me," he said quietly.

His friend studied him for a beat. "Wanna talk about it?"

No. He tugged off the gloves and moved to the bench.

"I heard your mom has a new nurse," Callum finally said.

Flynn froze, his gaze flying up. "What else did Tyler tell you?"

A smirk formed on his friend's face. "That she's pretty. And funny. That you hate it when he talks to her."

Asshole. "We kissed."

Callum's brows rose. "No shit. When?"

"Yesterday."

"And I'm guessing by the fact that you're here, beating the shit out of a bag, it didn't go well."

Flynn lifted his water and downed half the bottle. "Best damn kiss of my life."

"Big call."

Yeah, it was. That was the problem. Well, part of the problem. "Then she pushed me away and left."

She hadn't been able to get away from him fast enough, while he'd had to call upon every ounce of self-restraint to not tug her back and lose himself in her—a woman who was basically a stranger.

Her body hadn't felt like that of a stranger though. Her body in his arms, her lips against his—all of it had felt oddly familiar.

"Probably for the best," Flynn continued, shaking his head. "I don't know the details of what happened in Michigan."

"So find out."

"We dug up all the information we could on her. A hospital employee registered the complaint. The investigation was carried out. There wasn't enough evidence for it to stick."

Callum shook his head. "No, you idiot. Find out from *her.*"

Well, that would involve talking to her, and every time he did that, he lost himself in those blue eyes. Got distracted by those curves.

"Uh-oh."

Flynn's muscles tightened. "What?"

"You have that look."

He shouldn't ask. He knew he shouldn't. But... "What look?"

"You're falling for the woman."

"I just met her." Literally four days ago. And in that time, he'd fired her, rehired her under supervision, then attacked her with his lips in his mother's damn kitchen. Not exactly courting behavior.

"What about Victoria?" Callum asked.

"I broke up with her. I don't know what took me so long."

"When?"

"Two days ago." He bent down to lift his bag.

"Did you tell Carina you guys broke up?"

He paused. "No."

Callum gave him a pointed look, and he almost expected another "idiot" to fall from the guy's mouth.

"You think that's it?" Flynn asked.

One side of Callum's mouth lifted. "Only one way to find out."

Yeah, yeah, talk to the woman. Sacrifice his sanity and test his control. Got it.

Callum chuckled, tapping the doorframe. "See you in the conference room."

Flynn nodded before heading down to the bathroom. After a quick shower, he pulled on a T-shirt and jeans. When he stepped into the conference room, he found Aidan sitting at the table, typing away on a computer, and Callum reading something on his phone.

Flynn took a seat. "So, no sign of anyone stalking Simmons or his wife?"

Aidan's eyes remained on the screen while he spoke. "Actually, just before I left last night, I caught a guy in the backyard."

Flynn leaned forward. "Did you detain him? Where is he?"

Finally, Aidan's gaze met his. "Don't know where he is. I didn't catch him."

"What do you mean, you didn't catch him?"

After Project Arma, they were faster than any normal man. Catching a guy in a client's backyard should be child's play.

"I mean, I saw the back of him. Chased him. And when I got to the street, he was gone. It was like he disappeared or something."

Flynn swung his gaze to Callum. His friend gave nothing away. When he looked back at Aidan, Flynn paused for a second. "You think there's some truth to what Paul Simmons said? That the guy stalking them is like us?"

It sounded just as crazy from Flynn as it had coming from Paul.

"I don't know *what* to think, other than we should stick to the couple like glue. See if we can catch a glimpse of this guy again."

Flynn wanted more than a damn glimpse. Suddenly, he itched to get to Idaho Falls.

"Should we let Wyatt's team know?" Callum asked.

Wyatt Gray ran Marble Protection, a self-defense company in Marble Falls, Texas, with seven of his former Navy SEAL brothers. They were also victims of Project Arma. They should be the only other men in the world capable of what Flynn and his team could do.

"Let's wait until we have some concrete evidence before we drop a bomb on everyone."

He prayed that never came to pass, because if there were more men like them but on the wrong side of the law…that was just too damn dangerous to consider.

FLYNN'S GAZE had been on Carina all day. Like, *all* freaking day. It felt like a hot ray of sun beaming down on her. Burning her. But it wasn't just his gaze affecting her. At one point, the man had grabbed her arm and pulled her aside. So she'd done what any normal woman would do while trying to avoid intimacy with a taken man. She'd pressed her hands to his ridiculously muscled chest and pushed him away like he was the Antichrist.

He hadn't touched her again.

She paused while slicing a carrot, glancing over her shoulder. Their gazes clashed, splintering her calm, and she yanked her attention back to the food in front of her.

An involuntary shiver coursed down her spine.

What the heck was wrong with her? It was one kiss!

Yeah, one kiss, two days ago—and it had sent her into fight-or-flight mode. One kiss that had caused her to lose her damn mind. And the worst part was, every time she looked at him, she wanted to lose her mind again.

She gave herself a quick mental shake. No. She couldn't do that. Even if he wasn't in a relationship, *which he was*, he didn't trust her. And she knew that because he was still here. Still watching her. Still making sure she didn't take anything she wasn't supposed to take from his mother's medicine cabinet.

The scraping of a chair against the floorboards almost had her turning again. Almost.

"I'm going to go clean the gutters," he said in that too-sexy-for-her-own-good voice.

His mother, who was working at the stove beside her because she'd flat-out refused to sit down, turned with an exasperated sigh. "Flynn, will you just rest? Or better yet, go home. I'm okay. And I don't need your twenty-four-hour supervision."

Carina almost scoffed, half tempted to tell the woman it wasn't *her* he was supervising. But maybe she knew that and was just trying to lighten the heavy mood.

His steps sounded heavy as he moved closer.

"I want to be here." When he stopped, he was right behind her, so close, she could just about feel his heat penetrating her skin. "And if I don't do the gutters now, I'll just need to do them later."

She snuck a peek at him from beneath her lashes as he leaned in to press a kiss to his mother's cheek. She thought he'd walk away after that. He didn't.

Instead, that big warm hand, the one that felt like it took up her entire back, touched her there again, causing her to jump. The knife suddenly slipped from her fingers, slicing into her skin.

Flynn stopped the knife midslice.

Holy shit, the man moved fast! As in, faster than normal fast. *Again*. How had he—

"Are you okay?"

Before she could finish her thought, he was taking her wrist, studying the shallow cut. His brows were drawn together, and the muscles in his arms flexed. But that wasn't what really had her freezing. It was the way his thumb grazed the palm of her hand and how, in turn, her stomach quivered.

Quickly, she snatched her hand away, taking a hurried step back, her hip colliding with the counter. "I'm fine."

If fine involved teetering on the edge of madness.

The veins in Flynn's neck strained.

Patricia sidled up beside them, a worried look on her face when she saw blood on Carina's finger. "Oh, dear, that doesn't look good."

"It's just a small cut." She spun around, grabbing a piece of paper towel and pressing it to her finger. While her back was to Flynn, she used the moment to take a deep breath. When she turned back, she smiled. "You can go clean the gutters."

The man was still frowning. He reached out again, but she sidestepped the touch.

Too. Dangerous.

"I'm really okay. You should go."

One more glance her way, then he was exhaling loudly and running his hand through his hair. "I need to get some stuff from the shed down the hill."

Patricia's property was large and sloped, and the tool shed was at the very back.

"We'll be okay," she said. *And I won't steal anything.* Because she wasn't entirely sure what he was thinking right now.

The frown deepened. Crap. Could he read her mind? Then he was walking across the room. After the door closed behind him, Carina released a long breath.

Patricia's gaze softened. "Sorry. My son can be a bit intense. He's just like his father was."

She gave the older woman a polite smile. "I'm just going to grab a Band-Aid from the closet in the hall. Are you okay here?"

Patricia turned back to the stove. "Of course."

Carina eyed the meat in the frying pan before turning and heading into the hall. She knew everything that was in Patricia's first-aid kit because she'd checked it herself. It had been one of her first tasks when she started, confirming that everything she might need was here. She'd found that Patricia had more than enough stuff on hand. She was sure Flynn was responsible for that.

After opening the closet door, she pulled out the kit and rummaged around inside for a bandage.

Her brain still couldn't comprehend Flynn grabbing the knife. It happened so fast. Maybe she was mixing things up in her head, because surely, he hadn't moved as quickly as her mind was telling her. That was impossible. She remembered Superman-type speed. Absurd.

Grabbing the bandage, she quickly unwrapped it and stuck it over the cut.

She was just closing the door when a framed photo hanging on the wall caught her attention. It was the same one she noticed every time she passed it. Carefully, she traced the outline of Flynn's face. He looked young. Eighteen, maybe? He stood between a younger Patricia and a man she assumed to be his father. He wore a backpack over his shoulder, and he looked happy. Even then, he'd been handsome.

Was that the day he'd left for the military? He looked about the right age, and his parents seemed so proud.

For a moment, she wondered what might have been if he'd met her before everything happened in Michigan. Could he have fallen for her? Trusted her? Blowing out a long breath, she dropped her hand before heading toward the kitchen.

She'd only made it a few steps before the smoke alarm suddenly blasted through the house.

She took off, running the rest of the way. A gasp slipped from her lips when she saw smoke billowing from the burned meat.

Patricia had already grabbed the pan off the stove, so Carina turned to the smoke alarm on the high ceiling. It was between the open kitchen and dining room, right above a tall oak bookcase.

Moving on instinct, she grabbed a chair from the table and positioned it in front of the bookcase. After climbing onto the seat, she reached up, stretching on her tiptoes as she attempted to press the button.

So. Damn. Close.

Grasping the edge of one of the bookshelves, she used it to tug herself the last couple inches.

Almost there...

Finally, she pressed the little button, silencing the alarm—just as the chair slid from beneath her feet.

Carina grabbed the shelf to keep from falling, but the entire bookcase itself tilted forward, pulled off balance by her weight, and books and CDs clattering to the floor.

She screeched, then her breath was knocked out as she hit the floor hard—frozen in horror as the tall case fell toward her, books hitting her chest and legs.

She was seconds from being squashed when suddenly the door to the house flew open and Flynn was there, bent in front of her, catching the heavy piece of furniture with his back.

For a moment, she was still, fear and confusion swirling through her mind, stealing her voice. Not only because he'd just caught what was easily a two-hundred-pound bookcase like it weighed nothing, but because he'd literally been all the way across the room one second, and in front of her the next.

Patricia gasped from the kitchen. "Flynny! Oh, I'm so glad you caught it!"

Carina's limbs iced. What *was* he?

Flynn righted the bookcase and shot a glance at his mother. "Are you okay?"

"Yes! My goodness!" She shook her head, obviously shaken. "Who would have thought the time would come when I'd be grateful for Project Arma?"

Carina's breath sawed in and out of her chest. Project Arma? What the heck was that?

Patricia looked her way. "Dear, are you okay?"

Flynn stepped forward, reaching a hand out, but she scuttled away, not wanting the man—if he *was* even a man—to touch her.

That familiar frown returned to his face. "Are you hurt?"

"How did you do that?"

His expression remained the same. "What do you mean?"

What did she mean? Was he *serious*? "How did you move so fast? Why are you so strong?"

A beat of quiet passed. His words were oddly calm when he finally spoke. "You don't know about me being taken?"

"Taken? Where were you taken?"

He took another step forward, but she scrambled back again, her back hitting the leg of the dining room table. She used it to tug herself to her feet.

Patricia stepped forward. "Carina, it was all over the news."

She grabbed her bag off the table, edging toward the door while keeping as much distance between her and Flynn as possi-ble. "When everything started happening in Michigan, I stopped watching the news and listening to the radio, and I deleted all my social media accounts."

She still caught snippets of the news, of course. Hell, it was impossible to avoid in this day and age. But she'd never heard anything about men who were preternaturally faster or stronger.

"I was kidnapped," Flynn said quietly. "Drugged. My DNA was altered. Now I'm faster and stronger than I should be. I can hear things others can't. Heal faster. See in the dark."

Her heart gave a giant thud. That wasn't possible... Was it? There were no drugs in existence that could do any of that to someone.

"Who took you?" She couldn't believe those words left her mouth. She should be asking which psych ward he'd escaped from. Her brain must be malfunctioning.

"A military commander. He was trying to create his own army of elite soldiers."

That sounded like something from a sci-fi movie.

"I've got to go." Before her brain completely exploded.

Flynn moved forward, but Carina held up her hands to stop him. "No, no. I'm okay. I'll be back tomorrow."

Probably. Hopefully.

She turned on her heels and walked out, all but running from the man who had just told her he was barely human.

CHAPTER 7

*D*NA-altering drugs. Faster than a speeding car. Bullet wounds that heal in days.

What the hell was she reading? None of it could be true.

It is, a small voice whispered in her head. *You saw it with your own eyes.*

Carina massaged her temple. Shock ricocheted through her limbs. *Had been* ricocheting for the last hour since she'd gotten home, plonked her butt on the couch and started researching.

Her gaze danced over the words again. Abducted. Held hostage. Drugged. The man had been a prisoner, *a victim*, and now he was…well, something else entirely. It was crazy.

Her fingers trembled as she used the touch pad to open another website. It said the same. They all did.

Everyone had known. Everyone but her, apparently. Because she'd become a hermit over the last several months.

And it wasn't just Flynn. All the men from Blue Halo had been taken, held on some large, remote property, forcibly given drugs against their will.

No wonder the men were so close. To go through something like that, you'd have no choice if you wanted to survive. It also explained why Flynn felt so obligated to his mother. He hadn't said the words out loud, but she'd seen it in the way he looked at her. Doted on her. Visited every single day.

He felt guilty for not being there when she'd started her descent into Alzheimer's.

She clicked out of the latest article and rested against the cushions. Unbelievable. But true.

She rose from the couch and moved over to the kitchen. On the way, her gaze caught on the new note that had been slipped into her mailbox. This one read similar to the last. Something about getting out of town before it was too late.

Argh. Those damn kids.

Blowing out a frustrated breath, she opened the fridge. She wasn't hungry. Which was probably lucky, because there was diddly squat in terms of food. She could always order in. Or she could just eat a plate of cheese and crackers paired with a bottle of red. She smiled. Who was she kidding? That had always been the plan.

She reached into the fridge, lifted the cheese and wine, then grabbed the crackers from the cupboard.

Once she was settled outside, she leaned back in her seat. It was appropriate to drink an entire bottle of wine when you found out big, otherworldly information, right? Of course it was. If anything, it was expected.

She was already into her second glass and halfway through the cheese when her phone rang. Greg's name popped up and, for a moment, she considered letting it go to voicemail. But she'd already done that to his last three calls, not to mention the unanswered texts.

Setting down the wineglass, she answered the call. "Hi, Greg."

"Carina." There was a small pause. "I wasn't expecting you to answer."

She traced the rim of the glass with her index finger. "Sorry.

I've been dealing with the new job, new town and just getting everything organized."

"That's okay. How's it all going?"

Hm. Well, she'd learned about supersoldiers with crazy abilities. She'd been fired and then rehired under supervision. And she'd kissed a man she barely knew. So…busy?

"It's okay. Different."

For a moment, Greg didn't respond. She was on the verge of asking if he was still there when he finally broke the silence. "I miss you."

Her heart panged at his words. Their breakup had been one-sided. Her side. She'd done it only a week before leaving town. Which made her horrible, right? Because Greg had been nothing short of an incredible partner.

He was a doctor at the hospital where she'd previously worked, and when the accusation happened, he'd insisted he believed her. Assured her that everything would be okay. He'd even invited her to move into his place when she hadn't been able to pay her rent due to loss of income.

"I'm sorry, Greg. I know I didn't give you a lot of time to come to terms with our breakup."

"I don't even know what I did wrong."

Her eyes shuttered. "Nothing. You did nothing wrong. You were an amazing boyfriend. I just…I need some time away. A new town. A new start."

And just like she'd told Patricia, she hadn't felt that *thing*. The thing that made her excited and nervous and giddy.

The thing that Flynn made her feel without even trying.

Another stab of guilt hit her chest.

"I could have gone with you," Greg said quietly.

She shook her head even though he couldn't see it. They'd barely been dating six months. "We weren't at that stage in our relationship. We—"

She stopped when something from the side of the house caught her attention. A sound.

Wait… Was that…?

Another cracking sound.

No. Freaking. Way!

"I'm sorry, Greg. I'm gonna need to call you back."

Before he could respond, she hung up, rose from her seat, and rushed around to the side of the house that faced her less-than-welcoming neighbors' place.

Yep. Those damn boys from next door were throwing freaking eggs at her house again!

"Hey!" she shouted, marching forward.

They paused and turned to face her. But if she'd expected to see fear or hesitation, she didn't. They both faced her and smirked.

"Look who it is." The taller one scoffed. "You gonna call the cops on us again, bitch?"

Bitch? What the heck was wrong with these kids? "Yeah, damn straight I'll call the police. Get the hell off my property."

She was tempted to tell them to clean up their mess, but she didn't want them anywhere near her house.

"Or what?" the slightly shorter boy asked, anger blazing in his gaze. "You go crying to our mom again?"

They both laughed.

Carina lifted her phone. She'd had enough.

She'd only typed in the first number before the cell was yanked from her fingers. "Hey!"

The taller kid laughed and tossed it to his twin. She stomped up to his brother. "Give it back *now*."

He laughed in her face and tossed it back to his brother.

Okay. Now she was *really* pissed. She stormed back to the other kid and reached for the phone, but he lifted it above his head with one hand and shoved her back with the other. The shove was hard, causing her to stumble backward.

Closing her eyes, she braced, expecting to hit the ground for the second time today.

Instead, strong hands caught her waist, righting her.

The kid who'd pushed her gaped, and his eyes widened. "Where the hell did you come from?"

She shot a glance over her shoulder.

Flynn. His eyes were on her, and they were soft as he asked, "Are you okay?"

She gave a quick nod because that was about all she could muster. When his gaze rose to the taller boy, the softness dropped. And in its place was an anger so vicious it almost had Carina stepping away.

The man looked murderous.

ANGER POUNDED through Flynn's chest, heating his blood. He'd barely stepped around the house when he saw the kid push her.

Then he saw red.

He lunged forward, grabbing the kid by the shirt. "Give me the fucking phone."

The teenager handed it to him, and he quickly shoved it into his pocket. Then he lowered his head and his voice. "You and your brother are going to clean the shit off the windows. Then you're going to stay the fuck off her property. If you come *anywhere* near her or her house again, it won't just be the police you're dealing with." He lowered his head even further. "I'll fucking break you. Got it?"

The kid nodded, his body trembling in Flynn's hold. "Got it!"

Flynn shot a look at the other kid. "*You* got it?"

The boy inched backward, his eyes wide, looking just as scared as his brother. He nodded.

It wasn't enough. "Say it."

"I—I got it!"

"Good. I expect these windows to be crystal fucking clean in the next ten minutes."

He shoved the kid back in much the same way the boy had done to Carina. He hadn't even hit the ground before Flynn turned, took Carina's hand in his own, and led her around the back. He was about to step inside when she stopped, tugging her hand from his and grabbing a wineglass and half-eaten plate of cheese and crackers off the table. He snagged the wine bottle and trailed inside after her.

She quickly lowered the items onto the island before moving to the other side. Was she trying to keep space between them? Intentionally standing as far as she could without actually leaving the room?

"Have they done anything like that before?" he asked quietly, still feeling far too on edge.

Her gaze shot to the windows, and he had his answer before her words came out.

"Tell me."

She swallowed. "I came home to egg on my windows three days ago. I tried talking to their mother, but she didn't care."

He moved around the island slowly, testing to see whether she'd inch away. She didn't, and something in his chest loosened the tiniest bit. "The whole town knows about the Brown twins. They're assholes who like to cause trouble. Have they touched you before?"

There was the slightest widening of her eyes, and he didn't know whether she realized she was doing it, but her hands ran up and down her arms. "No. But I've never confronted them."

"I want you to tell me if they do anything like that again. Okay?" So he could murder the little shits. He took another slow step toward her.

"Okay."

For a moment, he studied her face, wondering how much of

the pale complexion was due to the Brown twins and how much was due to what she'd learned about him.

"How are you feeling after today?" he asked. She'd been scared when she left his mother's house. And he hated that.

"I'm okay."

"Are you okay with what I am?" He was now around the island, with nothing between them.

"Mm-hmm."

One side of his mouth lifted. "Not all that convincing, honey."

Her mouth opened and closed. "It's just...a lot to take in."

He took the final step forward so that she was within reaching distance. His hand twitched. "I'm still the same person I was. Just..."

"Stronger? Faster? A bit enhanced?"

He chuckled. "Yeah. A bit of all of that."

When she didn't step away from him, he raised his hand to touch her arm. The zing that shot through his system was immediate. A zing of awareness. Of desire.

She felt it too. He could tell by the quick intake of breath. The little flutter of her heartbeat.

When her gaze shot to his lips, his gut clenched. She needed to stop doing that. All he wanted to do was kiss the woman. Taste her again. Feel her soft body against him. And those blue eyes of hers, focused on his mouth, weren't damn well helping.

When his gaze went to her lips in return, her hand pressed to his chest, and she took a step back. "We shouldn't."

"Why?"

"Because you're taken."

Ah. So Callum was right. He moved forward. "Victoria and I broke up the night you saw us at the restaurant."

She took another step back. "Oh...well...you need time—"

"I don't. I should have ended it two months ago, after our first date."

Another step forward for him. Another step back for her.

"Okay. But you still don't trust me."

"I do." He tilted his head. "You're a great fit for my mother. I realized that after the first hour I watched you caring for her."

There was a slight crease between her brows. This time, when he invaded her personal space, she didn't back away. "But you've still been watching me."

"Maybe I couldn't stay away." He lowered his head, touching his lips to the skin just below her ear. Her shudder trembled against him. "Maybe I was desperate to spend time with you."

God, she smelled good. And the feel of her skin against his mouth... He pressed another kiss to her flesh, this time along her jaw.

"I'm going away for a job tomorrow. So you won't see me there for the next few days." It was a blow, when all he wanted to do was explore this. Explore *her*. "I'd like to see more of you when I get back, though." His breath brushed her skin with his words.

"You barely know me," she whispered.

His hand curved around her waist. He pressed a kiss to her cheek. "I know. But I feel something. And I know you feel it too."

On the next kiss, he touched the corner of her mouth. Her lips separated. She didn't pull away. In fact, she leaned into him.

He sealed his mouth to hers, plunging his tongue between her lips. She was just as fucking sweet as last time. And the kiss... It was heat and fire and a million other things. Kissing her was like nothing he'd ever experienced before, with anyone. And he wanted more.

His hands tightened on her hips, and he lifted her before sitting her on the island and shifting between her thighs. A whimper escaped her throat, making his hands tighten, his blood roar between his ears.

Fuck, but he burned for the woman.

His hand trailed up her stomach, her ribs, then his fingers closed around a plump breast. Another quiet whimper from

Carina. He swallowed it, finding her taut nipple through her shirt and brushing his thumb across the hard peak.

Her body jolted and trembled in his arms as her fingers held his ribs.

He trailed his lips down her cheek, landing on her neck. With a sigh, she ground against him, slowly, damn near destroying him. He was ready. So fucking ready to take her to the bedroom that it was a physical pain.

Her hand pressed to his chest.

"Flynn." Her voice was breathy. He sucked a spot on her neck, reveling at the shudder down her spine. "We should stop."

They should, but it was so damn hard when his entire body ached for her. Slowly, he unlatched his lips and pressed a final kiss to her skin before lifting his head. Her eyes were glazed, the light blue now looking close to navy.

Fucking radiant.

"What the hell do you do to me?" he rasped, stunned by what the woman made him feel.

Her mouth lifted into a small smile. "The same thing you do to me."

He lowered his head, eyes closing. "I'll be away for a few days. But I meant what I said. When I come back, I want us to pick up where we left off. No running from this, Carina."

He couldn't allow that.

When he opened his eyes, it was to see her bottom lips between her teeth. He almost groaned out loud. The woman was going to be the death of him.

CHAPTER 8

"Your father and I miss you, honey. Will you be coming home soon?"

Carina sighed as she headed into the kitchen. It had only been two weeks. "I miss you both too, but I'm not coming back. I'm not saying I'll be gone forever. For now, at least, I'm enjoying the change."

Understatement of the century. Not being in a town where every second person she ran into looked at her like she was a drugged-up felon was a breath of fresh air.

This time it was her mother who sighed. "Okay. Are you at least making new friends?"

Did the lady at the grocery store count? She used the woman's first name when she thanked her. Patricia was a patient so she couldn't really be classified as a friend. And Flynn…

Nope. Definitely not. He was something, but the term friend didn't quite fit.

"I'm meeting a lot of new people and am very happy." Yeah, that worked.

She opened the fridge. No food again. At least none that could be scrounged together and turned into dinner. God, she really needed to get better at that. She'd gotten so used to Greg taking care of everything those last few months in Michigan during the accusation nightmare, it was like she'd forgotten how to adult.

"Have you talked to Greg?"

Carina almost rolled her eyes. Her mother had all but fallen in love with the man, and her father hadn't been far behind. She was pretty sure the two of them had already started planning the wedding.

"I have. He's been checking in to make sure I'm settling okay."

She was careful to emphasize the "checking in" part because she *did not* want her mother getting any ideas about them getting back together.

"Oh, that man is so lovely. Your father and I were so sad when you broke up."

Another eye roll. *Like you've said a gazillion times, Mom.*

Carina crossed the room and picked up her keys. "I have to go now, Mom. I need to get to the grocery store before they close."

"Oh. Okay, honey. I love you."

"Love you too."

The second the call ended, Carina shook her head. She really did love her mother, but the woman had always thought she knew best when it came to Carina's life. And her mother's version of "best" rarely aligned with her own.

She walked into her bedroom, shooting a quick look outside and noticing it had just started to rain. Great. Quickly, she changed out of her sweatpants and into some jeans.

A couple of days had passed since Flynn left. Days of the man tormenting her every thought. Of flashbacks to the best kisses of her life.

Her cheeks heated at the memory.

She had no idea when he was returning, and she didn't want to text and ask. His job was sometimes dangerous, and she didn't want to distract him from that. He'd said he'd be away a couple of days, so he should be returning anytime now.

When she'd walked into Patricia's home this morning, she'd held her breath, hoping she'd see the guy sitting at the table. Maybe leaning against the kitchen counter with that sexy grin on his face.

Perhaps tomorrow. Her heart gave a little thump at the thought.

Quickly, she slipped on some shoes then headed out.

She was turning to lock the door when her gaze caught on the twins in their yard. They were walking up the steps of their front porch. Both watched her closely. And the way they looked at her... it had a chill sliding down her spine.

They're just teenagers, Carina, she quickly reminded herself.

She turned back and locked the door.

Over the last couple days, there had been one more letter but no egg on the windows. She wasn't sure she'd do anything about the notes or tell Flynn about them because they were harmless, right? Well, that was what she kept telling herself anyway.

Why she was trying to save the boys from the wrath of Flynn, she had no idea. Some ingrained need to protect kids, maybe? Her own aversion to violence?

Blowing out a breath, she turned to the porch stairs. She'd taken just one step when her foot slid on something wet. She swung her arms to try to save herself but fell down the steps quickly, unable to stop the momentum. Her knee collided with the concrete ground at an odd angle, quickly followed by her head.

She barely had time to register the pain when dots clouded her vision. The faint sound of laughter from the boys next door was the last thing she heard before darkness consumed her.

~

CARINA SUCKED SLOW, deep breaths into her chest. It was all she could think of to try to dull the pain. How much time had passed since she'd awakened to find herself in a hospital? She was sure it was only a few minutes, but every minute felt like ten.

Her head and knee ached. Especially her knee. The pain was a constant throb, which had her vision hedging.

She looked for the call button. It was too far. She could probably lean over enough to reach it, but God, just the thought had her breaking into a sweat.

She looked back to the hall, hoping—praying—that a nurse or doctor would enter the room. More minutes passed, and nothing.

Eventually, she shut her eyes and once again concentrated on her breathing.

"You're awake."

She jolted at the sudden voice, and a fresh wave of pain shot through her skull, causing her to scrunch her eyes tightly.

The nurse cringed. "Sorry. How are you feeling?"

Carina swallowed to wet her dry throat before focusing on the nurse again. "Not great. Can I get some pain medication?"

The nurse nodded. "I'll just call your doctor in."

Carina tried for a small smile but was sure it came off more like a grimace.

The nurse left the room, and less than a minute later, the door opened again. Carina's lips separated when she saw the woman who walked in.

Flynn's ex, Victoria.

Really? It wasn't enough she'd fallen down the steps of her porch, but she had to get this woman as a doctor?

Victoria gave a tight smile. "Hi, Carina. It's nice to see you again. In this hospital, I'm referred to as Dr. Victoria Astor, and I'm looking after you today."

Carina gave the woman a small nod.

"Do you remember what happened?"

She frowned. "Um, I think I just slipped on my porch." It had just started to rain, so that had to be it, right?

"You did. A neighbor across the street saw, said you landed

heavily and at a bad angle. She called the paramedics. You have a concussion and five stitches in your forehead. The worst of your injuries was the dislocated patella."

Well, that explained the knee pain.

"Your knee must have taken the brunt of the impact when you landed," Victoria continued. "The good news is, surgery wasn't required and the patella is back in place, but you've damaged the tissues around the knee, which has resulted in visible swelling and pain. We recommend you wear a knee brace for at least a week. I can give you the details of a store in Cradle Mountain where you can get one. You'll have pain for about a month."

Carina frowned, trying to take it all in.

"It's about four a.m. right now," Victoria continued. "In a couple of hours, I can discharge you and you'll be free to go."

She gave another small nod, the motion radiating pain throughout her skull. "That sounds fine."

"Great. Oh, and also, if your car is manual, I'd try to avoid driving it for a couple of weeks."

Well, that was just perfect, because her car *was* manual.

The doctor started to turn, but Carina stopped her.

"Could I get some pain medication?"

The corners of Victoria's eyes tightened. "I'll send the nurse in with some Tylenol."

Tylenol? Surely, she could get something stronger?

She opened her mouth to ask, but Victoria was already gone.

When the nurse stepped back in, she handed Carina the pills.

"Any chance I could get something stronger?"

"Sorry, Miss Murphy, this is what Dr. Astor has prescribed."

Carina opened her mouth, not sure if she was about to argue or ask for a new doctor, when the nurse spoke again.

"Get some rest if you can before you get discharged." Then the nurse disappeared before Carina could say another word.

Maybe if she just gave it a bit of time.

She closed her eyes, tried to clear her mind, but the pain radiating from her knee kept her wide awake. When the sun finally began to poke through the window, the nurse returned with discharge papers.

"I brought a phone so you can call someone to pick you up. Your cell is dead."

Someone to pick her up. Like a friend or family member. Neither of which she had at the moment. Not here, anyway. She slid the phone from the woman's fingers. "Um, do you have the number for Blue Halo Security?"

The nurse's brows rose. "No. But I can get it for you."

The woman returned a second later, handing her a piece of paper.

Carina bit her lip as she typed the number and put the phone to her ear.

"Blue Halo Security. Callum speaking."

"Um, hi." Carina watched as the nurse left the room. "This is Carina. I work for Patricia Talbot. I was just wondering if Flynn was back in town yet?"

"No, sorry, he's away right now. Would you like me to get in touch with him? Or leave him a message?"

Her heart sank. He was her only option. She was tempted to ask when he'd be back, but Callum hadn't willingly offered the information, so she was hesitant. "No. That's okay. I'll, um, call back later."

"Is Patricia okay?"

"Oh, yes. Sorry. I didn't mean to make you think she wasn't. She's fine."

Suddenly, she felt silly for calling. The last thing she wanted to do was make anyone worry about Flynn's mother, especially the man himself while he was working.

"I'll call back. Thank you, Callum."

She quickly hung up, staring at the phone. The pain continued to thrum throughout her body, this time mingling with exhaustion and frustration. Tears pressed at the back of her eyes.

The nurse stepped back inside the room. "How'd it go?"

She quickly blinked away the tears. "Someone's coming to get me."

She didn't know why she lied. Maybe because she felt sorry for herself, and didn't need anyone else feeling sorry for her, too. Or maybe she was just too tired and sore to say more than necessary.

"It wouldn't be possible to get another doctor, would it? To get some stronger pain medication?"

At the sympathetic look on the nurse's face, Carina already knew the answer to her question. "We've just had a bit of a rush in the ER. You're welcome to wait, but it might be an hour or two. Or I can see if a doctor could see you between patients."

Her heart sank. Squeezing her in would mean a longer wait for others. She didn't want to do that. And she didn't want to wait an hour or two, either. All she wanted was to get home, put on her sweats, and hide in bed. Maybe if the pain was still bad tomorrow, she'd come back. "Actually, I think I should be okay."

The nurse beamed. "Great."

Once she'd signed the discharge forms, the nurse helped her out of bed. The second she put weight on her knee, she almost crumbled at the severe pain. Getting dressed, even with help, was just as hard. She paused so many times to catch her breath that the process took ten times what it normally would.

She shuddered at the thought of doing this on her own at home.

The nurse disappeared from the room and returned a second later with a wheelchair. When they got to a waiting room near the entrance, Carina stopped the woman. "Here's fine. My ride will be here in a few minutes."

"Oh. Okay."

The second the nurse disappeared, she pushed to her feet. Pain. Mega-pain. It was instant. God, this was terrible. She had to grit her teeth and lock her knees to stay upright. Every step to the nurses' station had her breath catching in her throat.

When she reached the desk, the lady on the other side barely looked up from the forms she was filling out. "Yes?"

"I was wondering if I could use a phone to call a taxi or car service."

lynn took the stairs up to Blue Halo two at a time. It was mid-afternoon. He'd gotten back a day later than planned, only returning this morning. He'd gone home for an hour of sleep before coming to work, even though he was beyond ready to check on his mother. And Carina.

He pushed inside the reception area, not surprised to see no one at the desk. They'd had a receptionist for a short period of time, but that hadn't ended well, so now they just alternated admin duties. And with both their advanced hearing and the cameras they'd had installed, having someone at the desk wasn't really a priority, though they'd probably hire someone again at some point.

As he moved down the hallway toward his office, Callum called his name.

He stopped and turned back.

Callum sat behind his desk. "Welcome back. How'd it go?"

"No sighting of anyone. If Aidan hadn't spotted a guy in the backyard last week, I'd almost think they were making up their stalker."

Callum nodded. "We're continuing protective detail though, right?"

"Yeah. The guy's still desperate to keep us, so we'll stay." Logan and Jason were there right now. They'd keep alternating until the time came when they either found someone or Paul let their team go. "Everything smooth sailing here?"

Callum lifted a shoulder. He was the biggest of the team, but he was also the biggest softie. "No issues."

"Great. I'm just gonna check emails, then I'm off again to see Mom."

Flynn was moments from stepping away when Callum spoke again. "Almost forgot. Carina called for you this morning. Didn't leave a message though or tell me what she wanted."

Flynn frowned. "What did she say?"

"Just asked if you were back. When I said no, she sounded disappointed. Said she'd call back. I asked about your mom, and she said she was fine."

Flynn nodded. He hadn't told his team what had transpired between him and Carina the night before he left, but they knew *something* had. It would be hard not to, considering how well they all knew each other. "Thanks. If she's not at Mom's, I'll stop by her place after."

"Really?" Callum said it with that just-tell-me-you're-dating-already voice.

Flynn shook his head with a grin. "Bye."

He checked his emails and messages quickly, relieved to find there was nothing that couldn't wait. On his way out, he checked the time—after three in the afternoon. Maybe he could surprise Carina with some dinner.

In all honesty, he had no idea how the woman would react to food or a date or any of that. All they'd done was kiss. There had been no words spoken about moving the relationship forward, but God, he wanted to. Just a few days away from her had already confirmed that. Even though he'd been in the middle of a job, he'd thought about her every damn day.

When he pulled up to his mother's house, he noticed Carina's car wasn't there, but she often walked, so it didn't necessarily mean she wasn't.

He entered the house and found his mother sitting at the table doing a puzzle. She looked up. "Hello, honey."

Flynn swallowed his disappointment at Carina's absence. He moved over to his mother and pressed a kiss to her head. "How are you?"

"I feel really good today."

He lowered into a seat beside her. She *did* look good. Like the mother who'd raised him. Her smile was wide, and her hands looked steady.

He pressed a hand over hers. "I'm glad."

"How was the job?"

He smiled. His mother knew all about his work. Not the specifics of the jobs. But she understood what they involved... mainly protecting people. "It went well. Didn't catch any bad guys but the couple I was watching remained safe."

Patricia gave a sharp nod. "Good. I worry about you while you're away."

"No need to worry." His fingers tightened around hers. "Everything been okay while I've been gone?"

Her gaze lifted, her eyes warming. "Oh, yes. Carina has been an absolute angel." She frowned. "She should have stayed home today though. I told her to go, but she refused to leave until she'd prepared some food."

"Why should she have stayed home?"

"The poor thing hurt her knee and had a bandage over her head. She was limping all over the place and grimacing in pain at every step. I think she was trying to make it seem like it wasn't as bad as it was. I finally made her leave. She said something about a fall."

Unease slammed into his gut. "She was hurt?"

"Oh, yes. You should go check on her. I was quite worried when I saw her. I think she even called Clemence to take her home."

Clemence ran the only car service available in Cradle Mountain.

His heart rate tripled, every part of him wanting to go to her. He scanned the kitchen. "I'll get your dinner—"

She shook her head. "Flynn, it's almost four o'clock. I don't need dinner right now. But when I do, I'm perfectly capable of heating the stew Carina made for me."

"Sure?"

"Yes. Go."

Rising to his feet, he pressed a kiss to his mother's head before walking out to his car. Anxiety swirled through him. And questions. So many questions. Was she okay? Why had she gone to work while injured? And what the hell had happened?

CARINA MASSAGED HER TEMPLE. She lay on the couch, ice on her knee. The ice was doing nothing to numb the pain, and the Tylenol felt just as useless for her headache as it did for her knee. She was so damn tired. But she couldn't sleep through the pain. It was impossible.

Maybe she shouldn't have visited Patricia today. It definitely hadn't helped. Even though she'd called Clemence to get her there and back, the time on her feet had been agony. And the headache was now ten times worse.

But it was her job. And with Flynn away, she'd needed to make sure his mom was okay.

The ringing of her phone had Carina's eyes squeezing shut. Blindly, she reached for the cell from the coffee table and brought it to her ear. "Hello?"

"Hi, Carina. It's me."

Me, as in Greg.

"Hi, Greg," she said softly with her eyes still closed.

There was a small pause. "Are you okay?"

"Yeah, I just had a little fall yesterday." Was it yesterday? The last twenty-four hours felt like one big jumbled mess.

"What kind of fall?"

She breathed through the ache pounding from her knee. "I slipped and fell down the porch steps. Dislocated my knee."

"Christ. Are you okay?"

No. She felt far from okay. "Just resting."

"I'll take some leave from work and come help you."

"No, Greg, you don't—"

Knocking at the door cut her off. Carina almost groaned, not only because the sound was loud on her already aching head but because she would have to walk over there to answer it.

Lord, give her strength.

"Someone's at the door. I'll call you back, okay?"

She hung up before he could respond. Sucking in a sharp breath, she stood. Every step was slow and had her leaning heavily against any surface she could get her hands on. She really needed to get that knee brace.

The second she tugged open the door, her eyes widened. Flynn—looking tall and handsome and angry.

He frowned at the way she leaned on the door. Then he scanned her face. Her body. When he took a large step forward, his gaze stopped on her forehead. She'd taken the bandage off, so she was sure it looked bruised and ugly.

His finger grazed the area around the cut. The touch oddly soothing.

"What happened?" His tone was low. It reminded her of the calm before a storm.

"I slipped," she said quietly, still in shock that the man was here. "Fell down the steps."

He turned back, scanning the porch. "Here?"

She nodded. When she got home, she'd actually studied the wood where she'd slipped, just to make sure there was nothing there. That the teenagers hadn't coated it with some slippery substance. It had been completely dry. "It was raining."

His eyes darkened as he looked back at her. "When?"

"Yesterday evening."

Another stroke of his thumb. "Are you okay?"

No. "Yes." Another lie, just like the one she'd given Greg.

The corners of his eyes creased. "Where did you spend the night?"

"The hospital."

A small growl released from his chest as he closed the door behind him. She limped a step away, but that was as far as she got before he stopped her with hands on her hips. He slipped around her. "What happened to your knee?"

"It dislocated when I hit the ground."

His jaw clenched before he gently lifted her, cradling her against his chest. Even though he'd done it carefully, she still cringed at the sudden pain that radiated up her leg.

He cursed under his breath. "Sorry." Slowly, he laid her on the couch before crouching beside her. "What can I do?"

She swallowed. "You don't have to—"

"Carina. You need help, and I want to be that help. What can I do?"

She could have cried. She *did* need help, and the fact this man was offering it to her was almost too much for her fragile heart to bear.

"Right now, I just need some rest," she whispered. "But maybe you could order some dinner a bit later."

She'd never made it to the grocery store, so her kitchen was still empty. Not that she was very hungry. And even if she had groceries, she doubted she'd have the energy to prepare any food. Just making dinner for Patricia earlier had sapped her.

He gently pushed some hair from her face. "Done."

The man remained where he was for a second, his blue gaze bleeding into her. The fingers at her head trailed along the side of the cut again. "I'm sorry I wasn't here. Did you get home from the hospital okay?"

She nodded. "Once Victoria—I mean, Dr. Astor—discharged me, a nurse gave me Clemence's number."

Flynn frowned. "Victoria was your doctor?"

She gave a small nod, regretting it immediately.

The muscles in his arms bunched. "Where's your pain medication?"

"On the table." Fat lot of help they were doing.

Flynn turned, grabbing the small container. "This is only Tylenol."

"That's all Dr. Astor would prescribe."

If she'd thought he looked angry before, that was nothing compared to now. He looked murderous. "She would only prescribe you *Tylenol?*"

She swallowed. "Yes. And it's done nothing. I can't sleep. I can barely move."

His eyes closed as he took a deep breath, like he was trying to control his emotions. When he opened them again, he gave her cheek a final graze before rising and pulling his phone from his pocket.

"Hi, is Dr. Victoria Astor on?" There was a short pause. Carina cringed when the veins in his hand popped as his fingers tightened around the phone. "Okay, thanks."

A second later, he hung up. Then he was bending down beside her. This time when he lifted her, he did it so carefully that there was no added pain.

She grabbed at his shoulders. "What are you doing?"

"She's not on, but it doesn't matter. We're going back to the hospital, and we're not leaving until you receive the medication you need."

She opened her mouth to say no but then snapped it shut. She was exhausted. And her knee was throbbing so badly she felt it in every part of her body. There was no way for her to get the rest she so desperately needed like this.

Carina kept her eyes closed the entire drive there as she breathed through the ache in her leg. Flynn was silent, but the anger was just about bouncing off him, simmering in the air.

He parked, then was around to her side in a second, carefully lifting her out. She leaned her head against his hard chest and took a moment to appreciate the warmth and strength that surrounded her. The comfort that strength brought could almost make her forget the pain.

When he stopped at the reception desk, the nurse's eyes widened. Whether that was because he was so big, or she recognized who he was, or because he was carrying Carina, she had no idea.

"We need to speak to a doctor." Flynn's tone wasn't raised, but that deadly quiet was almost worse, and Carina didn't miss the way other nurses near the station stopped in their tracks.

"Oh, okay, um…sure." For a moment, the woman seemed flustered, but then she quickly organized for a nurse to usher them into a patient room.

Once Flynn had set her on the bed, he stood by her side, his jaw unbelievably hard, like he was preparing to fight a battle.

Usually, Carina preferred to fight her own battles. Lord knew she'd done it enough. But right now, being injured…it felt good to have someone else's help.

She was just lying back when Victoria walked past the room and glanced inside. She stopped, her eyes on Flynn, and a frown formed between her brows. Then she stepped inside. When her gaze touched Carina, her lips thinned. But they spread into a smile when her attention returned to Flynn.

"Flynn. I'm just starting my shift. What are you doing here?"

"What the hell, Victoria? You prescribe her Tylenol when she dislocated her fucking knee?"

"Flynn—"

"She needs stronger pain medication."

Victoria paused, and the smile slipped from her lips. "We can't do that, unfortunately. Not with her history."

A chill swept through Carina's insides, a gasp slipping from her lips. How did she—

"I know she stole drugs from her patient. I will not contribute to the woman's addiction."

Flynn stepped closer, and Victoria's eyes widened. She looked like she was about to step back, away from the clear threat.

"She was cleared of that accusation. She doesn't have an 'addiction', as you put it. Now do your job and prescribe her the damn meds she needs before I get you fired."

CHAPTER 10

"*O*h my gosh, I feel like a new person."

A new *tired* person, that was. With the stronger medication, the pain had finally dulled, but in its place came pure exhaustion.

She leaned her head back on the couch, and her eyes threatened to close. It had been nearly impossible to keep them open since Flynn had placed her there. But she forced herself to remain awake by sheer will, knowing she'd sleep better with some food in her stomach.

"Good." Flynn was in the kitchen preparing dinner. He was like an angel disguised as a man. "You shouldn't be in pain."

There was still that same edge to his voice.

She bit her lip as she watched him move around the kitchen. No one had ever stood up for her like he had in the hospital. Even in the middle of the drug case in Michigan, her parents and Greg had said they believed her. But her lawyer was the only one who'd actually fought for her.

Still, she couldn't help but wonder why Flynn *had* to. How had Victoria known about what happened in Michigan?

"What are you thinking about?"

Flynn's words cut into her thoughts. "I'm wondering how you're making dinner when I have no ingredients."

He gave her a look that said he didn't believe her, which was fair. She'd never been good at hiding the truth. But she also didn't lie. She honestly *didn't* have much in the house.

"You had some pumpkin and leek, so I've made a pumpkin soup."

Ah, that's what smelled so amazing. She'd always loved a good pumpkin soup. "So you're cute, kind, *and* you can cook. That's like the full package."

He chuckled, and his eyes crinkled at the edges. Her heart gave a little thud against her ribs. "I don't know about the whole package. I can be pretty damn grumpy sometimes. I've even been called an asshole on the odd occasion." Carina laughed. "But in terms of cooking, I got better when Dad passed away. Mom needed a lot of support, so I took some leave. I cooked for her a lot."

The smile slipped from her lips. "Your mom told me it was cancer."

He nodded. "We caught it too late. By the time he was diagnosed, we only had him for a few more weeks."

Carina pressed a hand to her chest. "I'm so sorry. What a horrible time."

Flynn's brows tugged together. "Sometimes I wonder…"

But he didn't finish the thought. "What?"

"Mom used to say she wished she could forget. That losing him was the worst thing to ever happen to her."

Carina's heart broke. "You wonder if her Alzheimer's is the universe's way of helping her forget sometimes?"

He poured the soup into bowls. "It's twisted, isn't it? That this disease, which robs her of so much, also wipes that time away. She's given these days where she doesn't know what it's like to lose her husband and her sister."

"It's not twisted at all," she said quietly. "Losing your dad must have been hard for you, too."

"It was the worst period of my life. My dad was, and still is, the best man I will ever meet. If I can be half the man he was, I'll be a lucky guy."

Flynn brought two bowls to the coffee table, then leaned over her, helping her rise to a sitting position. Now that the pain wasn't so all-consuming, she was able to appreciate the effect his touch had on her. The way her skin tingled from his hands. The way her stomach clenched at his closeness.

She expected him to move away once she was sitting. Instead, he paused, and their gazes clashed. Her heart gave another thud but this time for a completely different reason. For a second, she wondered if the man was going to kiss her. Her gaze lowered to his lips.

But then he slowly moved away, and it took everything in her not to show her disappointment. She *shouldn't* be disappointed. He wasn't going to kiss her when she'd just been in the hospital. He was here to take care of her.

Still, frustration snaked up her chest.

He reached for the bowls and handed her one before sitting beside her.

When she took her first sip, her eyes drifted closed in bliss. "Flynn! This is so good." Certainly better than anything she could have whipped up.

He lifted a shoulder. "I've made it a lot." He paused. "Mom told me you made her dinner today."

She didn't miss the disapproval in his voice. Her gaze lowered as she stirred the soup. "I didn't know when you'd be back, and I wanted to make sure she was taken care of."

He shook his head. "You just got out of the hospital. You should have been resting. You could have asked the guys at Blue Halo to check on her."

"I wanted to be there to make sure she wasn't having a bad day."

There was a small crease between his brows. "Thank you for looking after her."

"It's my job."

His expression softened. He glanced around the room before looking back to her. "I was thinking...maybe I should stay tonight."

Her brain misfired.

"On the couch," he quickly added.

Nope. That was not disappointment rising in her chest again. "Don't feel like you have to. I mean, I should be okay."

"You need someone with you, Carina. Not only because of your knee but because you had a concussion. Let me be that person."

He was right. She didn't need to be a nurse to know that. "Okay. Thank you."

FLYNN WAS JUST RINSING the last dish when he heard the light footsteps from the bedroom. He cursed under his breath when he turned and saw Carina, walking slowly, her face pained.

He moved across the room to her side. "What the hell are you doing?"

When she attempted to push at his hands, he grabbed her arms, keeping her still.

"Carina." There was definitely warning in his voice, but hell, the woman seemed to need it.

She looked up, and his breath caught in his throat because her mouth was too damn close to his, just like it had been on the couch.

"I was just going to the bathroom."

Her breath brushed against his face. His body tensed, every part of him wanting to lean in and kiss her.

Get yourself together, Flynn.

It took too much strength to tug his gaze away from hers. Then he lifted her, and her hand went to his chest.

"Next time, call me," he said through gritted teeth.

"Sorry. I didn't feel the pain, so I thought I'd be okay."

"Yeah, well, your knee's still three times the size it should be."

She frowned, glancing down at her knee as they stepped into the bathroom. Christ, even that little frown was cute. He lowered her to the floor slowly.

"I'm feeling pretty wrecked. I might brush my teeth and go to bed after this." She paused, fiddling with a small thread on her pants like she was nervous. "I, um, have a confession."

His limbs tingled. The way she said it made him think this little confession would do nothing for the fire racing through his veins.

"That shirt you gave me the other week, when I fell off the boxes? I've, um…been wearing it to bed."

Uh, fuck. The image of her in his shirt, and only his shirt…it had something primal rising up in his chest.

Christ, he was in trouble.

"I don't mind." No, he fucking loved it. Too much.

She gave a small nod. "Could you, uh, grab it for me? It's under my pillow. I'll get changed in here."

She wet her lips, and he had to clench his fist to stop from grabbing her again. He quickly turned, moved out of the room before he did something stupid, and reached beneath her pillow.

When he handed her the shirt, he was careful not to let their fingers touch. Not when he felt so damn weak. "You gonna be okay in here?"

She gave a small chuckle. "Yes. I'll manage."

Good. Because helping her change…yeah, he wouldn't survive that.

He fled the room quickly, pulling the door closed. He thought once he was out, he'd be able to breathe more easily. Apparently, it didn't work like that. All he could think about was her getting naked behind that door. Of his shirt touching her bare skin...

Fuck. What *was* it about this woman that had every part of him wanting her? Craving her? Feeling like she belonged with him?

He waited in the bedroom, not wanting her to walk out by herself. The second the door opened, a storm burst in his chest. A storm of heat and fire and need.

Mine. That was all he could think when he saw the woman. Her hair was down and tousled, her face cleanly washed, and he could just see the hard peaks of her nipples pressing against his shirt.

Sucking in a breath, he gritted his teeth as he lifted her and walked her over to the bed, her body too damn soft against his. The second she was on the mattress, it took everything in him to step back.

"Flynn?"

God. Now he had to look at the woman again without touching her.

His gaze trickled back to her. She was under the sheets, but that didn't stop the torment he felt.

She frowned, tilting her head. "You look angry."

"Because all I can think about is pressing you into this mattress with my body."

Her eyes widened. She hadn't expected his honesty. He hadn't either. But fuck the lies and the cordial pleasantries. He felt too damn much for that.

Her mouth opened and closed a few times. "I want you too," she whispered. "Maybe..." She wet her lips.

"What is it, honey?"

"Maybe you could *not* sleep on the couch."

He stepped back toward her, his hand curving around her

cheek. "You sure?"

She leaned into his touch. "Yeah. I mean, it's just sleep, right?"

Nope. With her, it was never *just* anything. "I'll go turn everything off and be back."

When his hand dropped, she snuggled into a pillow and shut her eyes. She was tired—so damn tired that he wondered how much sleep she'd gotten last night. Probably very little, if any.

For a moment, he watched her. Then he moved around the house, checking the doors and windows and turning everything off.

When he climbed into bed, he debated for a minute whether to touch her. He was a weak man, so he wrapped an arm around her waist and carefully tugged her back into his front.

Fucking heaven.

"Thank you for today," she said softly. "I should have made more of an effort to speak up, see another doctor, but I was so tired. So tired of fighting for myself."

What had she been fighting so long that was exhausting her? He tugged her a bit closer. "What happened in Michigan?"

"Nothing good. I started dating a doctor at the hospital. His name was Greg, and all the women loved him because he was charming. Charismatic. Cute."

His chest splintered at the very thought of her dating another man. But he was careful not to tense his muscles. He didn't need her knowing how much her words affected him.

"The change in my female coworkers was instant. Especially because one of them, Shelley, had been going out for coffee with him occasionally. She'd thought he was going to start dating *her*." She sighed. "They were just...mean. Bitter. I don't know which of them made the accusation. That information was never released by the hospital board. Probably Shelley."

He stroked his thumb across her belly through the shirt. "I'm sorry."

"Thank you. I'm just glad it's over."

It didn't take long for her breaths to even out. He continued to hold her, wondering if there would come a time he'd ever want to let go. He hated that she'd been through such a horrible ordeal in Michigan. What he didn't hate, though, was that it had led her here. Because the woman did something to him. Something no woman had ever done before.

And even though it felt good, it was also scary as all hell.

CHAPTER 11

"*S*o..." she said softly. "The doctor gave me the okay to drive my car and walk more."

Flynn shot a glance her way from behind the wheel. It had been a week since her fall. A week of sleeping in her bed, driving her wherever she needed to go...

Yeah. It had been a good week.

"That's good."

When she said *doctor*, she wasn't talking about Victoria. Her checkups had been transferred to a new primary care physician outside of the ER.

She fiddled with the hem of her dress. A nervous gesture? Her gaze slid up again. "So you probably don't need to stay with me anymore or drive me around."

There was a moment of silence. In that silence, he could hear her heart beating faster than it should be. "Do you *want* me to stop staying over and driving you around?"

Her mouth opened and closed. "Well...we're not even dating."

Not an answer to his question. And, yeah, they weren't officially dating, but they'd been sharing a bed. He'd been holding her while she slept. They'd kissed more than once. So, he'd say they weren't dating *yet*. And that was mostly because she was busy healing.

His hand shifted from the wheel to her leg, wrapping around her thigh. "I care about you, Carina."

There was a quick inhalation of breath from her. She opened her mouth, but before any words could come out, her cell rang.

Flynn frowned. Her phone rang every day. Multiple times. Sometimes it was her parents. But not always. "Parents or ex?"

She hesitated. So…ex.

She'd only told him a bit about the guy. He was a doctor, and she said they'd separated amicably, but Flynn had detected that as a lie. Considering how often the guy called, he guessed the breakup had been one-sided.

Regardless of how they'd separated, Flynn didn't like the guy solely on the basis of him being an ex. Probably never would.

He pulled into his mother's driveway, and Carina opened her door. When Flynn started to open his, she touched his arm. "You said you had a meeting this morning and probably wouldn't have time to come in."

"True."

"So you're only getting out to help me."

"Yes."

Her lips curved into a smile. "You don't need to do that. My knee is healing well, and I'm wearing my brace. I'll see you this afternoon."

This afternoon. After which, she didn't need him anymore. Too bad for him that he felt like he needed *her*.

She began to climb out, but this time it was Flynn who reached out. He leaned over and kissed her. They'd shared a few kisses over the last week. Not nearly enough.

His lips swiped against hers, and she all but melted across the middle console. Her fingers slid through his hair, tugging him closer, urging him to deepen the kiss. He slipped his tongue into her mouth, tasting her.

Always so sweet.

Even though they hadn't kissed often, he felt like he knew her mouth. In fact, it felt so familiar to him that he could trick himself into thinking they'd shared a million stolen kisses.

His hand slowly slid up her stomach, giving her the chance to pull away. When she didn't, he closed his fingers around her breast beneath her jacket, holding and massaging. Carina gasped. The gasp was quickly followed by a hum of pleasure.

God, he wanted her. All of her. Every little bit.

When her hand pressed to his chest, he slowly released her, his hand dropping. Her lips were a pretty red shade and her blue eyes were dark. The pitter-patter of her heart thudded double-time like background music to his ears.

"I'll see you this afternoon," he said quietly.

She nodded, her bottom lip disappearing between her teeth, then she climbed out of the car and entered his mother's house.

For a moment, he sat there, silent and listening. He could just hear the faint sound of his mother. She was okay.

With a smile on his face, he drove off, grinning like a goddamn lunatic. The woman had him good. Even though she'd been resting most of the last week, the time with her had just cemented what he was feeling. It was crazy—he knew it was. To barely know a woman and need her like he needed air to breathe. But he wasn't going to walk away from how he felt.

The smile slipped from his face when he thought about where he was headed. He hadn't been lying to Carina. He *did* have a meeting this morning. But before that, he needed to do something.

He parked outside Victoria's home and strode to her front door. He banged on the wood, hoping like hell she was here. He wasn't a patient man, so waiting wasn't an option, and he didn't really feel like traipsing around town looking for her.

He'd sat on this question for a week. It was a week too long. He needed answers, and he needed them now.

The door opened, and Victoria's eyes widened when she saw him. "Flynn, what a nice surprise. I wasn't expecting you."

"We need to talk."

A smile stretched her lips. "Of course. Come in."

He stepped into the living area, shoving his hands in his pockets. Her home was large and white. It was also clean. So clean, it felt sterile. He'd never seen a single speck of dust. Not a thing out of place. Damn, he'd always hated coming here.

"Can I get you some coffee? I just bought these new Brazilian coffee beans. They're gorgeous—"

"How did you know about Carina's drug charges in Michigan?"

Victoria stopped, her mouth slipping open. "What?"

"You don't have access to any medical history from doctors she visited back in Michigan, so it wasn't in her patient files. You also don't have access to employment files, because the hospital doesn't employ her. Not that the information would be in either of those files anyway. She *did* apply for a job at the hospital when she first moved here, but she wouldn't have disclosed that information in her application." He stepped closer. "So how did you know?"

All of that had been rolling around in his mind for the last week, and he knew Carina had to be wondering too. She hadn't said the words out loud but he'd read it on her face. The only reason he was confronting Victoria was because he didn't give a damn who he pissed off.

Victoria laughed, but the sound came out all wrong. "Come on, Flynn. Let me get you a coffee and we can—"

"*How*, Victoria?"

Her lips snapped shut and she exhaled loudly, looking out the window. When she looked back, the smile was gone.

"Fine. I knew she was hired as your mother's nurse before you told me. While you were in the hospital recovering from your bullet wound, and before she withdrew her application at the hospital, I heard around town there was a new nurse with your mother. Being your girlfriend, I wanted to look out for you."

She shuffled from one foot to another. "I called the University of Michigan Hospital, where she used to work, because I wanted to know who this woman was. I got to talking with a very chatty nurse called Shelley, and she told me all about the circumstances of Carina leaving the workplace." Victoria stepped closer. "I did nothing wrong. I was looking out for you. And I didn't ask the nurse to disclose that information. She did it freely."

Flynn's jaw clenched. "You *did* do something wrong. You should have reported the nurse for illegally telling a prospective employer the reason for Carina's job loss. You also shouldn't have withheld pain medication from a patient in need."

Fuck, he was angry. Angry for Carina. For the breach of her privacy. It wasn't enough that she'd already been through so much in Michigan, but a damn ex-coworker was still trying to keep her down. And now Victoria too.

He stepped closer. "You *will* be reporting the nurse for misconduct. And if you don't, I'll be reporting both of you."

"Flynn, you can't be serious."

"Try me."

He turned and headed outside. He couldn't even look at the woman any longer. Her footsteps sounded behind him.

"Flynn—I'm sorry!"

He unlocked his car door and finally faced Victoria before climbing in. "Tell me that the decision you made about Carina's pain medication was purely professional. Tell me her connection to me didn't sway your judgment."

She pulled back like he'd burned her. "The woman stole—"

"Was *accused* of stealing drugs. Then cleared. Just like we told you at the hospital. Did *Shelley* not share that part with you?"

Her tongue made a clicking noise. "In any case, my decision had nothing to do with you."

Her heart sped up and her pupils dilated. She was lying. It was like throwing gas on an already raging fire. "I want that nurse in Michigan fired by the end of the day."

Then he slid into his car and drove away from the woman, not caring if he ever saw her again.

❧

"DOROTHY, what on earth are you painting?"

Carina grimaced, and not because Patricia was calling her Dorothy again. They were sitting outside in the garden with paint and easels while Carina tried and failed at this art thing.

"It's a bee perched on a leaf." Carina tilted her head to the side. It wasn't that bad, was it?

Patricia leaned closer and squinted like she was trying to discern the leaf from the bee.

Okay, it sucked. But to be fair, art had never been her strong point, and this little activity was entirely Patricia's choice.

She cleared her throat, looking at Patricia's painting. "What about you? What have you painted?"

The woman looked back toward her own easel, and Carina subtly shifted her painting away.

"It's the little Italian restaurant David and I visited on our first date."

It was like a freaking photograph, and it wasn't even finished. No wonder the woman had looked so surprised at Carina's pathetic attempt at a painting. Her late sister Dorothy had probably been just as much a Picasso as Patricia.

The older woman pointed to the left window. "We sat at a table just there, by that window. I barely looked out of it the entire night. David was all I saw."

So romantic. "How old were you?"

Her sister probably would have known the answer to that, but Patricia didn't blink an eye. Maybe she just wanted to talk about her late husband.

"Thirty-five. Old in comparison to most women who meet their husbands, especially back then. I'd dated so many rotten eggs by that point that I'd just accepted marriage and kids weren't in the cards for me." She gave a quick shake of her head. "That night changed everything. David was like...he was the sun after endless rain. The fire on a cold winter night."

Carina's heart melted at the woman's words. "It sounds like it was love at first sight."

"Oh, it was. And every day after that, I've loved him more. Don't get me wrong, we've had our trials, but we always navigate our way through, coming out stronger."

The woman's use of present tense stung at Carina's chest. "How old were you when Flynn was born?"

"Flynn?" Patricia frowned.

A bolt of sadness coursed through Carina.

"Oh, Flynn," she said quietly before shaking her head. "Yes, ah, thirty-six... So, again, much older than most. I was terrified the entire pregnancy. I was expecting something to go wrong at every turn. David was my calm, of course. Whenever he'd see me anxious, he'd come over, whisper sweet things in my ear. Tell me to trust God's plan."

When Patricia looked up, there were tears in her eyes.

"He's not... He's not here anymore, is he?"

Wetness built in Carina's eyes, as well. This confusion and disorientation were normal for patients with Alzheimer's, but it was still heartbreaking.

"He's not." She reached out, closing her hand over the other woman's. "I'm sorry, Patricia."

A tear trickled down her cheek as she looked back to the painting in front of her. The woman traced the picture with her gaze, almost like she was taking herself back there. "Will you do something for me, dear?"

Carina swallowed the lump in her throat. "Anything."

"When you find a person who touches your heart like David

touched mine, live every moment you can with him, and don't take a second for granted. Because one day you'll blink, and those moments will be memories that only exist inside you." She paused. "And even then, they'll only exist when your brain chooses to remember."

This time, Carina's heart didn't just hurt. It rippled and tore. Not only at the woman's words but at the sadness that weaved through them. "I will."

Patricia swiped away the tear before patting her hand. "Good."

At the sound of the back door opening, they both turned their heads.

Flynn stepped into the yard. The second her eyes fell on him, her breath caught in her throat. If there was ever a man she wanted to remember every moment with, it was him.

He stopped beside his mother, pressing a kiss to her head. "Everything okay?"

Patricia gave a firm nod, suddenly looking fine again. "Of course, dear."

He held her gaze for another beat before turning to Carina. Just like he'd done for the older woman, he bent down, pressing a kiss to her forehead. Her skin tingled when his lips lingered.

Patricia rose from her chair. "I'm going inside to have a rest. You both go home. Spend time together."

They hadn't told Patricia that anything was going on between them, but Carina wouldn't be surprised if the woman knew. On her good days, she observed others closely, especially her son.

Carina stayed for another twenty minutes, packing up the paints and making sure everything was ready for Patricia's dinner, all the while much too aware of Flynn moving around her. Every so often, he touched her hip. Grazed her side.

When they reached her house, he walked her to her door. He didn't have anything inside. As the cleanest man she'd ever spent time with, he was always taking his stuff back to his place the next day.

"You sure you don't want me to stay the night?"

No. She wasn't. But he'd stayed with her because she'd been injured, and now she was okay. Well, as okay as she could be a week after a concussion and knee dislocation. "I'm sure."

He lifted a brow like he didn't believe her. Then he stepped closer. "Have you heard about the Cradle Mountain Street Party?"

She frowned. "No."

He shifted some hair from her face, and the air stalled in her lungs.

"It's an annual thing, and it's tomorrow night. I was wondering if you'd let me take you. You can meet some of my team. We could sit and have a drink. And when you get tired, I'll bring you home."

"That almost sounds like a date, Flynn Talbot."

His hand curved around her cheek. "Would you like it to be a date?"

Yes. With everything she had, yes. But her throat felt glued shut, so she gave a small nod instead.

One side of his mouth lifted. "Then it's a date."

His head lowered, and he nipped her bottom lip. She gasped. Then his lips pressed to hers. Even though the kiss lasted a total of two seconds, time slowed.

"I'll be here around six tomorrow night. Call if you need me before then."

Another nod. Then he was gone.

CHAPTER 12

*F*lynn pressed a hand to the small of Carina's back as they carefully negotiated their way through the crowd. The street was closed off for the party, and it was packed.

He leaned his head down, almost brushing her ear with his lips. "Remember, if your knee gets sore—"

"Tell you and we rest." She glanced up, and her smile was damn near soul-destroying. "I know. I remember from the ten times you told me on the way over."

His hand trailed to her waist, and he playfully tickled her side. Even though the street was loud, her laugh was all he heard. It filled his head and punctured his chest.

Wrenching his gaze away, he looked up to see four members of his team standing around one of the stalls. He lowered his hand to take hers and lead her over.

The guys looked up, all smiling.

Flynn smiled back. "Hey, guys, this is Carina. Carina, this is Callum, Aidan, Jason, and you've met Tyler."

She received a combination of nods and "hey" in return.

"You didn't have to come with this guy tonight out of pity," Tyler said to Carina.

The guys chuckled, and Flynn whacked him on the arm. "Don't even see a woman *willing* to take pity on you tonight."

Tyler laughed. "Yeah, the lucky lady hasn't found me yet. When she does though—"

"She'll run far and fast," Jason finished.

Callum shook his head. "Ignore them. How are you finding Cradle Mountain?"

"Amazing," Carina said. "So far, definitely living up to everything Joy Anderson said about it."

"What did she say?" Jason asked.

Tyler nudged Jason's shoulder. "Obviously, the woman told her about *us*—the sexy men who run the security business."

Carina chuckled. "Well, she definitely mentioned Flynn." Tyler scoffed, looking chagrined by her response. "And the pizza, and the coffee at The Grind, the place with the funny mugs. I've tried the pizza but not the coffee."

"What the heck, Flynn?" Courtney's voice sounded from behind him. "You haven't taken the woman to my shop? I have the best coffee in town! How's she been caffeinating?"

Jason's arm slid around Courtney's waist as she came to stand with them. He pressed a kiss to her head.

Flynn lifted a shoulder. "Plenty of time for that."

"Plenty of time tomorrow?" Courtney asked, lifting a brow with a hint of a smile on her face.

Flynn shook his head, all too aware of how persistent the woman could be. "Maybe. Carina might want to rest tomorrow after being on her feet tonight."

Carina shook her head. "The rest can wait. I want some of the best coffee in town in a funny mug."

Courtney leaned forward. "I'm Courtney, the owner, and the coffee's a-*mazing*." Then she nudged Jason's shoulder. "Tell her."

"It's okay," Tyler interrupted before Jason could get a word in.

This time, Jason leaned across and whacked him on the shoulder. Tyler clutched his arm, feigning injury. "You guys are going to give me a dead arm."

Carina's smile broadened. "Nice to meet you, Courtney. I'm Carina, Patricia's nurse."

Patricia's nurse? Sure as hell wasn't how Flynn would have introduced her.

"How are you doing after the fall?" Aidan asked.

Carina lifted a shoulder. "I'm okay. Still some pain in my knee, but nothing some medication can't dull. Flynn's been a lifesaver."

Callum smiled knowingly. "Has he now?"

Okay. Introductions were over. "Let's get a drink, honey."

He tugged Carina away from the group. They'd only taken a few steps when he felt her tense beside him before trying to pull her hand away.

Glancing at her, he frowned when he saw the worried look on her face. But he didn't release her hand. Not yet. "What's wrong?"

She turned her face toward his chest, and her words were low. "Victoria's here. You two only just broke up. Maybe we shouldn't be touching?"

He scanned the street, and sure enough, there she was on the other side of the road, standing with people he vaguely recognized from the hospital. The second he looked over, she looked away. But not before he saw the angry expression on her face.

His jaw firmed. "You don't need to worry about Victoria. We broke up. She's an adult. She'll be okay." And there was no part of him that wanted to stop touching Carina. He didn't think he could if he tried. Especially not when she was wearing those tight black jeans and that knitted sweater that showed a smooth line of midriff. The second he'd seen her tonight, he'd wanted to ditch the party and stay home with the woman.

When she still hesitated, nibbling her bottom lip, he lowered his head and whispered into her ear, "I don't want to let go of you, but if you really want me to, I will."

He swiped the pad of his thumb across the skin of her hand in a slow caress. He wasn't playing fair. But he didn't want to. Not with her.

She shuddered lightly and opened her mouth, but before she could say anything, Courtney was beside them, weaving an arm through Carina's.

"If you two lovebirds are finished, I'd like to steal Carina away and introduce her to the other women."

Flynn almost growled. "I haven't bought her a drink yet."

"So get her a drink. We'll just be over there." She nodded toward a small table, where Grace and Willow sat chatting.

Carina looked over at the table with both curiosity and longing. It suddenly dawned on him—she was new in town. Of course she would want to meet other women and make friends.

Reluctantly, he released her hand, but not before lowering his head and pressing a lingering kiss to her lips. He whispered against them, "Don't be gone long."

Or he'd damn well come for her. That was the pull she had on him.

He didn't take his gaze off her until she was seated. When he finally looked away, he returned to his friends—who were staring at him. "What?"

"You're really into her," Aidan said. He sounded surprised.

"Yeah. I am." There was no denying it. He knew what he wanted, and it was Carina.

Tyler shook his head. "He's been looking at her like that since the day they met."

Aidan frowned slightly. "Even when he thought…"

"She might be guilty?" Tyler finished. "Yep."

"I can't even argue with that," Flynn said. "It's true."

CARINA TOOK a sip of her drink. Flynn had gotten her a sparkling red wine in a fancy little bottle. Great choice.

She shot a quick look over to where he stood with the guys. When their gazes caught, she could have sworn she saw his eyes darken. Then he winked at her, and her stomach did a little somersault.

"You moved from Michigan, right?" Willow asked.

Carina smiled. "Yeah. I grew up there. It's a bit strange living somewhere else."

"Good strange or bad strange?" Courtney asked.

"Definitely good strange. Like a big gulp of fresh air."

The women chuckled. So far, they all seemed lovely. They were sitting around a small table on the side of the street. Willow seemed the nurturing-mother type. Grace was the quiet one with gentle eyes. And Courtney was the louder, more up-front personality.

"You'll love it here," Grace said. "Small towns are the best."

Courtney nodded. "And the guys aren't so bad either."

Carina laughed. They weren't wrong.

Willow nodded toward Flynn. "Are you guys dating?"

Carina bit her bottom lip. "Technically, I think this is actually our first date."

She got a variety of sighs and squeals in response.

Out of nowhere, a small girl ran up to the table. She had adorable brown pigtails and a wide smile on her face. A tall guy trailed closely behind. Carina already knew the man was on Flynn's team. He was everything Flynn and his other friends were: tall, muscular, intense.

The girl jumped onto Willow's lap. "Mama, can I have some cotton candy? Daddy said I have to ask you."

"Oh, did he?" Willow gave the man a pointed look , although there was a hint of a smile behind it.

The girl nodded.

"Hm. Okay. A small stick of cotton candy, but you need to share with Daddy."

Then she gave the man another look, this time as if to say, "You'd better eat most of it." Carina just held back her chuckle.

The man stood behind Willow, wrapped his fingers around her shoulders, and leaned down to press a kiss to her cheek. So sweet. All the guys from Blue Halo treated their women so well. "You got it, sweetheart." He straightened. "All right. Let's go, kid."

He reached over, lifted the girl from Willow's lap, and threw her in the air. The kid giggled. Willow touched his leg. "Before you go, this is Carina. She's looking after Flynn's mom. Carina, this is my daughter, Mila, and my husband, Blake."

She smiled at both of them.

"Are you dating any of Daddy's friends?" Mila asked.

Nothing like an upfront question from a child. "I am."

One date constituted dating, right?

Mila's eyes widened. "Tyler?"

The women around the table laughed.

"No, Flynn."

Mila opened her mouth to say something, but Blake got in before she could. "All right. Enough nosing around. Let's go get that cotton candy."

Mila's eyes lit up at the reminder of the cotton candy. Then she wriggled down Blake's body before grabbing his hand and dragging him toward the stall.

Yeah. The kid was definitely a cutie.

Carina spent another ten minutes talking and laughing with the women. It was awesome. Even in Michigan, she'd only had a few female friends, most of them from work, and the second she started dating a sought-after doctor, they'd turned on her.

She was just glancing around the street, taking in the sights, when she saw a familiar face.

Her jaw dropped to her chest. No. It couldn't be...

Greg. It was definitely Greg. God, what was he doing here? She'd told him not to come.

He was walking along the street, scanning the crowd like he was looking for someone.

Her, she assumed.

Carina touched Grace's arm without looking her way. "Sorry, I just saw someone I know. I'll be back in a sec."

Before the woman could respond, Carina stood and walked down the street. A few people stepped in front of her, blocking her view, and she quickly sidestepped, not wanting to lose him in the crowd.

When she finally reached him, he was facing the other way. She touched his arm, and his gaze fell on her. He sighed as if in relief, then he pulled her into a tight hug.

"Carina! There you are."

She pulled out of his arms. "What on earth are you doing here, Greg?"

He frowned, as if her question confused him. "You were injured and spent the night in the hospital. I *had* to come. I left as soon as I could. I tried calling yesterday."

She cringed. She'd ignored his call and hadn't listened to the voice message. She'd told herself she'd listen to it later, but later never came. And dammit, now it was biting her in the butt.

"Greg, that's crazy. Flying across the country to check on me when we're not dating is *crazy*."

He stepped forward and grazed the healing cut on her forehead just like Flynn had. But with Greg, it felt completely different. Clinical. All she wanted to do was step back.

She took hold of his arm, tugged it away from her head, then she pulled him to the side of the busy road. "You shouldn't be here. We broke up."

Something flashed in his light brown eyes. Hurt? "You said you wanted some time away from Michigan. I've given you that time."

Her mouth slipped open. For a moment, she was lost for words. "First of all, it hasn't even been a month. Second, this isn't a quick get-away-to-clear-my-head-and-I'll-be-back kind of thing. I'm not *going* back."

His brow scrunched before quickly clearing. He was just opening his mouth to say something when another familiar voice sounded from beside them.

"Who do we have here?"

Carina almost groaned when she saw the twins from next door.

"Is this *another* guy who's gonna fight your battles for you, bitch?"

Greg's gaze shot toward them. "What did you call her?"

She tightened her fingers on his arm. "Ignore them. They're just kids who get their kicks out of egging houses and threatening neighbors."

Greg's eyes flashed back to the kids, and he took a step forward. "You egged her house?"

The taller one smirked. "Yeah, we did. More than once. And we'll do it again if we have to."

They were drunk. They had that glassy look in their eyes. It had to be why they suddenly had the courage to threaten her in person, when for the last week, they'd barely looked at her.

The shorter kid suddenly whipped an empty bottle at her. It would have hit Carina in the face if Greg hadn't quickly swatted it away. The glass shattered on the ground, drawing attention from people nearby.

"You stay the hell away from her!"

"Don't hold your breath, old man." When their gazes roamed her body, Greg lunged toward them. The kids laughed as they ran away.

When Greg didn't immediately turn back around, she placed her hand on his arm.

Finally, he faced her and sucked in a long breath while his features slowly cleared.

"You shouldn't be here," she said quietly.

He touched her cheek. "I *should*. I love you. I've never loved anyone like I love you. Come back with me."

She stepped away and his hand fell. She swallowed before saying what she knew she needed to say. "I don't love *you*. I'm sorry if that's not what you want to hear, but it's the truth."

His jaw visibly clenched. He moved forward, grabbing her arm. "Carina—"

"I think she made herself clear."

The sudden heat at her shoulders had Carina's eyes fluttering closed. Flynn's hand pressed to the small of her back, the warmth from his touch penetrating through her top.

Greg's hand dropped. "Who the hell are you?"

"Flynn."

That was all he said, but it was enough to have Greg's expression darkening.

"Flynn's my patient's son," Carina explained softly.

He tensed behind her but remained silent. His hand never dropped from her back.

"You need to go, Greg," she continued. "Back to Michigan. That's your home, and this is mine."

For a moment, he didn't move. He didn't so much as blink. Then he shot Flynn a final look before turning and walking away.

"Are you okay?" Flynn asked quietly the second they were alone.

She nodded, mostly because she was in shock. Shock that Greg would come all this way for her. Shock that he'd told her he still loved her and wanted her back.

Flynn studied her for another beat before slipping an arm around her waist and leading her back toward the group.

CHAPTER 13

*C*arina watched the muscles in Flynn's back ripple as he moved inside the house ahead of her. Apart from their steps, there was silence. In fact, there had been almost complete silence between them since Flynn had seen her with Greg.

She walked around him to grab a glass from the cupboard and filled it with water, overanalyzing everything that had transpired. She was pretty sure she knew why he was being so quiet, but—

"How's the knee?"

Flynn's question cut into her thoughts as she turned off the tap. It was the only question he'd continued to ask since the scene with Greg. She gave him the same answer she'd been giving all night. "It's fine."

She lowered the glass without taking a sip and turned, watching him from across the room.

One small nod, and then that same quiet that had plagued them in the car. The man hadn't even turned on the radio.

He turned toward the door, and she wasn't sure if he intended to leave or just drop his keys on the small side table, but she stopped him with her question before he did either.

"Is it because I described you as my patient's son?"

Another ripple of those back muscles through the shirt. When he turned, his face was annoyingly unreadable. "It's because that's *all* you described me as. To both Greg and Courtney." He tilted his head. "I think we're a bit more than that. Don't you?"

He took a slow step toward her. Why did that step feel like an animal stalking his prey?

Her hands were now clenching the counter behind her, fingers digging into the wood.

"Do you always kiss your patients' sons?" he asked.

"No. But I was in shock. I didn't expect Greg to just show up out of the blue. I wasn't thinking straight."

Hell, her head *still* was a mess.

"So that's not how you feel?"

God, how had the man crossed half the room already? He hardly looked like he was moving.

She swallowed, and her next words came out quieter than the last. "What I feel for you is…it's unlike anything I've ever felt for any other person before."

That had him pausing. One side of his mouth lifted. "I feel the same, Carina."

When he finally reached her, his hands went to either side of her body, grabbing the counter to cage her in.

For a moment, words were lost on her. And it had everything to do with his musky, outdoorsy scent surrounding her. That hard, muscular chest almost touched her own.

His head lowered, and the kiss on her cheek was so soft, it had the fine hairs on her arms standing on end. "Where do you see this going, Carina?"

"Um…" Her eyes shut as another featherlight kiss brushed her cheek. What had he asked her? "I can't think when you're so close to me."

Another kiss—this time closer to her lips. "Okay. I'll tell you where *I* see this going. I see both of us having all of each other.

You getting all of me. Me getting all of you." Another kiss. "I'm all in."

She gasped at those last words.

And he dove, taking her mouth with his own, driving his tongue straight between her lips like he didn't have the time to lose.

A moan slipped from her throat, and her hands curved up his shoulders. Her knees had just started to shake when his hands went to her butt, and she was tugged off her feet, against his body. Her breasts pressed to his chest, cushioning his hardness.

He kissed her like he wanted to devour her whole. Exactly how she needed to be kissed.

Her hands burrowed into his hair, a fiery need growing low in her belly.

One of Flynn's hands slid up her hip, gliding under her top and up her bare stomach. When it closed over her breast, cradling the soft mound with a calloused palm, her hands stilled in his hair, clutching the strands. Her nipple hardened, and he found it immediately with his thumb and forefinger, teasing the sensitive bud.

Pleasure and need zipped through her body in a hot, heavy rush. The sensations were alive inside her, consuming her, throbbing from her breasts down to her core.

His mouth trailed down her cheek and throat as Carina's breaths became shallow, sawing in and out of her chest in quick succession.

Air whipped her flesh as he spun them around, lowering her to the kitchen island. She toed off her shoes before he stepped between her thighs, separating her legs. Then he tugged off her sweater. That mouth returned to her neck, but this time the kiss was slower. Gentle. He trailed his lips to her chest.

With one finger, he slipped the strap of her bra down her shoulder, his heated touch grazing her the entire time. It was like a line of fire burning her skin. Then the cup was down. When his mouth covered the tip of her breast, a loud cry tore from her throat.

He alternated between sucking the hard peak and flicking her nipple from side to side.

She was vaguely aware of the button of her jeans popping open. The sound of the zipper. Then his hand slipped inside, one finger grazing her slit.

Her entire body jolted, her cry more of a strangled moan. Heat flared in her core and lower belly. Then it spidered throughout her limbs. His finger continued to move and graze against her clit for endless minutes. Then it moved to her entrance, and her breath caught. Slowly, he pushed a finger inside her, causing a full-body shudder.

Carina rocked her hips, her fingers clutching his shoulders. "Flynn…"

The finger moved out, then slowly back in again, his thumb swiping against her clit the entire time. It was torture. When her nipple eventually popped from his mouth, his lips trailed back up her throat. When he reached her mouth, he kissed her one more time. Then he looked at her, his eyes stormy.

"Bedroom?"

His finger was still moving rhythmically inside her, his thumb pressing and rubbing at her clit.

It took a moment to make her voice work, then she breathed the single word. "Yes."

If possible, his eyes darkened further. His finger slid out of her slowly. She wanted to cry. Then he was lifting her against his chest, and the air shifted around them until they stepped into the bedroom.

With one hand, he undid her bra, allowing it to fall to the floor with a whisper of a thud. A small growl vibrated from his chest when her breasts sprang free.

Gently, he laid her on top of the bed. She watched as he

tugged his shirt over his head, his muscles rippling. Then he slipped his jeans down his legs.

Her mouth dried. The man was all power and sex.

He leaned onto the bed, gently removing her knee brace. Then he tugged her jeans and panties down her thighs. His eyes never left hers.

She'd thought she'd feel self-conscious being bare before him. Maybe want to cover herself. She didn't feel any of that. Not with the way he looked at her. Like she was all he needed. All he'd ever need.

Flynn bent down, pressing a kiss to her ankle. Then, slowly, his mouth trailed up her leg. When he reached the apex between her thighs, her heart skidded to a halt as he separated her legs.

At the first swipe of his tongue against her clit, her body jerked. It was like a bolt of lightning crashing through her system.

He swiped again, and her back arched, a moan slipping from somewhere deep inside her.

As his tongue continued to swirl and glide, the room around her hazed and darkened. Her mind became a red fog of heat and desire. Her chest moved up and down quickly. It was like there wasn't enough air reaching her lungs.

"Flynn, please!"

One more swipe, then those lips finally left her core, skimming up to her navel, her chest. He took a nipple into his mouth and sucked before allowing it to pop from his lips, then moved up her neck until he reached her mouth.

Then he went back to kissing her again with that same fiery need. Like if he stopped or slowed, they'd both disintegrate into nothing.

When she felt his hardness between her thighs, she reached down, slipping her hand into his briefs and wrapping her fingers around him. His body hardened and stilled. He was thick in her hand and continued to thicken as she tightened her hold. Slowly, she began to explore him, moving her hand up and down his length, loving the way his eyes clenched shut as if he could barely contain himself.

She took her time, relishing every rasping breath from his chest as she moved her hand from base to tip. Too soon, he was growling and rising from the bed, grabbing his wallet from his jeans and tugging out a condom.

When his briefs dropped, her mouth gaped. Feeling was one thing—seeing was another. The man was huge.

Her gaze trailed up to Flynn's, and his eyes were still as dark as ever. The expression on his face... It claimed her. Destroyed her.

Once he'd donned the condom, he slid back over her body and settled between her thighs, his length right there, pressing at her entrance.

He leaned down, whispering words against her cheek. Words that were lost to the roaring blood between her ears. Then he pushed inside—and every single muscle in her body seized.

His mouth claimed hers again, his tongue dancing with her own as he began to thrust, filling her completely before pulling out again.

Carina's eyes closed in pleasure. Every time he returned to her, that pleasure built, tipping her closer to the edge. Her fingernails dug into his shoulders, and when his hand once again cradled her breast, pinching her nipple, she bucked and shuddered. She was holding on for dear life, every tilt of his hips brought her closer to the edge.

She wrapped her legs around his waist, tugging his body back to her on each thrust.

He rolled to his side and pulled her with him, his thrusts never stopping, now driving into her from a new angle. It was both heaven and torture. Her body rioted against the sensations flooding her core.

Her eyes clenched shut. It was too much. All of it.

When the hand around her waist tugged her closer, and he took a pebbled nipple between his lips, her body finally spasmed, clenching and rippling around his length.

A deep growl reverberated from Flynn's chest as he claimed her lips once again, a hand replacing his mouth on her breast. He thrust harder. Deeper. Prolonging her orgasm, drawing it out.

Then he tensed, his body tightening.

Oxygen moved in and out of her chest in slow, deep breaths as he stilled. When she opened her eyes, it was to see Flynn looking at her like he was seeing her for the first time.

"You're incredible," he whispered, the hand on her breast still grazing her peak.

She swallowed, leaning her head against his and just breathing. "That was…"

"Everything," Flynn finished when she couldn't.

Yes. It was everything.

CHAPTER 14

*F*lynn watched the rise and fall of Carina's chest beneath the sheet. The sun was just glinting through the curtains, but he'd been awake for a while. He should get up. Shower. Dress. But moving away from her felt impossible.

Last night had felt different to him. *She* felt different to him. And like everything else he felt about the woman, last night's intense connection scared the hell out of him.

He'd never been the type of guy to easily give himself to another person. Trust had been given rarely and with caution. In Delta, he'd seen the worst of humanity. Then being taken by Project Arma, treated like an object... Hell, if the guys from Marble Falls hadn't broken his team out of there, he'd probably be a robot soldier right now, fighting someone else's war.

That sort of thing would rock anyone's faith in humanity.

His gaze traced the contour of her neck between her hairline and shoulder. Her head turned, and a piece of golden hair fell across her face, causing her eyelids to twitch. Unable to stop himself, he reached out, pushed the lock away, and grazed her skin in the process.

So damn soft.

Three of his friends had found love. Logan, Jason, and Blake. How had they learned to trust again after the military and Project Arma?

He'd been so sure love wasn't in the cards for him. Marriage. A forever kind of connection with a single person.

Had that changed?

Carina's eyelids scrunched, and her fingers twitched. A second later, those beautiful blue eyes opened, looking straight at him. It was like an arrow to his fucking chest. She pierced his soul with a single look. That was the depth of her effect on him.

That was why, alongside the desire, came that emotion he rarely felt. Stark fear.

A smile stretched her lips. "Hey." She almost sounded shy. Her hands went to the sheet, tugging it higher over her chest.

He pushed his thoughts to the back of his mind. "Morning, honey." His hand curved around her shoulder as he leaned in, pressing a long, lingering kiss on her lips, something he'd been wanting to do since the moment he woke. Her kisses were like little flecks of perfection.

When he pulled back, her eyes were closed once more. He caressed her shoulder. "Sleep well?"

She looked at him. "I think so. I can't remember."

He lifted a brow. "You can't remember?"

"Well, I'm not used to being with someone like you." Her gaze roamed down his bare chest before rising to his face again. "You kind of empty my head."

He chuckled. "Yeah, I remember you saying that before."

"Literally nothing up there right now."

His smile widened. "You do the opposite to me." Bending toward her, he dropped a kiss beside her mouth. "You take up so much space in my head, you shove everything else aside."

His mouth trailed down her neck. He was seconds from tugging away the sheet and sliding the woman beneath him when banging sounded on the door.

He lifted his head. "Expecting visitors?"

She shook her head, frowning.

Who the hell was it then?

Flynn tugged on his jeans, then moved to the door. His hand was wrapping around the knob when another bang sounded—this one harder than the last. Then a woman's voice shouted.

"I know you're in there! Open the fucking door!"

He tugged it open to find a very angry-looking middle-aged woman standing there. Her bleach-blonde hair looked like it had been pulled up in a rush, and she wore jeans and an oversized sweatshirt.

Anger sparked in her eyes. "Where are my boys?"

"Your boys being the Brown twins?"

He was making an educated guess here. He'd never seen the woman before in his life.

Carina's quiet steps sounded behind him.

The woman took a step forward, and Flynn inched to the side to block her from entering the house. "Don't play dumb with me!" Her gaze shot behind him to Carina. "Did your boyfriend follow through on his threat and do something to them last night?"

Carina touched his arm while her words remained aimed at the woman. "Excuse me?"

"You think I didn't hear?" Her eyes flashed back to Flynn. "I was right there by my window when you threatened them. I saw you grab my son! Then last night, people were talking about how they threw some shit at her at the street party. Now my boys haven't come home. What did you do?"

His blood boiled. The kids threw shit at Carina? He wanted to turn and ask her about it, but he pushed the urge down. It would have to wait. "Did you also watch as they egged Carina's house, took her phone, and shoved her too?"

Her eyes flared.

So, yes.

"Where are they?"

Flynn kept his expression neutral. "I haven't had any interaction with them since that day."

"Bullshit!" she sneered.

Carina tried to step forward, but he put his arm around her body, stopping her. "I don't know what you're trying to accuse him of," she said. "But I've been with him since your boys approached us last night. He had nothing to do with them not coming home."

"Why the fuck would I believe anything you say? You're probably in on the whole thing!"

Carina frowned. "Whole thing?"

Okay, time for this little altercation to end. "I'm part owner of Blue Halo Security. I'd be happy to look into the matter for you?"

For a moment, the woman looked somewhere between shocked and disgusted. "You stay the fuck away from them. And if I find out you did anything, I'll make you pay!"

Then she stormed back across the yard to her house.

Flynn shut the door and turned to find Carina nibbling on her bottom lip.

"Do you think they're okay?" she finally asked.

With a hand on the small of her back, he led her to the kitchen. "They're teenage boys with very little parental supervision. There are a million things that could have kept them out all night."

He stepped closer, slipping his arms around her waist and tugging her against him. "What was she talking about them throwing shit at you?"

Her eyes widened, her lips separating. "Oh. It was nothing."

Lie. Why was she protecting them? "Tell me. Please."

"They just threw a bottle at me. Greg swatted it away."

Yep. The second they turned up, he was going to kill them. He should have kept a closer eye on her last night. "You okay?"

She gave a small chuckle. "Trust me, those kids with their eggs and low-level threats are the least of my worries."

Flynn's muscles tensed. "Threats?"

She shook her head. "It's nothing. I received some notes in the mail. I'm sure it was them."

What the hell? Okay, now he was really losing his calm. "What did they say?"

"That I'm not welcome here, and to get out of town."

His hands tightened on her waist. He didn't like the sound of that. "Do you still have them?"

"Um. I don't think—" She stopped. "Wait, I might have one."

She slipped away from him and rummaged through a small pile of mail on the kitchen counter. "Got it."

Flynn took the sheet from her and studied it. Damn, it was typed. He'd been hoping for a handwritten note. At least then he could have compared it to something the boys had written.

His gaze skimmed across the words.

Why are you still here? Go home before you make me do something you'll regret.

"Me," Flynn read quietly.

Carina frowned. "What did you say?"

"The note reads *me*." He looked up. "If it had been the boys, I would have thought they'd say us. Make *us* do something you'll regret. I'm guessing there was no return address?"

She shook her head.

"Was the envelope handwritten?"

"Uh, yeah, but I didn't keep it. Sorry. I'll keep the next one."

His gut kicked. "Next one?" She just expected more. "Why didn't you tell me?" he asked quietly.

She lifted a shoulder. "Because I assumed it was the boys next door, and I thought they were harmless threats."

Those boys had some questions to answer. His hands went back to her hips, and he tugged her closer. "Next time, tell me."

He scanned the front door. "Maybe I should upgrade the security on this place." He'd been thinking about it anyway.

She shook her head. "You don't need to do that."

"I want to. Especially since I have to go away again tomorrow for the job in Idaho Falls. I'll probably be gone for a couple of days." He made a mental note to organize the security system and get his team to look at this letter, before lowering his head for a kiss. "I have to get to work now, but I'd love to come over tonight. Maybe we could grab takeout. Watch a movie."

His hands snaked up her shirt and trailed across her warm skin.

Her hands went to his chest. "Okay, but instead of takeout, I'll cook. I make an awesome ragu."

He groaned. "She cooks too." Another kiss to her lips. "Too damn perfect."

It was an hour later when he finally got to his office. He spent the day talking potential projects with a couple of big companies and organizing the new security system for Carina's place. After a lengthy phone call, she'd finally agreed.

He was almost done for the day when his cell rang. "Tom, what can I do for you today?"

Tom was a police officer at the station. Flynn and his team had helped him out with local crimes on a few occasions.

The man sighed. "Flynn, I've received three calls and a visit from a very angry Eadie Brown."

Flynn frowned. "Who?"

"She lives next door to Carina Murphy. Mother to the Brown twins."

Flynn scrubbed a hand over his face. *Christ.* "The kids still aren't back?"

"No. Not answering their phones and haven't made contact with anyone all day. We're not declaring them as missing persons just yet, but the mother is pretty worked up."

"And the mother thinks I did something," Flynn said, more to himself than to Tom. "Look, about a week and a half ago, I arrived at Carina's house to find them egging her windows. Then they snatched her phone and shoved her. I scared them off and made sure they knew if they did it again, there'd be consequences. But that's it. Last night, I was at the street party and then at Carina's. My whereabouts can be verified."

"I know you didn't do anything, Flynn."

He and Tom had been friends in high school. They went way back, and the guy knew that hurting kids wasn't something Flynn would do or allow. Still, as local law enforcement, he had to do his due diligence.

"We're happy to use our resources here at Blue Halo to do what we can to find the kids," Flynn said.

"That would be great. Get the other guys to take care of it though…not you."

"Gotcha. Stay out of it. We'll let you know if they find something."

CHAPTER 15

Carina stepped into The Grind and gave herself a moment to soak it all in. The café was bright. And colorful. And so busy. Just about every table in the place was taken, which was fine. She was just planning on getting coffee to go.

Slowly, she slipped between the tables, making her way to the counter where Courtney stood. The woman's lips widened into a smile.

"Carina! You finally made it in."

She took a seat on a stool. "I did. Sorry it's taken me so long."

Courtney shook her head. "Don't be silly." She shot a glance over Carina's head. "Flynn isn't with you?"

"No, he's away for a couple of nights for a job."

"Ah, yes. The job in Idaho Falls."

Carina tilted her head to the side. "Jason told you about it?"

"Not all of it. Just that some guy's convinced someone's stalking him and his wife, but they haven't found much evidence of it."

"That's strange."

Courtney lifted a shoulder. "If someone's stalking the family, the guys will find him. Now, what can I get you?"

"Just a coffee to go, please."

Courtney pulled back like Carina had offended her. "To go?"

She cringed. "Sorry. I need to be at Patricia's place in twenty minutes."

"All right, I guess I'll forgive you." She turned toward the coffee machine. "It means you miss out on the funny mugs, though."

"No jokes on the to-go cups?"

"Afraid not. The mugs were my grandmother's before she passed away. Well, most of them. I've become somewhat of an addict since, buying whatever I can get my hands on. Amazon loves me."

Carina chuckled. "What was the last purchase?"

Courtney's eyes flicked toward her feet before she set down the milk she'd been heating and disappeared beneath the counter. She pulled out a mug but had her hand over the front so Carina couldn't read it.

"Okay, so there's this guy who comes here a lot. Like, *a lot* a lot. And I should preface this by saying I love all my customers. But he always orders pickles with his meal, and he's the loudest open-mouth eater I have ever heard in my life, so it just..." She closed her eyes like she was trying to calm herself. Carina chuckled. "The sound grinds my gears a little bit."

By *a little bit*, Carina was assuming the woman meant *a ton*.

Courtney turned the mug around.

If I can hear you chew, I have fantasized about your death.

Carina's eyes widened. "You give that to him?"

"No. Sometimes I give it to the customers around him, because he barely seems to read his own mug."

Carina threw her head back and laughed. The woman was hilarious and fearless.

Courtney put the mug back before finishing the coffee, telling another hilarious customer story as she went. When she placed the to-go cup on the counter, Carina pulled out her debit card, but Courtney shook her head.

"Nope. First coffee is always free. Consider it a welcome-to-town drink."

"Oh. Thank you."

Courtney's smile widened. "You're welcome."

"Do I get a free coffee?"

They both turned their heads to see Jason standing behind Carina.

"You, my darling, get all the free coffee your heart desires," Courtney said, leaning over the counter and kissing him.

Okay. Cute. But also her cue to go. Carina stood. "Thanks again, Courtney."

She was turning toward the door when she bumped into someone.

No, not just someone. Greg.

Her eyes widened. "What are you doing here?"

He offered her a small smile. "Same as you, getting a coffee. Are you going now?"

"Ah, yeah. I have to get to work."

"I'll walk you out."

Not her preference, but she wasn't going to cause a scene, so she gave a small nod. When she turned and said goodbye to Courtney and Jason, she didn't miss the narrowing of Jason's eyes or the smile-less wave from Courtney.

They stepped out of the shop, then spoke at the same time.

"Greg—"

"Carina—"

She shook her head. "You first."

He shoved his hands into his pockets. "Okay. I know what you're going to say. That I need to leave. That we're over. But I wanted to remind you that we were friends before we were anything more."

"That's true. But once you've dated someone, you can rarely

go back." Especially after that someone tells you they still love you. That kind of squashes any chance of a friendship.

"I can't just turn it off though. I, um…I've decided," he started slowly, "that I'm going to stay for a few more days. Maybe a week. If you want to catch up during that time, I would love that. If you don't, that's fine too."

Was it, though? His hopeful expression said otherwise.

"I just…" He sighed. "I can't leave until I'm *really* sure you don't want this."

They stopped at her car.

His words confused her. Hadn't she already made herself perfectly clear that she was really done?

His gaze skittered between her and a point in the distance. "If you really don't love me anymore, if you really don't want so much as a friendship, I'll leave at the end of the week." He took a small step closer. If her car wasn't right behind her, she would have stepped back. "But…if you want to remember what we had, explore what we *could* be, then you have my number, and you know I'm close."

"Greg, I appreciate the offer, but I don't need a week, or even a day, to think about it. I'm not going back to Michigan. I'm happy where I am. And…I'm exploring feelings for someone else."

His eyes narrowed. "Someone else?"

"Flynn."

Greg's jaw tightened, and an expression came over his face that she hadn't seen before. There was definitely anger. Not to mention jealousy.

"I'm not going to lie—I don't like that. But regardless, I'm not a man who gives up on what he wants, and I know what I have to offer. So I'm staying the week, Carina. I hope you get in contact."

God, the guy didn't stop.

He bent closer to kiss her on the cheek, but Carina quickly pressed a hand to his chest, pushing him away.

Another flex of his jaw. Then he blew out an exasperated breath. "Bye, Carina."

He disappeared down the street. Carina was just about to climb into her car when she looked up to see Jason watching her from inside the café. And he didn't look happy.

~

FLYNN STOOD SILENTLY inside Paul Simmons's home. Paul wasn't here tonight.

They were trying a different tactic to draw the guy out. If there *was* a guy. Paul had entered his home this afternoon in broad daylight before sneaking out the back, through a neighbor's yard, and getting into Tyler's car.

Tyler was spending the night with Paul and his wife at the hotel, while Flynn remained here, hiding inside the house. They were counting on this guy having seen Paul enter alone.

Flynn treaded the carpet lightly. Fuck, he was tired. He'd already been awake for the last thirty-six hours, and he was going to be awake for another twelve. His body could handle less sleep than most, but tomorrow he'd sure as hell be crashing.

It wasn't just the lack of sleep or the job that was making him frustrated though.

It was Jason's message about Carina's ex trailing her out of the café—and trying to kiss her.

It shouldn't make him so annoyed. He knew that. But the fact that he wasn't there... Yeah, it made his chest feel tight as hell.

He scrubbed a hand over his face right as his phone vibrated from his pocket. Tugging it out, he wasn't surprised to see it was Tyler.

Any activity?

Flynn sent a quick reply.

Nothing yet. But it's only midnight.

He was just tucking his cell back into his pocket when he

heard it. The light rustling of feet on the ground outside. It was almost silent.

Almost.

Flynn held very still. Made sure his breathing and heartbeat were even. The footsteps drew closer to the house. They hadn't put anyone on the street intentionally. Any time they'd surveilled the street, the asshole hadn't shown. So now it was just Flynn.

He moved out of the bedroom. All the curtains were drawn, ensuring there was no way the asshole would see him. He reached the stairs and moved down slowly.

Suddenly, glass shattered somewhere in the house, closely followed by footsteps.

Footsteps moving *away* from the house.

Flynn took off, dropping down the last of the steps and leaping through the broken living room window, not caring about the shard of glass that cut through his clothes and slashed his skin.

The guy was on the street, running. When he turned his head, Flynn got a glance at his face. Saw the angry sneer.

Flynn cursed under his breath. The asshole *was* fast. A hell of a lot faster than he should be.

Paul was right. This guy wasn't normal.

Flynn pumped his legs, ignoring the whip of the air on his face and movement of a car zipping past.

The guy turned a corner, and by the time Flynn followed, he was already turning another. He was too damn fast. Not faster than Flynn, but definitely his equal. All Flynn could do was keep pace.

At the next corner, Flynn saw him run into a backyard.

From his distance, he could hear the blasting of music and people. A party.

Flynn ignored the beeping of a horn, speeding across the road and into the yard. He watched as the guy jumped the fence into the yard of the next house behind. Flynn did the same.

That's when he realized this was the place the music was coming from.

Fuck.

He ran around the house. There were cars all over the road. People everywhere. In the house. Out of it. In their cars.

He scanned the faces, but it was like picking a needle out of a haystack. All he'd caught was a glimpse of the guy. And right now, there were too many to single out his face, and worse, there were cars coming and going. He could be in the house. In a car. Already running again.

"Goddammit!" Flynn shouted, shoving his hands through his hair in frustration. He wasn't going to catch him. Not tonight. But he had achieved one thing. He'd confirmed what Paul had told him. This guy wasn't normal. Flynn wasn't sure if he was exactly like them, but he at least had their speed.

And that was dangerous for a man on the wrong side of the law.

CHAPTER 16

*C*arina smiled as she turned onto Patricia's street. Heck, she'd been smiling all morning. A smile that lifted her spirits and had little parts of her soul doing a happy dance. Because Flynn was coming home today.

How was it possible that she could miss a man when a few weeks ago, she didn't even know him?

Maybe there'd been an empty section of her heart, a section she hadn't known existed. And now that he'd filled it, brought attention to it, there was no going back.

The raindrops started just as she was pulling up at Patricia's house. Big, fat raindrops that splatted across the glass. The sky had been gray all morning, so it wasn't a surprise.

She reached across to the passenger side and grabbed her bag before stepping out of the car. At the twinge in her knee, she cringed. Crap. She'd forgotten to put on her knee brace. Not good. Especially with the slippery, wet ground. Most days, the brace was the only thing that kept her knee feeling stable.

Well, not much she could do now.

Carefully, she walked up the stairs. *Don't slip* was pretty much on repeat in her head the entire way.

She was just opening the door when she heard it. Loud clattering. Pots and pans, maybe?

Frowning, she stepped inside. Her mouth dropped open at what she saw.

The house was a mess. It looked like someone had broken in and trashed the place. Cushions covered the floor. Every drawer in the living room and kitchen was open and empty, the contents tossed everywhere.

Her gaze shot over to Patricia in the kitchen. She had her head in a cupboard and was midway through emptying the containers.

What the heck was going on?

Carina dropped her bag by the door before moving across the room and bending down beside her. "Patricia, what are you doing?"

The woman looked up, and Carina almost pulled back at the wild look in her eyes. "Where are they, Dorothy?"

Carina frowned. "Where are what?"

"My car keys! Where are my keys?"

Patricia didn't have a car—not since her Alzheimer's had progressed and her license had been canceled. "Why do you need your car keys?"

"To find David! I've searched the entire house. The entire yard. I even tried calling him, but the number didn't work!" Patricia rose to her feet, her gaze skittering around the room in an almost manic way. Whether she was looking for her keys or her late husband, Carina wasn't sure.

Carina touched her arm. "How about we have some tea?"

She was scared that if she reminded the older woman her husband was deceased right now, that would just upset her further.

"Tea?" Patricia stepped back, and Carina's hand fell. "Did you hear what I said, Dorothy? David's *missing*! I can't have tea when David's missing. I need to find him. He might be in trouble!" The older woman pressed a hand to her chest. "I have this awful feeling inside me. Like he's not okay. You need to help me find him!"

Oh, gosh. "Okay. I will."

Patricia frowned. Carina's chest tightened with unease as the woman took another step back. "Why aren't you panicking? Do you know where he is?"

Carina was careful to keep her voice calm. "No." God, she'd always been a terrible liar, and by the angry look on the woman's face, she saw right through her.

"You're lying! Where is he?"

"Patricia—"

"Did you take my keys?"

"How could I have taken your keys? I just got here." Carina took a small step forward, her hands raised. "Why don't I try calling him? Maybe I'll get through."

Carina was hoping and praying that if Patricia was calling her Dorothy, she might be confused enough to think Flynn was his father.

"I already told you," Patricia shouted in obvious frustration. "He didn't answer."

Patricia turned, moving out of the kitchen and toward her bedroom. Carina followed, watching as the older woman tugged clothes out of drawers. She wasn't going to stop.

Carina grabbed her phone from her pocket. "I'm going to call him. I'll be back in a second."

Patricia didn't even acknowledge her words. Quickly, Carina stepped out of the room and called Flynn.

Usually, he answered on the first ring. This time it took three. "Hey, honey."

The man sounded tired. He was never tired. Guilt flooded her at disturbing him when he'd just finished a two-day job.

"I'm sorry to call."

"You don't need to be sorry. What's wrong?"

Could he hear it in her voice? "It's your mom."

Suddenly, the exhaustion left his voice. "What happened? Is she okay?"

"She's not good today. She's pulling her house apart looking for her car keys because she wants to go search for your dad."

Flynn cursed over the line. "Okay, I'll—"

A bang sounded from the other room, cutting off Flynn's words. Carina raced back into the bedroom and gasped at the sight of Patricia on the floor, clutching her wrist.

"Oh God." She ran over to the woman and dropped down beside her.

"What happened?" Flynn asked. A whoosh of air sounded over the line, like he was running.

"She fell. She's holding her wrist." Carina touched Patricia's elbow. "Patricia, are you okay?"

"I just… I need David!" A tear fell down the older woman's cheek as she continued cradling her wrist.

Carina's heart broke for the woman.

"I'm in the car. I'll be faster than an ambulance."

"Okay. See you in a second." Carina hung up.

She leaned closer, inspecting the wrist. Just by the swelling and tenderness when she probed it, Carina was almost certain it was a break. Her fingers were moving though, so there was circulation. She needed an X-ray.

Quickly, Carina rose to her feet. "I'll be back in a moment, Patricia." She raced into the kitchen and hunted through the recycling until she found a sturdy piece of cardboard. She also grabbed a small towel from the hall cupboard before running back into the room.

"I need to immobilize the joint, so I'm going to make a splint for your wrist. Is that okay?"

The woman gave a small nod, her eyes still foggy with confusion.

Carefully, Carina wrapped the wrist with the towel to cushion the joint before placing the cardboard beneath her arm. Then she grabbed a shirt from the floor and used it to fasten the splint. She tied it tightly enough to keep the wrist still but not tight enough to cut off circulation or hurt the woman.

Once she was done, she looked back at Patricia. "Flynn's going to be here in a second, and then we need to get you to a hospital."

"Flynn? I don't..." Patricia shook her head, the tears once again building in her eyes. "I'm confused."

This poor woman. "I know. I'm sorry." So damn sorry, her chest felt like it was bleeding. "But I'll be here with you until he gets here, okay? You won't be alone."

She didn't know if that offered the woman any comfort, but she hoped so. A lot of the time in hospitals, when older patients came in, company in times of pain helped.

It wasn't long before she heard the front door open, then Flynn ran into the bedroom. Carina inched back as he bent down in front of his mother, his eyes pained when he glanced at her wrist.

"Mom?"

Finally, some of the confusion slipped from Patricia's face. "Flynny. You're here."

"I'm here, Mom. Let's get you to the hospital."

Carina picked up her bag and followed, locking the door behind them. She sat in the back with Patricia, helping to keep her arm stable as Flynn drove. When they arrived at the hospital, he carried his mother to the reception area and then into a patient room, where he lowered her to the bed.

It was about five minutes later when Victoria stepped into the room. Carina's stomach cramped, but she was careful not to show it. This wasn't about her—it was about Patricia.

"Good morning, everyone," Victoria said, her gaze brushing over Flynn before landing on Patricia.

He shook his head. "No. I want a different doctor."

The corners of Victoria's eyes creased, her lips thinning. "It's a very busy day in the ER, Flynn. Every doctor is working with other patients right now."

The veins in his neck bulged.

Carina remained silent. She was sure his mom would be fine with Victoria. As far as they knew, the woman didn't have anything against Patricia. But this was Flynn's decision.

Victoria stepped forward. "I promise you, your mother is safe with me."

Patricia groaned. He looked at her, taking in her pale face.

"Fine," he said through gritted teeth.

Victoria nodded, stepping beside the bed and lifting Patricia's arm. "Patricia, can you tell me what you're feeling?"

"My wrist hurts."

Victoria gave a small nod as she started to unwrap the wrist. "And can you tell me what happened?"

Patricia frowned before shaking her head. "I don't... The morning's a blur."

Carina pushed off the wall. "She slipped. There was a lot of clothing on her bedroom floor, so I assume she tripped on them."

Victoria turned cold eyes toward Carina. "You assume?"

"I was turned away and on the phone with Flynn."

There was a slight thinning of the woman's mouth before she turned back. "Based on the deformity of the wrist and the swelling, it looks to be a distal radius fracture, but I'll order an X-ray so we can know for sure."

She lowered Patricia's wrist carefully. "I'll just go check when they can do the scan."

Carina took a small step back as Victoria left the room.

Flynn stepped forward, talking quietly to his mother. She'd never seen him this worried—or this tired. It had her heart tearing with guilt. The fall shouldn't have happened. It was her fault for not following Patricia when she left the kitchen. She shouldn't have taken her eyes off the older woman.

When tears welled in Patricia's eyes again, Carina stepped into the hall, wanting to give them some privacy.

Her finger clenched the strap of her purse. *Her fault.* The words continued to repeat in her head. Maybe she should have tried harder to calm Patricia. Maybe she should have offered to drive the woman to find David and taken her to Flynn.

It was probably better that she stay in the waiting room. Scrubbing her hands over her face, Carina turned and walked straight into Victoria.

"Oh, my gosh." Carina took a quick step back. "I'm sorry."

Victoria gave her a tight smile. "It's fine." Then she stepped around her and headed into Patricia's room.

Carina blew out a long breath. She'd only taken a few steps toward reception when she heard Flynn.

"Carina. Can you come in?"

She hesitated. The guilt was eating at her. And surely, Flynn felt what she felt. That this was on her.

But she wasn't going to walk away from him when he was asking for her.

Turning back, she stepped into the room. When Flynn held his hand out for her, she almost sighed in relief. She dropped her bag by the lone chair, and moved to his side. His fingers wrapped around hers. Maybe he didn't feel the same.

CHAPTER 17

*F*lynn leaned his head back against the wall. Damn, he was tired. The waiting room was busy and loud, and every little sound ground at his skull. All he wanted was silence. He hadn't slept in forty-eight hours and, fuck, he was feeling it.

Anger tore at his chest, suffocating him. Anger that he hadn't been there to stop his mother from falling and breaking a bone. Anger at the goddamn disease that was riddling her mind. And anger at himself for not catching the guy who had gotten away last night. He'd missed time with his mother to get this guy, and he hadn't even done that.

His fingers tapped the arms of his chair in quick succession, so agitated he could barely sit still. A soft hand covered his, and his eyes flew open to see Carina in the seat beside him.

"Hey." Her quiet voice soothed some of the unease coiling in his gut. Not all of it, but some.

"Hey."

Her eyes searched his. "How are you doing?"

"I hate seeing her like this. I hate her being in pain. I'm all she has left. I should have protected her from this."

"You can't be there all the time."

"She needs someone."

Carina bit her lip, and whatever she was about to say, Flynn knew he wouldn't like.

"It might be time," she said quietly, "to start looking into full-time care."

His entire fucking chest clenched. "You're saying I should move her into a care facility?"

"Maybe."

Shredded—that's how the idea made him feel. His mother had been living in that house for a long time. It was her home. The place where she'd lived with his father. The place where she'd raised Flynn. Taking her away from that would be taking her away from everything she knew.

Carina's fingers tightened around his. He leaned his head back again and was about to close his eyes when she spoke.

"I'm sorry."

When he looked at her again, he saw it. The guilt. The pain. "For what?"

"For taking my eyes off her when I called you. I knew she was throwing her clothes everywhere. I should have recognized she was at risk of falling."

He turned his hand over and threaded his fingers through hers. "It's not your fault."

She opened her mouth, but before she could speak, Victoria stopped in front of them. "Patricia's back in the room, and I have the results."

He nodded. When Carina started to stand, Victoria turned to her. "I need to speak to Flynn alone for a moment."

Immediately, he shook his head. "I'm okay with her being there."

"No. There's something else. Something that needs to be discussed alone."

Now the woman was just pissing him off. He stepped forward. He wasn't in the mood for bullshit right now. He spoke slowly so she understood every word he said. "Carina is Patricia's nurse. And I want her there."

He was fully prepared to battle the woman on the issue, but then Carina touched his arm. "It's fine. If Victoria—I mean, Dr. Astor—wants to talk to you alone, then I'll just wait here."

She gave him a quick smile before lowering back into the seat.

Flynn's chest brimmed with frustration, but he needed to get to his mother. He turned to Carina. "I'll call you in a couple minutes."

Another small smile from her, then he followed Victoria into the room. There was another woman in the room as well, a nurse, but he went straight to his mother's side. Her eyes were closed, and her chest was moving with even breaths.

"We gave Patricia a sedative for the pain and exhaustion," Victoria said before turning to the woman beside her. "This is Nurse Kalli."

"Hi." He barely spared the nurse a glance. "How's her wrist?"

"Fractured distal radius, like I suspected. The radial distal is the long bone in the forearm near the wrist. The good news is, it looks like it will heal on its own. The bad news is, we needed to put a cast on her, and the cast will need to remain for six to eight weeks, so she may need extra in-home support."

Flynn nodded. He already planned to be there more and call Home Care Agency to request a second nurse be there when Carina couldn't.

"Because no one actually witnessed the fall, I'd like to keep her overnight just for observation to make sure she's okay," Victoria added.

"That's fine."

There was a small pause. "There's something else."

Flynn's gaze left his mother, and he scanned Victoria's face, but the woman gave away nothing. Then he looked at the nurse. Unlike Victoria, she gave away *everything*. She was clearly uncomfortable.

His gaze shot back to Victoria. "What is it?"

"Carina left her bag in here on the floor. When Kalli came in, she saw something."

His eyes narrowed on the nurse. "What?"

The nurse was holding her hands tightly in front of her, fidgeting and looking nervous as hell. "Prescription pain medication."

"It's not the medication I prescribed her. I was careful to order her a different kind of med than prescribed to your mother. Not that Carina should be taking it anymore, anyway. The medication in her bag is the same kind your mother has for *her* knee—and the same kind Carina was accused of stealing in Michigan," Victoria added.

Flynn straightened, every muscle in his body tensing. "Maybe she keeps it in there for my mother."

"There are two bottles in there, Flynn. And the labels have been torn off."

When he remained both silent and still, Victoria nodded toward the bag. "Check for yourself."

He walked over to her bag, and sure enough, two small containers of pain medication sat inside. And just like Victoria said, there were no names on the bottles, just the name of the medication.

He ran a hand through his hair. "I don't believe it. Someone put them in there."

"I'm sorry," the nurse said quietly. "I wasn't trying to be nosy. I just saw them and had to say something."

"I need you to say the words," he said, watching the young woman closely. "I need you to say that you found the drugs in Carina's bag."

He watched her closely to see if her pupils dilated. Listened to the beating of her heart. He blocked out everything else. Everything but her.

Kalli swallowed. "Her bag was open, and I saw the prescription pain medication on the top. I mentioned it to Dr. Astor, not realizing..."

Truth. She was telling the truth. His entire chest seized.

Flynn scrubbed a hand over his face. He was so fucking tired, and his head felt foggy as hell. He yanked his phone from his pocket and sent a quick text to Carina, asking her to come to the room.

Every second they waited, his chest grew tighter. His gaze shot to his mother again. She looked so small and frail under the sheet. She was his to protect. And at this moment, he couldn't help but think he might have let her down.

THE SECOND CARINA stepped into the room, she felt it. The heavy energy that had her stomach dropping. The thickness in the air that almost choked her.

Her gaze shot around the room. To Patricia sleeping. To Victoria and the nurse beside her. And to Flynn. He still looked tired and frustrated and angry, but there was something different about him.

"What is it?" she asked quietly, unease trickling down her spine. "Is Patricia okay?"

Oh God, was it worse than a broken wrist? Had she hit her head or something?

Flynn held up two small bottles of pills. It took Carina a second to recognize them as Patricia's pain medication. "What were these doing in your bag, Carina? And why is the label with my mother's name torn off?"

For a moment, Carina's entire world slowed. Not just at the questions or at the way they pulled her back to the worst time in her life, but at the way Flynn asked. With a cold, hard voice. A voice she barely recognized.

She took a step forward. "Flynn—"

"Just answer the questions, Carina." His voice rose, and the muscles in his arms flexed.

Her feet stopped. And little parts of her heart, the parts that had been learning to trust, splintered.

"I don't know," she said quietly.

He watched her like he was searching for the truth. But the thing was...he shouldn't have to search. He should *know*. Yes, they'd only known each other a short amount of time, but in that time, she'd fallen for him. Let him into her bed. Her heart. And if situations were reversed, she never would have questioned his integrity.

He ran a hand through his hair, turning to look at his mother. "I don't know what to fucking believe."

His words sliced at her insides like razor blades. Tears pressed at her eyes, but she straightened, blinking the wetness away. She wanted to fall apart. To crumble. But she owed it to herself to speak on her own behalf.

"If I really stole drugs, do you think I'd be so stupid as to leave my bag unattended in this room?" Her gaze swung to Victoria. "Maybe someone else put them in there."

Victoria's eyes narrowed. "I haven't been unattended in this room with your bag. That can be verified."

Flynn also watched Victoria closely as she spoke. He was listening for a lie. Did he find one?

"You need to leave," Flynn said quietly.

He wasn't looking at Carina, but she knew his words were meant for her. For a moment, she couldn't breathe. The air just wasn't reaching her lungs.

This wasn't real. It couldn't be. He didn't actually think she'd stolen medication from his mother. Just three nights ago, he'd told her he was all in...

"Flynn, I didn't—"

"Just *go*."

She flinched at his words. And this time, they were more like a dagger straight to the center of her heart. More tears stung, and again, she blinked them back. She would not stand here and cry. She would not let the man witness the depth of her devastation.

Grabbing her bag, she walked out of the room and then the hospital.

She breathed deeply the entire time. Because that was all she could do to keep herself together. To keep from completely falling apart.

It was happening again. Only this time, it was worse. So much worse. Because even in Michigan, at least Greg had believed her. Offered her sanctuary. And she felt things for Flynn she'd *never* experienced with Greg. But Flynn had made a choice. A choice to *not* believe in her.

And in doing so, he'd shattered her heart.

The second she stepped outside, rain soaked her hair. Her clothes. She barely felt it. She didn't have a car, but she couldn't stay at the hospital and wait for a ride. But she needed to get out of here. Needed to be away from him.

So she walked, ignoring the rain. Ignoring the way her insides felt raw. And now that she was alone, she finally let the tears fall.

She didn't know how long she'd been walking when a car slowed beside her. "Carina?"

Greg.

She kept walking. Even though her tears had mixed with the rain, her eyes had to be red and puffy. She probably looked like hell.

"Carina, stop. Get in the car."

She couldn't even respond to him. She didn't want his help or anyone else's. The only thing she wanted was to crawl into a dark space and let the world disappear for a while.

The car stopped. When Greg ran out and grabbed her arm, her knee jolted and gave way, causing her to stumble. A small cry slipped from her lips. Greg put an arm around her waist, keeping her on her feet.

"Christ, Carina! Are you okay?"

She grabbed his shoulder to steady herself, breathing through the pain. "I'm fine."

"You're not. You're crying, your skin feels like ice, and your knee just gave out." He squinted at her through the rain. "Please get in the car."

She swallowed. "No. I'm almost home."

"You're not. You have at least another fifteen minutes of walking before you get there."

She knew he was right. And there was no way she'd last that long, not considering how numb her limbs had become, and her now aching knee. Swallowing the self-pity, she turned and let him help her into the car.

The second they started moving, she felt Greg's eyes on her. "What happened?"

"Nothing." Not nothing. Her world had once again imploded. But the last thing she wanted to do was put her ugly reality into words right now.

"Carina, let me in. I might be able to help."

Help? No one could help her. It was done. Flynn believed what he chose to believe. And she was breaking.

She swallowed, looking through her side window, not wanting him to see the fresh tears building in her eyes. There was no rain to hide them anymore.

A few minutes passed. Then Greg sighed. The rest of the drive was silent. When they got to her house, she didn't even have a chance to tell Greg not to come in because he was already out, and, God, she didn't have the energy to argue.

When they stepped into her house, he went straight to the kitchen to turn on the kettle. She lowered onto the couch, not caring that she was soaking wet. A second later, he sat beside her, gently lifting her knee.

"How's it feeling?"

"It's fine."

He tsked before feeling around the area.

"Greg." When he didn't react or lift his head, she repeated his name, this time louder. "*Greg.*"

Finally, he looked up.

"Thank you for driving me home, but I really want to be alone right now." She needed to crawl into bed and wish this awful day away. She needed space to drown in her misery.

He studied her for a long moment before finally nodding. "Okay. I'll go. But I'm going to keep checking in on you. I need to make sure you're okay."

She didn't have words, and if she tried for them, she knew her voice would break.

He rose to his feet before pressing a kiss to her forehead. The kiss just made her sad. Because it wasn't the kiss her body craved.

The second Greg left, the room fell silent. And even though she was soaking wet, even though her skin was ice cold and her knee ached, she dropped to her side, lying on the couch. Her eyes closed, and she tried to clear her mind, but all she could see was Flynn. All she could hear was his cold voice as he told her to get out, like he could no longer stand the sight of her.

CHAPTER 18

lynn stepped into the Blue Halo building and moved up the stairs. He'd woken up with a pit in his stomach, and it was still fucking there. All he could think about was the expression on Carina's face in the hospital room yesterday. That look of disbelief mixed with hurt and anger...

It tormented him. Tore at his damn soul.

He'd tried calling her. He'd even gone to her house this morning, but she hadn't been home. Probably for the best. He didn't know what he would have said. He still had no idea what happened yesterday. And when he'd gone back to his mom's house, there had been no pain medication anywhere. So *had* she taken his mother's pain pills? Had she pulled his mother's name off so no one could prove who they belonged to?

Shaking his head, he pushed into the reception area and moved down the hall. When he passed the gym, he was tempted to stop and hit the bag for a while. Let out some of his frustration. Instead, he moved into his office, all but slamming the door behind him.

Settling behind his desk, Flynn leaned back in his seat and

scrubbed a hand over his face. Footsteps sounded down the hall before they stopped outside his office. Then the knock came.

"Go away," Flynn shouted.

The asshole didn't. Aidan pushed the door open before stepping inside and crossing his arms. He lifted a brow. "You look like hell."

"Yeah, well, I look how I feel, then."

"Wanna talk about it?"

"Nope."

For a moment, Aidan was silent. "What about a coffee?"

Fuck, he could use ten right now. He checked his watch. He had some work to do before picking his mom up from the hospital, but, yeah, he could use some caffeine.

His friend was silent as they left the office. It wasn't until they were on the street that Aidan finally asked the question Flynn had been waiting for. "This about Carina?"

"Mom broke her wrist yesterday."

Aidan cursed. "Is she okay?"

"Yeah. Hospital kept her overnight as a precaution, but I'm picking her up after lunch."

Aidan nodded. "What else?"

Of course, his friend knew there was more. They all saw every little part of each other.

He ran a hand through his hair. "A nurse found prescription pain medication in Carina's bag. Two bottles. The same medication Mom takes for her knee—and the same one Carina was accused of stealing in Michigan."

For a moment, Aidan was silent. It was a silence much like the one he'd felt in that room yesterday. Bursting with disbelief. Confusion.

"You think she took them?"

"I don't know what the hell to think. I watched and listened to the nurse when she said she found them, and Victoria when she said she'd never been alone in the room with her bag, and both of them told the truth. And Mom didn't have any medication in her house."

"What about Carina when you asked her if she took them?"

Flynn paused. Had he actually asked her that exact question? "I asked her what they were doing in her bag, and she said she didn't know."

"Was she telling the truth?"

Was she? He'd been so damn tired... Had he actually looked at her closely, like he had the nurse and Victoria? "I don't know. My head was a mess. I'd just gotten off the forty-eight-hour stakeout in Idaho Falls. And I was pissed about losing that guy and worried about Mom."

"I think it's worth asking her again and really looking at her when she answers."

He blew out a long breath. "Hell, I don't think she did it. I have no idea *how* they got there, or why Mom has no medication in the house...but I know she wouldn't do that." Jesus, what the hell was wrong with him? "You should have seen the look on her face when I questioned her. When I told her to get out. It was like I tore out her fucking heart."

Was the damage irreversible?

"So make it right," Aidan said quietly as they crossed the street. "If I still had a shot with Cassie, I'd sure as hell take it."

Flynn glanced at his friend. "I heard you flew over to Pinedale, Wyoming, last week."

Aidan stopped outside The Grind. Flynn didn't miss the way the muscles in his arms tensed. "Who told you that?"

"Tyler saw the boarding pass on your computer."

Aidan shot a glance at the coffee shop door, then back at him. "I had to see her. Just once. I had to make sure she's happy and safe."

Flynn's heart hurt for his friend. He'd been dating a woman before he'd been taken by Project Arma. He'd loved her. In fact, while they were held at the compound, he'd talked about her every damn day. But by the time they got out, two long years later, Cassie had married someone else. And she hadn't reached out to him once since the world learned of their ordeal.

"And?" he asked quietly.

Aidan lifted a shoulder. "They were out for lunch, and she did —look happy."

"Did you talk to her?"

He laughed but there was no humor behind it. "So I could torture myself further? No. I just needed to make sure she was okay. And she was." He swallowed, his head dipping to his chest. "She's been friends with the guy she married since they were kids. I never thought it was anything more than that."

Flynn still thought it was worth talking to the woman. But he could see Aidan wasn't ready. Not yet.

Aidan opened the door. "Let me know how it goes with Carina."

Flynn followed him inside The Grind. And that was when he saw her.

Carina, sitting in a booth near the window.

With her ex.

CARINA LET the heat from the coffee mug seep up her arms and into her chest. Greg sat opposite her, talking about some medical journal article he'd read recently. She was struggling to follow. Not because she couldn't understand what he was saying, but because she'd gotten basically no sleep and woken up feeling just as groggy as she'd felt yesterday. She wasn't even sure why she was having coffee with him. Maybe because he'd just shown up this morning, and she'd been too tired to say no? Or maybe she'd been feeling so damn heartbroken that a bit of company from someone who had always been on her side felt nice.

"Awesome mugs," Greg said, holding his up.

They were. And on a normal day, she was sure she'd be able to appreciate them. His said, *And here we go again. I mean, good morning.*

She glanced down at hers. *I can't be held responsible for what my face does when you speak.* Both were pretty fitting for her mood today.

"Courtney's shop's pretty great." She took another sip of her coffee. It was almost finished, and the second the mug was empty, she planned to return home. What she was going to *do* at home, she had no idea. "Are you still going back to Michigan once the week is up?"

The smile slipped from his lips. "I don't know. That depends on you."

She swallowed. "Greg—"

"I want you to come with me."

Oh God. She did not have the energy for this again. Not today. "Even if I left Cradle Mountain"—which was looking very likely—"I'm not going back to Michigan."

A frown creased his brows. "Why not?"

"You know why. I feel like every person I run into knows what happened in that town. I don't want to go back and have people stare at me like I'm a terrible person while I'm doing my grocery shopping. Not to mention, no one would ever hire me to work as a nurse there again."

Although, after yesterday, she might not be able to work *anywhere* as a nurse again. Would Flynn go so far as to report her? If he did, she didn't know if she had the strength to defend herself a second time. The case in Michigan had gone on for two months, and it had drained her, almost costing Carina her sanity.

Greg swallowed before giving a quick nod. "Okay. Well, I can go where you go."

Her mug landed heavily on the table. How many times did she have to tell this man no?

She was moments from losing the last fragments of her

patience when Courtney stepped up to their table, her smile tight.

"Hey. Just wanted to come over and check that everything's okay. See if you need anything else."

Greg smiled at the woman. "It's great, thank you. Nothing else for me."

Carina nodded. "Same." Her gaze caught on the door as it opened behind Courtney, and her heart started beating a million miles an hour. Aidan. Closely followed by Flynn.

Flynn's gaze caught hers immediately. When it flicked to Greg, his eyes darkened.

Okay. Coffee time was officially over. She gulped the last bit of coffee, ignoring the burn in her throat. She was no longer looking at Flynn, but she could feel his eyes on her, watching from where he sat at the counter.

Carina pushed up from the booth. "I need to get going."

"I'll come with you." Greg started to rise.

"No." She held up her hand, stopping him.

"But I drove you."

"I'll walk."

He huffed. "Your knee—"

"I'm really fine, Greg. I'll text later, okay?"

She walked toward the door before he could say anything else, and she was almost certain she saw Courtney inadvertently blocking his way out of the booth.

She wasn't sure why she cared about Flynn seeing her with her ex. Maybe she *didn't* care. Maybe she just didn't want to be in the same room as either of them. Who the hell knew? The hurt was so strong it muddled up everything else inside her.

The second she was far enough away from the shop, she slowed, letting the limp take over. The jolt to her knee yesterday had definitely set her back in her recovery. The pressure was now a dull throb, and this walk wouldn't make it any better.

She tugged her phone from her pocket to call a car.

149

"Clemence speaking."

"Hi, Clemence, this is Carina. Any chance you're free to give me a lift?"

"Won't be available for another hour, I'm afraid."

"Oh. Um. Okay. No problem. I can walk."

Her house wasn't that far. She quickly hung up and tucked the phone back into her jeans.

"Why are you limping?"

She jerked in surprise and spun around. In the process, her knee hitched *again*, and she cried out as she almost fell.

Flynn grabbed her by the arms, holding her up. "Jesus, Carina. Are you okay?"

"I'm fine." She snatched herself out of his hands. His touch burned her, and for once, it wasn't in a good way.

"You're not fine. Your knee's worse than it was yesterday. Why?"

She could have laughed, even though there was nothing funny about any of this. "Yesterday you were accusing me of stealing your mother's medication, and today you're worried about my wellbeing?"

"I didn't accuse you. I asked what the bottles were doing in your bag."

She shook her head. It was the same thing.

"And yes," he continued. "I'm worried about your wellbeing."

"You don't need to be."

She tried to step away, but he grabbed her arm. "Carina—"

"What, Flynn? What do you want from me? Because I'm not going to lie, I was on top of the world yesterday morning, but you kind of shattered me a few hours later. And I know you had a lot going on with your mom and just getting back from a job, but I needed more from you. I needed your trust!"

"Just listen—"

"*No.* You don't get to worry about my wellbeing or care about my knee when you care so little about the rest of me. I need you to leave me alone. It's the only way I can mend my heart before any more of it breaks."

Something flickered across his face. Pain, maybe? Remorse? Her gaze shot away, because looking at him was just too hard for her fragile mind right now.

He held her for a moment longer, then slowly, his fingers untangled from her arm. And for just a second, she was hit by a massive wave of longing. Longing to have his touch return. To have him return to *her*.

But she gritted her teeth and limped down the road. She had no idea how long it would take her to get home. She just knew she needed to get away before any more of her disintegrated.

CHAPTER 19

Flynn had just parked outside the hospital to pick up his mother when his phone rang.

"Callum, you get anything?"

His team was still helping search for the Brown twins. Neither boy had shown up yet. And every day that passed had Flynn thinking more and more that this wasn't a simple case of the teenagers having some fun.

"We spoke to a couple of their friends this morning. They said the boys went to their car after the street party and were supposed to be driving to one of their places but never showed. We also spoke to Tom. He said there's been no activity on their phones since that night. Both numbers are just going straight to voicemail."

Shit. Something had happened to the boys. And the longer they were missing, the less likely it was they'd be found alive.

"We did learn something interesting though."

Flynn took off his seat belt and climbed out of the car. "Tell me."

"Their car was spotted on street surveillance footage driving down Highway 75 toward Bald Mountain that night."

Flynn paused beside his car. "I'm guessing none of their friends live near Bald Mountain?"

"Nope."

He shook his head. "I don't like this. Any of it."

"Me neither. We're going to spend a few days searching the area, see if we can find anything. We'll let you know if we do."

"Appreciate it."

"Before you go, got some more bad news for you."

Dammit. Not what he needed today. "Hit me with it."

"There were no prints on the note left for Carina."

"So it probably wasn't the twins, then." Because they sure as hell weren't smart enough to not leave prints. "And we have no other leads." *Fuck.*

"Sorry, brother."

"Thanks for looking into it."

Tucking the phone into his pocket, he headed into the hospital and down the hall toward his mom's room. The news about the note was annoying as hell, but he'd suspected as much. And the fact the twins were still missing... Yeah, that was worrying as hell.

Ideally, he would have liked to help look into the twins' disappearance. But with Tom's warning, and the mother still breathing down his neck, that was a no-go. Even if Tom hadn't warned him, it was smarter for him to stay away from it and let his team take over.

He stepped into his mother's room to see her fully dressed and standing by the window. Her silhouette took him back to his childhood. She used to do that often. Stand by the window, letting the sun wash over her.

He'd always wondered what she thought about when she stood there. He knew she loved nature, and she appreciated the little things that most didn't pause to notice. The bees that congregated around the flowers. The way the leaves turned upside down before a storm.

He took slow steps forward, not wanting to pull her out of whatever she was thinking about. It wasn't until he was standing beside her, and she didn't react at all, that he suspected she'd known he was there the entire time.

"Did I make a noise?" he asked.

Her lips tilted up. "You're my son, Flynn. I knew the second you stepped into the room, no noise needed."

He wasn't sure how that was possible, but he knew better than to question the woman. "How are you feeling?"

"Ready to go home."

"Do you remember what happened?"

Her brows scrunched. "Little bits and pieces." When she looked up at him, her eyes turned sad. "I'm sorry."

He frowned. "What are you sorry for?"

"Every time I forget you, I feel like I let you down."

Her words had his chest clenching. "Not true at all. You could never let me down, Mom."

She smiled, but just like her eyes, the smile was sad. "That's very kind of you to say, honey. Even if I don't believe it."

She obviously didn't view her struggles the way he did. "You've looked after me your entire life. Now it's my turn to look after you."

She wrapped her fingers around his arm and squeezed. "I appreciate it. I appreciate everything you do for me." She blew out a long breath before shooting a glance behind him. "Do you know when Carina's due to arrive? Or is she meeting us at my place?"

Dammit. This was the part he'd been dreading.

He was careful not to react to her words, but before he could say anything, his mother continued.

"I like her. And I may be old and senile, but I know something's going on between you two."

Flynn looked out the window, trying to figure out a way to

word it without his mother looking at him like he'd run over Bambi.

His mother angled her body toward him, already knowing something was wrong. "What is it?"

There was no best way to say it. Every option made him look like the asshole he was. "When we brought you in, a nurse saw some drugs in Carina's bag. It was the same pain medication that you take."

There was a beat of silence. Then, "Oh, Flynny. What did you do?"

Nothing good.

He scratched the back of his neck, not wanting to say it, because saying it made it more real. "I told her to leave."

And that told his mother everything she needed to know.

There was a long sigh. He lifted his gaze to see her shaking her head. "That woman would not have stolen a penny from me, let alone my pain medication—which she's always encouraging me to take."

His jaw ticked. Yeah. He'd messed up big time.

"You've always had trouble trusting," she said quietly. "Especially this last year. And I'm not saying I blame you. Being taken and going through everything at the hands of men who were supposed to be trustworthy...I don't even have words."

It was true. His entire life had been the military. He'd been a Delta Force soldier, only to get snatched from his hotel room before a mission by men who were former SEALs. Held hostage by a man who was a former military commander. It had shaken his trust in everyone.

"Eventually," his mother said quietly, "you'll need to decide. Give your whole trust to another person or live alone. Because I guarantee you, you can't have both."

His muscles twitched. She was right. He'd tried to convince himself that the decision not to trust Carina had been about his exhaustion, and it partly was. But it also wasn't.

Just a few nights earlier, he'd told her he was all in. But when crunch time came, when he'd had to prove himself, he'd let her down. Christ, he really was an asshole.

"I know. I'm going to fix this." He had to.

His mother patted his arm, and he glanced at the door just as Victoria passed.

"I'm going to talk to Victoria about your discharge," he said, stepping away.

His mother scoffed, remaining where she was. "Good. Better *you* talk to her than me."

He chuckled to himself, almost certain she'd given the woman hell today. She always did.

He moved into the hall just as Victoria fished her phone from her pocket and turned a corner. He trailed behind her and turned the same corner quickly enough to catch her slip into another room as she pressed the phone to her ear.

He frowned. No. Not a room. A supply closet.

He kept moving, stopping a few feet away. With his advanced hearing, he heard every hushed word she spoke.

"Hey. Just leaving a message to check in and see whether you want to grab a drink later. I need a big glass of wine after this week. I can't believe it actually worked. She came in, and I just… did it. Kalli saw the drugs, and everything went to plan. Call me back."

Disbelief and anger roared in Flynn's blood.

The door opened, but before Victoria could take more than a step, he was in front of her.

Her eyes widened. "Flynn. Hi."

"What do you mean, Kalli saw the drugs and everything went to plan?"

Her jaw dropped, and her face paled. And that was the last bit of confirmation he needed.

"You set her up," he said quietly, his face heating with rage. "You planted the drugs in her bag. How?"

"Flynn! You know I wouldn't—"

"Don't fucking lie to me, Victoria." His voice rose, and it had her mouth snapping shut. He'd had enough. "I know you did it, and I want to know *how* and who you're working with."

Her back straightened, and the fear cleared from her face, replaced by a vicious sneer. "If you think I'm going to stand here and admit to a goddamn thing, you're an idiot. Now get out of my way."

"Tell me you *didn't* do it, then."

Her gaze skittered between his eyes. "I don't have to do anything!"

She tried to walk away, but Flynn grabbed her arm. "Victoria—"

"Unless you want me calling security, take your goddamn hands off me."

For a second, he stood there, fingers still wrapped around her arm, rage making him see red. But she was right. Unless he planned to force the words out of her right here in the hospital hallway, he had to let her go.

He'd find another way. There were cameras in this hospital. If she'd done something, they would have caught it.

Slowly, he released her. "This isn't over, Victoria. I *will* find out what happened—and you will pay."

HYPOTHETICALLY, if she cried over spilled milk, did that mean her emotions were a mess?

Okay, maybe it wasn't so hypothetical, but it also wasn't just the spilled milk she was crying over. It was *what* she'd spilled it over. Flynn's shirt. The one he'd given her the day she'd fallen off that box. She'd washed it a couple of times since he'd given it to her, but she'd still managed to convince herself the thing smelled of him.

Yep, it was ridiculous that she was upset. For one, his scent had disappeared after the first wash. Two, the shirt needed another wash anyway, milk or no milk. And three, she shouldn't *want* a shirt that smelled of the man.

She wiped a tear off her damp cheek as she rinsed the shirt in the sink.

Big. Fat. Mess. That's what she was.

For the second time since arriving in Idaho, Carina had spent the entire day searching for jobs. Only this time, she hadn't looked for them in Cradle Mountain. Because she couldn't. Even if there was another nursing job here, there was no way she could remain in the same town as Flynn. Seeing him every week but not being with him... It would crush her.

So, yet again, she needed a new start. And yet again, it was because she'd been accused of something she didn't do.

She blinked away the tears. Once the shirt was rinsed, she took it to the laundry room and bent down to throw it in the washer. Her knee tweaked as she stood, and she cringed at the shot of pain.

Damn it. She really needed to remember to wear her brace, even if she was home all day.

Sucking in a few deep breaths, Carina moved into the kitchen. She was just about to start rinsing dishes when the doorbell rang, causing her to straighten.

Great. Just what she needed—a visitor to see her red, blotchy face.

Scrubbing her cheeks, she went to the door and looked through the peephole, then immediately jerked back. For a moment, she froze, unsure if she had the strength to talk to him today. If she cried over spilled milk on his shirt, what would she do if he told her he'd reported her for stealing drugs? Or was he in the process of making sure she never worked as a nurse again?

She'd probably fall into a heap on the floor and cry.

The guy had already tried to call her multiple times. She

hadn't answered any of the calls or listened to a single message. Because she was a coward.

"Carina, can we talk?"

She bit her bottom lip, wrapping her arms around her waist. Even hearing Flynn's voice had her body fighting between running and tugging the door open.

Maybe if she just ignored him—

"I can hear you breathing," he said almost gently. "And your heartbeat."

Her breath stopped, even though she knew it was too late. She couldn't do anything about her heart though.

"I don't blame you for not wanting to talk to me," he continued, his voice pained. "I'm an asshole and wouldn't want to talk to me either. But I need to apologize, and I want to do it in person."

"Apologize?" she asked quietly, all too aware that if he were a normal man, he wouldn't have heard.

"Yeah, honey. Apologize."

Maybe it was the endearment. Or maybe it was because she was feeling weak. But she took a small step forward, opening the door.

"There you are," he said quietly, a sad smile on his face.

"What do you want to apologize for?"

His hands were shoved into his pockets, and his biceps rippled as he spoke. "I was wrong. So wrong that I don't know how to make it right."

"Wrong about what?" She knew. But she needed to hear him say it.

"You didn't do it. Victoria slipped the drugs into your bag. I don't know how—"

"She bumped into me in the hall," Carina interrupted. "I've gone over and over it in my head, and I'm almost certain that's when she must've slipped them in."

She'd replayed her movements that day a hundred times, and

if it was true that Victoria hadn't been alone in the room with her purse, the bump in the hall was the only time she could have done it.

His jaw ticked. "I'll see if I can access any video footage."

"So you can confirm I'm innocent."

"I know you're innocent."

She tilted her head. "How do you know?" Because he certainly hadn't known the other day.

"I overheard Victoria saying everything with Kalli went as planned. She didn't admit to it specifically, but she may as well have."

The small hope in Carina's chest died. He hadn't come to this conclusion on his own. He didn't really trust her. He'd simply found evidence.

Her face must have shown her devastation, because he took a quick step forward, his hand rising. She took an equally quick step back. She couldn't allow him to touch her. The second he did, she'd give in.

Another click of his jaw. "But even if I hadn't heard what she'd said, I would have come. The second I got some sleep, I knew I'd messed up."

His smell intoxicated her. Drowned her.

"I was exhausted that day," he continued. "My body can survive on little sleep, but after two consecutive nights of no sleep at all, my head was a mess. And it doesn't help that I struggle with trust. I'm sorry for that. It's something I promise you I'm working on."

She swallowed. "You said you were all in. But you weren't. I can't just forget that."

She couldn't just...trust again. Trust that he'd have her back next time. Because that's what a relationship was built on. Trust. And no matter how tired a person was, if they loved you, they trusted you.

"I know. And I'm not asking for you to forgive me. Not yet."

Her heart gave a little thud at the way he said *yet*. Like it was a promise that the time would come when he would ask for her forgiveness. "But I'd like you to come back and work for my mother. I've got a second nurse lined up for the times you can't be there. But she needs you, too."

For a moment, Carina didn't speak. If she stayed, there was every possibility she'd fall even harder. Because this was Flynn. The man who'd pierced her heart in only a couple short weeks.

But he was right about one thing. She wasn't willing to forgive and forget. Not yet.

This time, when he lifted his hand, she didn't step back. Instead, she let the heat of his skin penetrate her flesh as he caressed her cheek.

At that single touch, it was like the little fractured parts of her soul realigned. *That* was his effect on her.

"Please stay," he whispered.

It took three seconds to gain the strength. Three seconds to come up with words that made sense. Finally, she stepped back, letting his hand drop. She didn't miss the hurt in his eyes or the way the muscles in his arm tensed.

"Okay. I'll stay. But only for your mom."

The lie was like a whisper in the air. A lie she had to pray he didn't call her out on. Not now, when her mind was jumbled, and her heart was hurting.

CHAPTER 20

*C*arina took two small pills from the bottle and handed them to Patricia. Once the pills were in the older woman's mouth, she handed her the glass of water.

Patricia took a sip and swallowed the pain medication before handing back the glass. "Thank you, dear."

She helped Patricia ease into her bed. "You're welcome. How's the wrist feeling today?"

"It's fine. I've had worse, like these wretched knees of mine. At least with the wrist, I can just not use it. With the knees, I have no choice if I want to get from A to B."

Carina gave a small smile. "We could always get you a—"

"Do *not* say it. I am not at the wheelchair stage yet. I will walk for as long as my legs hold me."

Carina dipped her head. Fair enough. She'd probably feel the same if someone tried to force her into a wheelchair.

Patricia had only returned from the hospital a couple of days ago. Carina had been nervous on her first shift back, unsure whether the woman would also believe Carina had taken her medication. They'd never discovered where her previous pills had gone.

She should have known Patricia would be nothing but lovely.

As if she'd read her mind, the older woman's gaze softened. "I said this yesterday, but I'll say it again. I never thought you stole anything from me. And the second I heard others did, I was outraged."

"They *all* thought I did."

Patricia scoffed. "Well, I'm the only one with any sense then, aren't I? I'm a good judge of character, and I can tell you're not the type of person to do that."

She could have used Patricia in her life several months ago.

The woman touched her hand. "My son's had a tough time since his rescue. I know he can be a lot of work, but he's worth it."

Carina's smile faltered. "I just... I don't want to get my heart broken." She almost heard her heart laugh. *Ha. Too late for that.*

"But, dear, if someone can get close enough to your heart to break it, then maybe they're worth the risk."

God, this woman was wise. And it was true. No one had ever touched her heart like Flynn. And in such a short amount of time. Maybe that was the real reason she was scared. Because imagine what she'd feel for him after a year. After *two*. And then what if he hurt her again when she was in even deeper?

She smiled through her fear. "Maybe you're right."

"I'm definitely right."

Carina chuckled. "Will I be as wise as you one day, Patricia?"

"Oh, you have to live through a whole lot of years before you get this wise."

She shook her head. "Well, I look forward to that day. I'm going to let you get some rest now. Sally should be here in ten minutes and will stay overnight. So, if you need anything, just call her in."

Some of the light left the older woman's eyes. Carina could tell she hated that she needed so much help. "Thank you, dear. Now go home and get some rest yourself."

She gave the woman one last smile before she moved across the room, switched off the light and stepped out.

Sally would be looking after Patricia when Carina wasn't. She only lived a town over and had just finished her last placement, so the timing was perfect. She'd briefly met the other woman on shift changeover yesterday, and she seemed kind.

Carina pulled out her phone as she walked to the kitchen table. No messages from Flynn. She ignored the little flutter of disappointment. She was here for Patricia. She was no longer dating Flynn. She shouldn't be disappointed.

Quickly, she shut off the phone, knowing if she didn't, she'd just keep checking.

Patricia's words came back to her in a whisper. That he was worth the work. Worth the risk to her heart. Her sanity.

Blowing out a long breath, she turned—almost jumping out of her skin when she saw the man himself standing in the living room.

"Oh, my heart! *Flynn!* What the heck are you doing standing there in the shadows like some kind of ax murderer?" She pressed a hand to her chest, not entirely certain her heart wouldn't break right through her ribs.

Flynn stepped forward. "Sorry, I was sitting on the couch, waiting for you to be done with Mom. I thought you heard me when I got up."

"I didn't." No, she'd been too eager to see if the man had messaged her and then too disappointed when he hadn't. "How long have you been sitting there?"

Oh, God. Had he heard what she'd said to his mom?

There was a moment of pause. Her stomach dropped.

"Maybe twenty minutes."

So he'd heard everything. Including her comment about being scared of getting her heart broken. At least she hadn't told his mother anything crazy...like she was already in love with the man.

Flynn took a small step forward. There was only a dim light coming from the corner lamp in the living room, and somehow the shadows on his face made him look bigger. Fiercer. More of everything that made him…Flynn.

"How's your knee today?"

"It's fine."

He took the final few steps to reach her. Then his hand gently grasped her hip.

Her next breath stalled in her chest. Quickly, she inched to the side, letting his hand slip away.

Do not let him touch you again, Carina.

She dragged her bag across the kitchen table, making sure she didn't look at him on her way to the door. She couldn't. Because everything about the man spoke to her heart in a language only known to them. It was too much.

"Now that you're here, I'll head out," she said quietly. "Sally shouldn't be far off."

She didn't even hear Flynn move, but when she put her hand on the doorknob, she felt his warmth surround her, his hands on her waist, holding her.

"I miss you," he whispered, his mouth far too close to her ear.

Her entire body heated. "It's only been a couple of days."

His thumb swiped her ribs—a thumb that was far too close to the underside of her breast.

"I need you."

When he moved closer, and his lips lightly touched her neck, her eyes drifted shut. She felt the touch in every little part of her body. It zipped through her like a shot of electricity.

His lips were feather-light, like if he pressed too hard, he'd risk scaring her away. She *should* walk away. She knew that. But, God, it was like asking a starving woman to walk away from her first chance of nourishment.

The light grazes became kisses pressed to her neck. Her hand tightened on the doorknob. Her breath shuddered from her lips.

The kisses trailed up her neck, behind her ear.

She tilted her head, giving him better access, his lips now touching her jaw. When she turned her head toward him, he moved quickly, his lips pressing to hers.

A hum vibrated from her chest.

His hands went to her hips and turned her. She was swiftly lifted against his body and pressed to the door.

Her blood heated in her veins, and a dull throb began in her core. She wrapped her fingers around his neck, grazing his hair, as his tongue dipped into her mouth.

This was what had been haunting her dreams these last few days. This intoxicating desire to touch him. Have him. The scream in her head that this was it. This was her everything.

He drew her bottom lip into his mouth, suckling and nibbling, causing the dull ache in her core to ripple and vibrate.

His fingers grazed the skin at the base of her shirt, slipping beneath the material and gliding up. Her breath caught. When his hand snuck inside her bra and closed over her breast, she lost his mouth, throwing her head back and using all her strength to silence her cry.

She writhed as his thumb grazed across her nipple, grinding her core against him and returning to his kiss.

When his hand suddenly stilled and his mouth released hers, she wanted to cry. To tug him back and make this moment last longer.

His forehead pressed to her own. "Sally just pulled up."

Sally. Because she was at Patricia's house. With Patricia sleeping in a room down the hall while she writhed against the door that the next nurse was about to walk through.

Reality was like a bucket of cold water on her head.

She lowered her arms and wrapped her fingers around the wrist of the hand still holding her bare breast.

The muscles in his forearm rippled. Then he released her. He slid his hand from her breast and eased her down to the floor.

He'd only just stepped back when there was a soft knock on the door. She moved to the side seconds before it opened.

Sally smiled. "Oh! Sorry. I almost hit you. Evening."

Carina almost sagged in relief when the woman immediately headed to the kitchen.

Good. She didn't notice the suffocating thickness in the air.

She cleared her throat. "Hi, Sally. Patricia's in bed. Everything's clean and tidy. Call if you need anything."

She didn't wait for a response or look at Flynn. Nope. She was getting the hell out of here before she did something else stupid. She ducked her head and slid out the door.

God. How could she have done that? How could she have let him touch her, kiss her like that, just days after what had happened? How could she have kissed him back?

She silently cursed herself the entire way to her car. She was reaching for the handle when Flynn stepped between her and the door.

"Carina, please. You felt that too." His voice was pleading.

She swallowed. "Flynn, I need more time."

And she couldn't put an exact number on that time. All she knew was that now was too soon.

He touched her cheek. She didn't move away, but she didn't lean into the touch, either. "I screwed up. And I'm so damn sorry. I want to make this right."

She nibbled her bottom lip. The cautious side of her brain screamed at her to say no. But the other part of her knew that the second she'd agreed to remain in town, this was inevitable.

She opened her mouth, not sure what words were about to come out, when a car drove past. It wasn't the car that had her pausing, though. It was the way Flynn turned his head to watch the back of it as it drove slowly down the street. His eyes narrowed, and the veins on his neck stood out.

He reached into his pocket but cursed under his breath when

his hand came out empty. Was he looking for his keys? His phone?

"What?" she asked, turning to glance behind her. The car was already gone.

He looked down at her, smiling. But the smile didn't reach his eyes this time. "Nothing. Drive safe, honey."

She gave a small nod and was about to slip into her car when he touched her arm.

"Make sure you lock your house up, okay?"

She frowned, about to question him, but then just shook her head. It was late, and she needed to get home. "Okay."

THE SECOND CARINA DROVE AWAY, Flynn ran back into the house and grabbed his keys.

Sally looked up from where she was putting the kettle on. "Everything okay?"

"Make sure you lock the doors and set the alarm."

A small frown marred her brows, but she nodded. "Okay."

He ran back out and slipped into his car. He couldn't believe he'd left his keys inside. He could have gone after the car in Carina's vehicle, but that would have either left her to walk home alone, in the dark, or he would have had to take her with him. Neither of those choices was viable.

He called Callum as he hit the road.

"Yo, Flynny, what's up?"

"Can you remind me what Alex Brown's license plate is?"

Callum quickly recited the plate numbers, as well as the color, make, and model of the car.

That was the one. "I just saw the car drive past my mom's house. I'm on the road looking but can't spot it."

He'd lost the guy.

"Shit. Did you see who was driving?"

"No. There were tinted windows, and I only looked up once it had passed." He'd been too distracted by Carina.

"So either Alex and his brother are still here in Cradle Mountain and okay. Or—"

"Someone took them *and* took their car." Although, why you'd take local kids and then drive their well-known car around, Flynn had no idea.

"I'll call a couple of the guys to search the streets, and we can look into street cameras tomorrow, see if we can get an image of the driver's face."

Flynn gave a small nod even though his friend couldn't see him. He pulled up in front of Carina's house and turned off his car.

"Why would he drive past your mother's house?" Callum asked.

"No idea. Her place is alarmed though. I'll be notified if anyone breaks in, and I'm not far away." Carina's house was alarmed too, but he had a bad feeling in his gut about this.

And that bad feeling had led him to Carina.

"Good. I'll call the guys. We'll talk tomorrow."

Flynn leaned back in his seat. "Thanks, man."

He didn't put his phone away. Instead, he sent a text.

Flynn: You get home okay?

Her car sat safe in the driveway, but he wanted to see her text. Connect with her in some way. A full minute passed before he received a response.

Carina: I did. Just getting ready for bed.

Before he could respond, another text came through.

Carina: We shouldn't have kissed tonight. That was a mistake.

No. It wasn't. It was the best thing he'd done in days. But he'd messed up. Damaged what they had. And Carina needed time to heal and forgive him for that.

Flynn: It wasn't. It couldn't be. Not when every time I touch you, everything feels right again.

Not just right with *her*. Right with the whole goddamn world.

For a moment, there was no response. At one point, three dots showed that she was typing a reply, then they disappeared.

Flynn: I hope that one day soon, we can kiss and it won't feel like a mistake to you.

No response.

Flynn: Make sure you lock your house up, honey. I'll see you tomorrow. X

He clicked out of his phone. But instead of driving away, he remained where he was, not entirely sure he'd be leaving anytime soon.

CHAPTER 21

*C*arina stepped into the busy bar. God, the music was loud and people were everywhere. Sitting in booths. Gathered around bar tables. Moving on the dance floor.

Rising to her toes, she searched for Courtney and Grace. There—standing at a high bar table, drinks in hand. Carefully, she weaved her way through the crowd, trying not to fall in her high heels.

Courtney had texted her earlier today asking if she wanted to come for drinks tonight. At first, she was going to say no, mostly because she'd been contemplating a long night of self-pity with a bottle of wine. Then she was hit with a bolt of sense. Why punish herself when she'd done nothing wrong? If she was going to drink, she might as well do it with some nice women.

When Courtney looked her way, the woman's lips stretched into a smile.

Carina smiled back as she approached, every step she took slow and careful.

Why the heck did you wear these heels, Carina?

She glanced down and the reason came back to her. Because they matched perfectly with this figure-hugging gold dress. And the dress made her feel pretty and feminine and gave her just a bit of a lift—both physically and mentally. She really needed the latter right now.

The second she reached the table, Courtney whistled. "Look at you, woman. You look hot!"

A laugh burst from her chest. "Probably because I'm wearing something other than jeans and a T-shirt for once."

To be honest, this was one of the few dresses she owned. One she rarely wore. But pulled at her hips and breasts in just the right way, so what the heck, maybe she should wear it more often.

Grace leaned over and kissed her cheek. "You look beautiful."

"Thank you."

Courtney shook her head. "That Flynn Talbot really messed up."

Grace gave Courtney a pointed look. "Carina might not want to talk about it."

She shrugged. "I'm guessing Logan and Jason told you guys everything, anyway."

Grace shook her head. "Not everything. Just that something happened at the hospital and Flynn messed up."

"Messed up *big time*," Courtney said, leaning over the table.

She was pretty sure the women knew more than that, but it was nice of them to pretend they didn't. "A nurse found some pain medication in my bag. It was the same as Patricia's, and because I was accused of drug theft in Michigan—"

"No!" Courtney gasped. "Do *not* tell me Flynn thought you stole the meds from his mom?"

Okay, maybe they *hadn't* known.

Courtney pushed her cocktail in front of Carina. She didn't even hesitate. She took a large gulp, letting the sweet alcohol warm her insides.

"He did." She lowered the glass. "I was accused of stealing from a patient in Michigan, so it wasn't a far stretch, I guess."

Grace tilted her head to the side. "Something tells me you didn't do that, either."

"Why do you say that?" Was she asking because she needed the validation that she didn't come across as a terrible person?

Courtney laughed. "With that sweet smile, there's no way."

Grace nodded. "She's right. One conversation and everyone would know it wasn't you."

See? This was why she'd come out tonight.

She went to push the drink back but Courtney shook her head. "Keep it, I'll get another. You need it more than me."

Well, she wasn't wrong. "Thank you." She took another sip.

"How did it happen in Michigan?" Grace asked.

"An anonymous complaint. The hospital takes all complaints seriously, so I was forced to take leave without pay and hire a lawyer until it was resolved. In the end, there wasn't any evidence for the complaint to stick."

Courtney shook her head. "Whoever made that complaint's a scumbag. They should have been named and shamed."

"I'm pretty sure it was one of the nurses. From the day I started dating Greg, they hated me." She shook her head. The worst part was the relationship hadn't even been worth it. "It's actually kind of funny, really, how both times I was accused or set up by jealous women working in hospitals who like the man I'm dating. Maybe the universe is telling me I shouldn't date at all."

The hermit life wouldn't be so bad, right?

"Or it's telling you that some women are bitches," Courtney scoffed.

"That too."

Grace leaned forward. "Don't let anyone make you feel like you don't deserve someone to love you. You're allowed to be loved and to fall in love with whoever you want."

Carina's eyes softened. "Thank you." With everything the universe was throwing her way, she wasn't sure she agreed, but maybe she would in a few days, when she wasn't feeling so raw.

Courtney grinned. "Grace thinks everyone's meant to find their soul mate and fall in love."

"Is that so terrible?" Grace asked.

"Talking about falling in love, where are your guys?" Carina asked. For some reason, she couldn't imagine them leaving their women alone in a bar crawling with men. Not because they didn't trust Grace and Courtney, but because they didn't trust the men around their beautiful partners.

Courtney nodded her head toward the corner. Sure enough, when Carina looked that way, she saw them. Logan, Jason, and Tyler, sitting in a booth. "We told them they needed to stay home tonight. They refused, so we compromised and here they are."

Grace shook her head. "I was very clear on this being a girls' night, and Logan said that was fine, he'd sit in the corner."

Carina's heart clenched. Some women probably found that suffocating, but by the looks on their faces, both women loved it. Because they loved their guys.

Grace looked back to Carina. "Both Courtney and I have found ourselves in a bit of danger over the last year. It's the only reason they're so protective."

Courtney rolled her eyes. "That's a lie if ever I heard one. Each one of them have 'protective' programmed into their DNA."

"I love that," Carina said quietly. "Having someone around to make sure you're okay. To watch your back. Everyone should have that." Even though she hadn't known Flynn for long, she'd kind of hoped he would be that person for her.

Grace's smile slipped. "I'm sorry about Flynn. I think sometimes it can be hard for the guys to trust after what happened to them."

Carina nodded. "Flynn told me that. So did Patricia, actually."

She fiddled with the rim of the glass, yet again questioning her decision to keep him at a distance. Was it supposed to be this hard?

Courtney opened her mouth, but before she could speak,

Jason was there, sliding his arms around her waist and tucking his face into her neck.

Logan also popped up, standing beside Grace and slinging an arm around her hip.

"Disgustingly cute, aren't they?" Tyler said, setting his elbow on the table beside her. "They can't go five minutes without touching."

Carina chuckled. "I think it's adorable."

Logan punched Tyler in the shoulder. "Jealousy doesn't suit you, my friend."

Tyler scoffed. "Yeah, okay. We'll pretend that's what I'm feeling."

Carina was just taking another sip of her cocktail when she saw him—Flynn—stepping into the bar, Aidan by his side. His gaze went straight to her. It was like a beam drilling into her.

For a moment, he remained still, watching her through the crowd, his eyes boring into her own.

It took everything in her to look away. Holy hell. Maybe she should have been a hermit and stayed home tonight.

A second later, he and Aidan were at the table. Flynn didn't stand beside her, but she was sure that was only because there was no room. She said a silent thank you to Tyler and Courtney for standing so close.

"Didn't know you guys were stopping in tonight," Tyler said.

Aidan lifted a shoulder. "A drink and some music never hurt."

Carina's eyes remained firmly on the cocktail for far too long. She would not look up under any—

"Good company never hurt either."

Her gaze whipped up at Flynn's words. Her heart crashed into her chest.

Yep. He was looking straight at her with eyes that were too dark and an expression that was too intense.

Time to escape.

"I'm just going to grab my own drink." She pushed the half-finished cocktail back in front of Courtney before leaving the table.

She skirted through the clusters of people, twitching with the need to look over her shoulder and check if he was still there, still watching her, but refused to allow herself to do so.

God, she should have known he'd be here. Where Courtney and Grace were, the guys were never far behind.

When she reached the bar, she sagged in relief. Maybe she should give herself a pat on the back for making the distance and not succumbing to the urge to look.

Suddenly, body heat flared on her side. Her breath stuttered. But when she looked up, it wasn't Flynn. It was a guy she'd never seen before, who had dirty-blond hair and a piercing in his left brow.

"Hey there. Can I buy you a drink?"

Her brows rose. "Ah, no, thank you. I can buy my own."

She turned back to the bar, but the guy nudged her shoulder. The contact had her jerking and felt far too intrusive on her personal space.

"Come on. One drink. Doesn't mean I'm going to demand you go home with me or anything. Although, a dance wouldn't go astray."

Argh. A man who couldn't take a hint. Just what she needed.

She opened her mouth to tell the guy no a second time, but suddenly, Flynn was there, towering over the man and looking far from happy.

"The woman said no."

The guy turned, opened his mouth, and looked like he was on the verge of telling Flynn to get lost, but the second he saw him, he paused. His mouth snapped shut.

Carina didn't blame the guy. Flynn was tall, standing at six four, at least. And he wore a black shirt that stretched across his wide chest and pulled against his bulging biceps.

Massive. That was the only way to describe him. Definitely

not sexy though. No. Carina *would not* be admitting that to herself right now. Not even in her head.

"Whatever." The guy straightened before walking away.

Carina quickly turned back to the bar, already knowing Flynn wasn't about to leave her side. The hairs on the back of her neck rose as he leaned against the bar. He stood closer than the other guy had, his entire side touching hers. But where the stranger's closeness had made her feel uncomfortable, almost claustrophobic, Flynn's made her heart race and her skin go tingly and hot.

"What are you doing here?" she asked, her eyes never leaving the bottles on the shelves at the back wall.

"I wanted to see you."

Her stomach dipped at his honesty.

The bartender stopped in front of her. "What can I get you?"

"Red wine, please. Whichever you recommend."

The bartender nodded before turning to Flynn. "Nothing for me, thank you."

"You're not going to have a drink?" she asked.

"No. I like a clear head."

When she finally turned to look beside her, her heart thundered. He was right there, his lips so close to her own it would only take the smallest shift to touch.

No. She could not think about kissing right now.

Swallowing, she dragged her eyes away as the bartender pushed the drink in front of her. She was reaching for her card when Flynn held his phone out, paying before she could.

Carina frowned. "You don't need to buy my drink."

"I know."

He turned to angle his body toward her, making her breath catch. His hard stomach and chest now touched her side, and when he placed a hand on the small of her back, it felt like he was touching her everywhere.

"You look beautiful tonight," he said quietly.

"Flynn..."

His head lowered, his breath brushing against her ear. "Dance with me."

"No." The word was out faster than was polite. But she couldn't dance with him. Not when he looked and smelled as good as he did. And definitely not when she was on the verge of tugging down those walls and giving herself to him.

The man didn't trust her. She needed to keep her distance. It was the only way she could protect herself.

"Please." Again, his breath brushed her ear, and it sent a wave of desire straight to her core. "Let me hold you for one dance. That's all I ask."

She closed her eyes against the desire to be held by him. It was strong. Too strong. Even the thought of it had ice thawing in her chest.

The hand on her back curved around to her hip. His mouth brushed her ear as he pushed into her hair. "Please, honey."

It was the endearment that had her head dipping and the soft word finally releasing from her chest. "Okay."

She could have sworn she heard a sigh of relief. Then his hand took hers and led her through the crowd. They stopped for a second at the table so she could set her drink down. She got a smile from Grace and a wink from Courtney, then she was tugged the rest of the way to the dance floor.

She wanted to keep some distance. Her brain damn well screamed at her to do so. But the second his arms skirted around her waist, she leaned into him.

"I'm sorry," he said quietly.

Her eyes closed, and she allowed herself to be held by the man. "You've said that already." *Multiple times.*

"I'll repeat it as many times as I need to, to make sure you know it's the truth."

Do not give in, Carina. "You didn't trust me until you learned the truth."

"Not true. I had this pit in my stomach the entire time. Like I was making the wrong choice. That's what those unanswered calls were about. But I didn't go to you and beg for your forgiveness, because I'm a stubborn asshole." He dipped his head, and his breath brushed against her neck. "I'll never let you down like that again."

A shiver traced down her spine. She expected him to lift his head. Instead, he pressed a light kiss to her neck.

His kiss... It was everything she'd been craving. She should push him away, but in this moment, swaying to the music, with the lights dimmed, she just...couldn't. It was like a spell had been cast.

"God, I miss you," he whispered.

"We've hardly been broken up. And before that, we'd hardly been together."

"I know. It's crazy. I've never felt anything like this before." Another swipe of his lips, accompanied by the tightening of his arms around her. "This all-consuming need to touch you. Hold you. Hear your voice. It's destroying me."

She sucked in a shaky breath at his words, having none of her own to return.

He lifted his head, and his gaze bore into her. "Have dinner with me tomorrow night. Come to my place. Let me cook for you. Let me prove to you I can be better."

She wanted to say yes. Her heart pleaded for her to say yes. But there was so much fear. Fear that he'd let her down again. Fear that her feelings would grow while his would stall because of his trust issues.

"I know you're scared," he said, as if reading her mind. "But I promise you, Carina, you and me—we're real. And if you let me, I can be everything you need."

His head lowered again, and this time it wasn't one kiss pressed to her neck, it was a series of them. All light. All burning and trilling across her skin.

Her breathing became labored, her skin singing.

She dipped her head to his chest, causing his lips to leave her. She took a moment to breathe. To collect herself. Then she looked up. His eyes were pleading just as strongly as his voice. So she let the weak part of her soul win.

"Okay. But just dinner."

His arms tucked her closer. "Thank you."

CHAPTER 22

*C*arina watched the fat raindrops pound the windshield. It just had to be unseasonably wet when she needed to go places, didn't it?

She sighed. Every window was fogged up, but that was probably because she had the heater on full blast. She'd been waiting for the rain to stop, or at least slow, so she could make a run to Flynn's front door.

Ha. Didn't look like that was happening anytime soon. But then, what was the bet that as soon as she made it to the house, it stopped?

She'd decided to come here straight from Patricia's house, so now she was early. Only by five minutes, but that was still early. And so far, Flynn hadn't opened the door or called for her to come in.

She grabbed her bag before putting her hand on the door, still hesitating for no other reason than, you know…rain.

God, stop being a wuss, Carina. Just do it.

Sucking in a quick breath, she opened the door and ran to the house. Even though she was wearing her brace, she was careful not to move too fast, because there was no way she wanted to jolt her knee again.

When she reached the door, her wet hair stuck to her forehead, and her clothes were well and truly damp. Thank God there was cover over the door.

A shiver rocked her as she knocked. She waited a moment. Then another. She was about to knock again when her phone rang from her pocket.

Flynn.

She frowned, answering it. "Hey."

"Hey. I'm sorry, I had a meeting with a client that ran over. I'm only just packing up now."

"Oh. That's okay."

"Wait, are you outside?" Before she could answer, he cursed under his breath. "You're already at my place, aren't you?"

"Kind of. But it's okay. I'll wait in my car." She eyed her vehicle. Argh, she'd have to run back through the rain.

"My home security system is linked to an app on my phone. I'll unlock it now."

Her brows rose. Okay, that was a bit James Bond.

"Okay, it's unlocked."

She reached for the handle, and yep, the door opened. "Wow. I'm a bit impressed."

Flynn chuckled.

She stepped inside and almost sighed in relief. Not just because the place was dry, but because it was warm. The man must leave the heat on all day.

"There's a small alarm pad to the right." Flynn recited another code, and she typed it in.

"Done."

"Good. I won't have to kick my own ass now for letting you sit in the rain or a cold car."

She chuckled, closing the door behind her and finding the

nearest light switch. "My car was warm, but being inside is better."

Much better. The big wooden staircase, along with the open-plan living room and kitchen, was beautiful. And like, three times the size of the small place she was renting.

"I'll be there in ten minutes. Just leaving the office now."

"'K. See you soon."

She hung up, and her gaze rose to scan the staircase. It sat to the left of the hall and was huge.

"Beautiful," she whispered to herself. And so grand.

The place she was renting was dated, with beige walls and ten-year-old fittings. This place had character, with the big fireplace, the shutters on the windows with wide trim, and the kitchen...

She moved through the living and dining rooms, then grazed her fingers along the thick stone countertop when she reached the kitchen. It was the perfect mix between character and modern.

Turning, she placed her bag on the table before checking out the fireplace. The house was warm, but with the dreary rain outside, her heart called to her to start a fire. It was a wood fireplace, so there was no way she could. Firstly, because she didn't know how. Secondly, she didn't have anything to start it with.

Instead, she ran her fingers along the mantel. They stopped at a framed photo. It was of Flynn and his seven teammates standing outside Blue Halo Security. They looked happy. Was that their first day in business?

They were all good-looking. All tall and strong. But only Flynn stole her attention.

What is it about you, Flynn, that calls to me so much?

Everything. It was everything.

Setting the picture back on the mantel, Carina moved into the kitchen. He wouldn't mind if she made herself coffee, would he?

The heat took the edge off, but the dampness of her clothing made a hot coffee sound heavenly.

She smiled as she moved over to the coffee machine. It was big and fancy. Would she even know how to use it? One way to find out.

She rummaged through the cupboard, found the coffee, and got to work.

Flynn letting her into his home without him was a good indication, right? Because you didn't allow someone inside your home, tell them what the home alarm code was, without trust.

She'd just finished the coffee when a sound from the entrance snagged her attention. That was quick.

Smiling, she turned, expecting to see Flynn in the hall.

The smile slipped when he wasn't there. No one was.

Had she left the door ajar?

Frowning, she slowly crossed the living room, only stopping once she reached the hall.

Not only was the door ajar, but the knob was broken, almost hanging off the wood.

The fine hairs on her arms stood on end, and her skin chilled. She took two large steps back—and hit something behind her. Something big and hard.

With a yelp, she spun around.

A man she didn't recognize. He stood several inches taller than her, a ski mask over his head, so all she could see were his eyes and mouth. He was broad and muscular and dressed all in black.

It took three tries to get words out. "Who are you?"

He smiled, but there was nothing nice about it. "Ilias."

He took a step forward. She took a quick step back. "How did you break the door?"

No normal person would have been able to break it like that. Not in so little time and so quietly. Unless he *wasn't* normal…

"Let's just say I'm special."

Another step back. Her back hit the door, and it made a little thud as it hit the frame. She wrapped her fingers around the side of the wood, itching to tug it open and run. "What are you doing here?"

That sinister smile widened, and terror flooded her limbs. "It's funny, really. I saw your boyfriend chasing me when I was on a job. A day later, I get a call about *another* job. Way more money. And now, here I am. In his house."

A job? As in...her? Was she the job? Or Flynn?

On his next step forward, she turned and yanked the door open, ready to run. Before she could move more than a step, she was wrenched from behind and thrown.

Her head hit the bottom of the stairs—hard. Oh, God. The pain in her skull was instant and had her vision hazing.

She tried to push up, but her arms trembled. Suddenly, her hair was jerked painfully, and hot breath brushed her ear. "I was pleasantly surprised when you didn't alarm the house. Made my job a little easier."

Then he threw her head into the stairs again.

Her vision blurred, but she forced herself to move, crawling up the steps. She didn't know where she was going, and she knew she couldn't run from him. But every little part of her screamed to get away from the threat. Disappear.

She'd barely moved at all when those punishing fingers gripped her hair again, yanking her head back, shooting pain through her skull.

FLYNN TURNED RIGHT onto his street. He was late. On the night he actually needed to do well and make things better between him and Carina.

It was annoying as hell.

He'd planned to be early. Light a fire. Get a start on dinner and greet her with a glass of wine. But his meeting with Paul Simmons had gone over. The man wanted them to step up their security. Instead of two men, he wanted four. Not because he'd seen anyone or that anything new had happened, but because Flynn had told him about chasing the asshole from his house, and now he was even more uneasy.

Flynn pulled into his drive and stopped beside Carina's car. He was moments from pressing his remote to open his garage door when something caught his eye.

The front door. It was open. Only slightly—but that wasn't what had his muscles tightening.

It was the way the doorknob hung from the door.

What the fuck?

Once the engine was off, he quickly reached for his gun beneath the seat before running up the walk. The second he stepped inside, his blood iced in his veins.

Carina cried out in pain from upstairs.

He took the steps three at a time, and the second he reached the top, he saw the man holding her.

Flynn aimed his weapon. "Release her!"

The man had a thick arm around her neck, and it took everything in Flynn not to react to the fear in Carina's eyes.

"Or what?" the guy sneered. "You'll shoot?"

"Yes. Bullet straight to the head." He'd kill the man anyway. He'd touched Carina. Bruised her. He needed to die.

The arm around Carina's throat tightened, and Flynn was moments from shooting when Carina's words stopped him.

"He's like you!"

Flynn frowned, scanning the man's face. That's when recognition blasted through him. The eyes. The same eyes of the man Flynn had seen running from Paul Simmons's house.

"You."

"Me," he sneered quietly. "So you already know I'm just as fast as you. I'm also just as strong. Just as quick to heal." The guy smirked. "Surprised there are more of us?"

Flynn's muscles tightened further. "Us?"

"Yeah. Us. Paid guns. Bought on the black market. So you shoot, and I'll shift her in front of the bullet so fast you won't even see her move."

His insides coiled.

Flynn took another step forward. "Let her go."

"No." He laughed. "Don't you want to talk for a bit? Come on, ask me whatever it is you want to know."

Flynn ground his teeth. "How are you one of us?"

A slow smile inched over the guy's face. "Hylar had some guards. All of us former soldiers who'd been dishonorably discharged."

Hylar. The old military commander who'd run Project Arma. The man responsible for the changes in Flynn and his teammates.

"A few of us weren't on shift the day the facility was raided and you guys were freed," he continued, that damn arm still around Carina's neck. "We disappeared. Hylar either didn't have the resources or didn't care to find us. Heard you killed him though. Thanks for that."

Only it wasn't Flynn's team that had killed Hylar. Not that he'd be sharing any details with this asshole. It was the guys in Marble Falls, Texas. They'd found the former commander. Killed him and his men.

"How's it feel?" the guy asked quietly. "Knowing I could snap her neck right in front of your eyes in less than a second?"

Wouldn't happen. Flynn would shoot the second his arm tightened. "How about you leave her alone and fight someone your own size."

"I could. Or I could just kill you bo—"

Flynn pulled the trigger.

The guy ducked his head, but the bullet grazed his skull.

Flynn was already moving, catching Carina before she hit the floor and pushing her behind him.

The guy moved just as quickly, grabbing Flynn's hand and pointing the gun away from him before throwing his elbow into Flynn's face. He barely felt the hit as he shoved the man into the wall, hard.

The asshole swung them around, bashing Flynn's hand against the wall. The gun fell.

Flynn lifted his leg, kneeing the guy in the gut and sending him back a couple steps. He followed it up with a fist to the face.

The asshole grunted as he fell to the floor.

Flynn dove on top of him, throwing one punch, then another. He was about to land a third when the guy flipped them over and jabbed. Flynn moved his head, narrowly avoiding the hit.

When he managed to roll the guy onto his stomach, Flynn pinned him to the floor, holding his wrists with one hand and shoving his head down with the other. "Who sent you?"

The guy bucked, but Flynn slammed his head against the floor again. He caught a glimpse of Carina lifting the gun.

"Tell me who sent you before I break your fucking neck," he growled.

"I'm not telling you shit!" He threw his head back so quickly Flynn couldn't dodge it. It glanced off the side of his face and stunned him long enough for the man to shove him off and stand.

Flynn saw Carina point the gun at the man. He charged her, moving inhumanly fast.

"No!" Flynn jumped to his feet just as Carina shot the guy in the gut—and he shoved her over the stair rail.

Flynn lunged over the railing and grabbed Carina's arm with one hand and a baluster with the other. Footsteps pounded through the house as the man raced out.

Flynn pulled them both up and over the railing. The second

they were on the landing, he cradled her cheeks between his hands, careful to avoid the bruise on her temple. "Are you okay?"

She swallowed, giving a quick nod. "I'm okay. Go."

He gave her a final look before running down the stairs and out of the house. The blood led to the street, then stopped.

He was gone. Again.

When he returned to Carina, it was to find her looking at the trail of blood left behind. It was a lot of blood. And a bullet wound like that would kill a normal man.

Unfortunately, their assailant wasn't normal.

CHAPTER 23

lynn scrubbed a hand over his face as he sat on the couch. The last of their FBI liaison's guys, along with Steve himself, had just left. They'd taken samples of the blood from the floor, so with any luck, Flynn and his team should know the asshole's name in a few days. While that was happening, Flynn also had someone fix the broken doorknob.

Callum, Tyler, Aidan, Blake, and Jason stood around his living room. Logan and Liam were in Idaho Falls, watching Paul and his wife.

"I need to be quick," he said quietly, looking around at the guys. "I need to be with Carina."

His gaze shot to the stairs. She was staying with him tonight and had just gone to his bedroom. He could hear her moving around up there. She was far from okay. Being attacked and shooting a man had shaken her.

"I'll call Wyatt," Jason said, tugging out his phone. "Let him know the latest information on this guy." Flynn's team had kept the guys in Marble Falls up to date on the information about a potential enhanced suspect in Idaho Falls.

Wyatt answered on the first ring. "Jason, what's going on?"

"That man we told you about," he said. "The one just as fast as Flynn? He broke into Flynn's home today and confirmed he was part of the project."

There was a beat of heavy silence. "What part?"

Flynn leaned forward. "He claimed he was a former guard of Hylar's. He wasn't at the facility the day your team infiltrated the place and broke us out. Said there were a handful of them who weren't. That they're now basically guns for hire on the black market."

Wyatt cursed. "Where is he now? Has anyone interrogated him? Found out where the others are?"

"Carina shot him, but he got away," Flynn said quietly. "I had to choose between saving Carina and chasing him. I chose Carina." And he would choose her every time. The same as the rest of them when it came to an innocent person...or a woman they loved.

Blake stepped forward. "The FBI took a sample of his blood, so we should have a name soon."

"Got it. At least that's something," Wyatt said. "I'll let my team know. We'll search for information on others from this end."

"We'll do the same here," Callum said.

"Thanks for keeping us updated. You need anything else from us?" Wyatt asked.

Flynn shook his head, even though the other man couldn't see him. "Not at the moment. But we'll let you know if that changes."

"Okay. Talk later."

When the call ended, Flynn blew out a long breath and leaned back in the seat.

"So," Aidan said quietly. "Who was the hit on, you or her?"

"That's the fucking question." And it was tearing him up. "I would have assumed he saw my face in Idaho Falls when I chased him, and he came to eliminate me. But the guy said to Carina that he was here for a job, just like he was doing a job there."

"Does she have any enemies?" Callum asked.

"None that I can think of, except..." He paused before shaking his head.

"Victoria?" Tyler asked.

"She wasn't happy when I broke up with her, and she was even less happy when I started dating Carina. Hell, she tried to frame Carina for drug theft."

The damn hospital footage—both from where the drugs were stored and the hall where Victoria bumped into Carina—had been wiped for that day. He didn't know how she'd done it, but he suspected Victoria was responsible.

"Do you think she'd go so far as to hire a hitman to kill her?" Aidan asked.

"No. But then, I wouldn't have thought she'd frame her for drug theft and erase the footage, either."

"We'll find this guy and ask him ourselves," Tyler said, pushing off the wall. "In the meantime, we make sure Carina's protected, and you watch your back."

"Want us to stay?" Aidan asked.

Flynn shook his head. "I'll alarm the house. I don't think we'll receive any more visitors tonight, but I'll be ready if we do." He could go from asleep to awake in seconds.

Once they left, Flynn took his time going through the house and checking that every door and window was closed and locked, then set the alarm.

His team had brought over some food. Food that Carina hadn't so much as touched, and he'd had very little stomach for. He quickly put the leftovers in the fridge before moving up the stairs.

The floor was silent as he made his way to his room. The second he stepped inside, he heard the steady heartbeat. The quiet breaths. Sounds that were already achingly familiar to him.

He stepped up to the closed bathroom door. There was no sound of movement. No running water or rustle of clothing.

He lifted his hand and knocked softly. Her breath stuttered.

"Carina? Can I come in?"

There was a short beat of silence. "Yes."

He cracked the door open slowly. She was facing the mirror wearing one of his shirts. It drowned her, making her look ten years younger than she was. In her right hand was a bloodied antiseptic wipe.

"Did it start bleeding again?" he asked quietly, studying the cut on her temple. They'd already cleaned and covered it. He'd pushed for a hospital visit, but she'd insisted she was fine and didn't want to go back there. He couldn't blame her, given her experiences so far.

"Yeah. It's okay, though."

Nothing about tonight was okay.

His hands went to her hips, and he gently turned her before lifting her to the bathroom counter and stepping between her legs. He took the wipe from her hand. "How are you feeling?"

A large bruise bordered the cut. Fuck, but he hated that.

"I'm all right."

He paused from dabbing her head. His voice lowered. "You're not. And you don't need to pretend you are. But you will be."

Her brows tugged together as she looked at his chest. "Do you think I killed him? I know he ran out of here, but do you think the bullet wound will kill him?"

He wasn't sure if she was worried about the asshole dying at her hands or worried that she hadn't killed him and he'd come back. But he couldn't lie.

He lowered the wipe and took her face between his hands. "He's like us. Fast healing. So he'll probably live. But he won't get near you again. If you *had* killed him, it would have been okay, because the man doesn't deserve the air he breathes."

Not a single fucking breath.

"I know. I just... I've never shot another person before, and it feels..."

"Wrong," he finished for her. "I remember feeling the same the first time I shot a man."

She gave a slow nod. "I'm sorry you had to choose between saving me and chasing him."

The woman didn't need to say sorry. There was nothing to say sorry for.

He lowered his head, touching his forehead to hers. "I would choose you again. Without thought. Without hesitation. Every time."

Her hands rose to his neck. The first kiss she pressed to his lips was soft. Almost more of a graze. Yet, it stole into his heart, taking every good feeling he had and making it her own.

He itched to take her into his arms and devour her. But *she* needed to choose now. The pace. The touch. What happened next.

She kissed him again, her fingers threading through his hair.

On the third kiss, her tongue slipped inside his mouth.

Blood began to pound through his veins. He slid his hand under her shirt, gently digging his fingers into her flesh.

She continued her slow exploration of his mouth while wrapping her legs around his waist, pressing her softness into his hardness. His chest rumbled at the feeling.

Slowly, so slowly that she could stop him at any time, his hands went to the hem of her shirt before pulling it gently over her head. She was naked beneath the shirt, save for panties, and it almost had his control snapping. Almost.

She did the same to him, tugging his shirt off, their lips only separating for a second. Then they returned to each other.

When he wrapped his fingers around one soft breast, she hummed, pressing into his hand, her fingers tightening around his neck.

After what had happened tonight, this was everything. *She* was everything. She soothed the fire that had been raging since he'd opened his door. She was the peace that had been stolen from him.

His thumb grazed her peak, and she whimpered, her fingernails now scraping down his chest.

His mouth trailed along her neck, her chest, stopping at the breast he hadn't yet explored. He took her hard nipple between his lips. Her cry was loud, echoing through the room. He sucked and nibbled, absorbing every little whimper and jolt.

His other hand lowered, slipping inside her panties and grazing her slit. He lifted his head and took her lips again, swallowing her cry. He swiped and played with her as her fingers dug into flesh. Then he placed a finger at her entrance and slowly eased inside.

This time her head tilted back, her lips separating, drawing a long breath into her mouth.

So damn beautiful.

He thrust his finger in and out, all the while swiping at her clit with his thumb. When he pushed a second finger inside, her nails dug deeper into his biceps.

"Flynn..."

He kissed her neck. Nibbling. Tasting. "What do you need, baby?"

Her hands lowered, stopping at his jeans, unbuckling and unzipping. Then her fingers reached inside his briefs, holding him.

Everything in him stopped. His movements. His breath. His heart. When she stroked, just once, the fire inside him ignited and flared. The blood roared between his ears.

For a moment, it was all he could do to force his lungs to work. The air to move in and out of his chest. She stroked and grazed him, moving her hand from his base right up to his tip.

It was too damn much. With desperate fingers, he opened the drawer beside them, whipping out a condom and donning it. He easily tore her panties from her body. Then he returned to her, pressing himself at her entrance and pushing inside.

Her eyes shuttered as he caught her mouth, plunging his tongue between her lips. Then he thrust, filling her each time, pulling out to the tip.

She consumed him, drove him crazy. But she was also his sanctuary.

Everything in Flynn knew this woman belonged to him. That they belonged together. It was this voice deep in his soul, which had once been a whisper but now was a shout. Demanding he keep her close. Demanding he protect her. Protect *them.*

His hand rose to her breast while the other wrapped around her waist, tilting her hips and changing the angle.

She moaned as he rolled her nipple between his thumb and forefinger.

That sound… It tormented him. He did it again and again, rewarded every time. He thrust harder. Faster.

It was on another roll of her peak that her back arched, her lips tore from his, and she shattered.

Flynn continued to rock inside her, but at the feel of her walls tightening, his entire body tensed, then he broke. He cried out as he recaptured her lips.

When he finally stilled, it was only their chests that moved. He held her close, making a promise there and then. This woman was his to keep and protect. And he would destroy any man or woman who tried to take her from him.

CHAPTER 24

Carina helped Patricia out of the car. She scanned the hospital parking lot, spotting Aidan emerging from his car a few spots over. There had been a different guy following her each of the last few days. Some of the guys stayed close. Aidan didn't. He liked to give her more space. Which was fine with Carina.

"Thank you, dear," Patricia said once she was out. "I don't know why I need to come back here. I just left."

Carina gave the woman a sympathetic smile as she helped her across the lot. "They just want to check that the wrist is healing well. They might have a look at your knee too."

"Pfft. I'm fine."

Carina bit the inside of her mouth to stop the smile. Of course she was.

They were just stepping up to the doors when Carina saw Victoria and a man round the corner of the hospital and step out of sight. Good. At least if the woman was finished for the day, it meant Carina wouldn't run into her.

"Are you okay?"

Patricia's words jerked Carina's attention back to the older woman. "Yes," she answered, ushering her charge inside.

Over the next half hour, she waited with Patricia until she was finally taken to have an X-ray. She hadn't seen Aidan during that time. It was like the guy could just disappear. But she knew he was there watching.

When she stepped into the hall to wait as Patricia was escorted away, she finally spotted him leaning against a wall.

"You don't need to stay so far away, you know," she said, stopping beside him.

He lifted a shoulder. "It's good for you to feel safe while also feeling normal."

"True." She crossed her arms and watched another patient being led down the hall. "Tell me, why's a tall, handsome, sensitive man like yourself single?"

The smile slipped from his lips, and Carina wanted to take her words back. Oh God, had she said the wrong thing?

"There was a woman," he said quietly. "She's married to someone else now."

For a moment, Carina was silent. There was real pain behind his words, and it had her at a loss as to what to say. "I'm sorry."

He tipped his head in acknowledgement. "That's life. Full of highs and lows. And completely out of our control."

She would argue that it wasn't *completely* out of their control. But that wouldn't be helpful to him right now.

"What did you love about her?" she asked before she could stop herself. That probably wasn't the appropriate thing to ask a man when he was still so clearly grieving the loss.

Aidan smiled slightly, not seeming to care whether it was appropriate. "So many little things. She was confident. Happy. Whenever I'd come home from a bad day, she knew exactly how to make me laugh. She was a live-every-day-like-it's-the-last kind of person. And the way she looked at me... It was like she really saw me. Like she was the only woman who *ever* really saw me."

Heartbreak. It riddled his face and voice. "Maybe you'll return to each other one day."

Unlikely if she was married, but maybe…

One small nod. That was all he gave her. And it told her everything. That he didn't believe they would, either. That in his mind, he'd lost her long ago.

But the woman still meant so much to him. He didn't need to say it for Carina to know.

A minute of silence passed before she tugged her phone from her pocket, checking for any messages from Flynn. There were none. Not that she was surprised. He was working at Blue Halo today. Probably busy saving the world, one bad guy at a time.

Surprisingly, there hadn't been a message from Greg in a few days, either. Whether that meant he'd finally left town, she wasn't sure. She hoped so.

"How are you doing after the other night?" Aidan finally asked.

She pushed her phone back into her pocket. "I'm okay."

She'd woken in a pool of her own sweat after a nightmare the night of the attack, but none since, thank God. She hated that Flynn had seen her wake up like that. She felt like she should be stronger. Flynn hadn't batted an eye. Yes, he was former Delta. He was in the security business. But he was still human, just like her.

When she looked up, it was to see Aidan watching her closely.

"You don't need to lie to me," he said. "After being attacked like that and having to shoot someone…you're not *supposed* to be okay."

"That's good. Because I'll admit, it's been hard. I also feel so guilty that the guy got away while Flynn saved me."

"Don't feel guilty. Saving you was never in question for him." Aidan's gaze skittered between her eyes. "One way or another, we'll find this guy and bury him. If Flynn had lost you, it would have destroyed him."

She swallowed, feeling the small acceleration of her heartbeat.

When his phone rang, he straightened and pulled the cell from his pocket. "Callum, what's going on?"

The muscles in Aidan's arms bunched, and Carina held her breath. Oh Lord. What now?

"Got it."

When he hung up, she was almost too scared to ask, but knew she had to. "What is it?"

He looked down at her, and her stomach suddenly felt like it had a huge rock inside, pressing on her organs.

"They found the twins."

That was good, wasn't it? "Where?"

"Ruud Mountain, in Ketchum. They've been dead for almost two weeks."

∽

FLYNN RAN a hand through his hair. "We can help, Tom."

He looked up, his gaze passing over Callum, Tyler, and Liam. They stood in the Blue Halo conference room, and they looked just as frustrated as him. Tom was on speaker, so he could hear all of them.

"Your guys have done enough. The boys were shot in the head. This is a homicide now, and I want you as far away from this as possible. The mother is already breathing down my neck, wanting you locked up."

"I have an alibi," he said through gritted teeth.

"An alibi with the woman you're dating."

Yeah, okay. That wasn't optimal. But it was what it was.

Callum pushed off the wall. "Let the rest of us help, then. Two teenage boys have been murdered in our own hometown. We found the bodies We can help find the asshole who killed them. We *need* to find him."

Tom's exhale was loud over the line. "I can't. I've got a few people I'm looking into. But I need you guys to stay away from this now. Hell, I shouldn't have let you help in the first place. I'm sorry."

The line went dead.

Flynn paced back and forth. "It's connected. I know it is. The dead kids. The letters Carina received. The man who damn well tried to kill her."

"Maybe even her fall off her porch?" Tyler said quietly.

Flynn stopped. Every muscle in his body tightened. "You're right. That could be fucking connected. It was raining, so we just assumed it was that. But maybe someone set it up."

Goddammit.

"What about that ex of hers?" Liam asked.

Flynn scrubbed a hand over his face. "We've done a background check on him. There were no red flags. Nothing in his past. He has a stable job at the University of Michigan Hospital. Grew up with divorced parents, both of whom also worked in the medical field. Nothing in his history to suspect any issues."

Liam frowned. "Maybe he's just good at covering his tracks."

"Where was he the night the boys were killed?" Tyler asked.

Good question. "I don't know. But according to Tom, we're not allowed to ask."

"We can't," Callum said quietly. "But Carina can."

Flynn shook his head. "No."

He didn't like anything about Carina's ex, particularly not the fact he was here to get her back. There was no way he wanted her talking to him, especially to pry information from the guy.

Callum stepped forward. "She could talk to him in a public place like The Grind. You drive her there. We watch them. She'd be safe. And she might be able to learn something we can't."

Christ, he was right. And he fucking hated that. "I'll think about it."

When his phone vibrated in his pocket, he yanked it out and saw a message from Carina.

Carina: Just packing the last of my things. Want Aidan to drive me to yours?

He shot a look at the time. Almost five. He hadn't seen the woman since early this morning, and damn, but he missed her.

Flynn: Wait for me. I'm coming to your place now. x

She was staying with him for a while. Partly because he had better home security. But, more than that, he wanted her close. Plain and simple.

Flynn pushed the phone back into his pocket. "Okay, guys, I'm going. I'll let you know about the Greg meetup."

It was the only idea they had. And she *would* be protected. Didn't mean he hated it any less.

The drive to her place was quick, and Carina and Aidan were already standing by the door with her bag at their feet when Flynn arrived.

He wrapped a hand around Aidan's shoulder. "Thank you, brother."

Aidan dipped his head. "You got it. Call me if you need anything."

The second Aidan left, Flynn tugged Carina into his arms and kissed her. "Man, I've been thinking about this kiss all day."

He felt her smile. "You kissed me this morning."

"Yeah. It's been too damn long." He kissed her between each word. His gaze shot down to the bag. It was huge. "That's a lot of stuff."

"So either I'm staying a while, or I'm just high maintenance."

"Hm." His mouth hovered over her lips. "I'm thinking the former."

One last kiss, then he lifted her bag and placed a hand on the small of her back to guide her outside. He waited as she locked the door, then they headed down the stairs.

They were halfway across the yard when the door to the house next door opened. Then came the angry voice.

"Hey!"

He tugged Carina behind him as Eadie Brown marched across the yard. Her eyes were red, her hair a mess, and her clothes rumpled. "You're a fucking murderer! You killed my boys!"

"I didn't—"

She shoved him. He didn't move an inch, which just seemed to enrage her more, so she shoved him again. "Don't you lie to me! I know it was you!"

"Ms. Brown—"

"I swear, I'm going to make you pay for what you've done!"

Carina tried to step around him, but he swept an arm out, halting her where she was and preventing her from moving forward.

She reached a hand out. "Ms. Brown, I'm so sorry—"

"Don't! You were probably in on the whole thing, you little whore! Did you plan it together? Drag my boys off to the mountains?" Her gaze flew back to Flynn. "She watched while you shot 'em, right?"

He gritted his teeth against the accusation. He was tempted to tell the woman her kids were abusive assholes who'd pissed off a lot of people. He didn't. She was grieving—and her sons clearly hadn't had the most nurturing upbringing.

"No," he answered simply.

She shook her head and moved back slowly. "Mark my words. Both of you will regret *ever* hurting my family."

CHAPTER 25

*C*arina rapidly tapped her foot beneath the table as she watched the door of The Grind. It was taking everything in her not to look at Flynn. He sat in the far corner of the coffee shop, while Aidan sat behind her, with his back to her. Both were listening. The shop was busy, so with any luck, Greg wouldn't see either of the guys.

Callum was also sitting in a room in the back, watching through a video surveillance camera. He'd be watching the guy's face as he spoke. Looking for signs of a lie.

Nerves trickled up her spine. Greg wasn't a murderer, and she was certain he wasn't part of any of this. There was no way he'd hurt kids. She just needed him to confirm that today so the guys could hear and rule him out.

Her gaze dropped to her phone. One o'clock on the dot. Greg was always on time, so he'd be here any second.

Before her attention went back to the door, almost involuntarily, she looked at Flynn. The second they made eye contact, he winked. There was also a slight tilt of his lips.

Some of the crippling anxiety that had been churning away in her gut all morning eased. Everything would be okay. She'd ask

Greg her questions, confirm he had nothing to do with anything, then they'd part ways, and all would be fine.

Ha. She almost laughed at that. When did anything in her life work out that easy?

She'd just started strumming her fingers against the table when the door to the shop opened and Greg walked in. She almost sagged in relief when he didn't look across the room in Flynn's direction. The smile on his face was wide when he spotted her. He headed straight to the table.

Okay. Keep calm, Carina. You've got this.

"Good morning." He bent down, pressing a kiss to her cheek before lowering onto the seat opposite her. "I was so glad to read your text. How are you?"

She forced a smile to her lips. "I'm okay."

Before Greg could respond, Courtney stopped at their table. "Hey, guys. Coffees?"

Carina turned to look at the other woman. "Yes, please. One sugar."

When Courtney's gaze switched to Greg and her eyes narrowed. It was only slight, so slight she was sure Greg wouldn't notice, but Carina did. Courtney didn't like the guy. But that was probably because she and Jason were so close to Flynn, and, well…Greg wasn't Flynn.

As it was, Greg didn't look at her anyway. "I'll have the same."

When Courtney left the table, Greg tilted his head to the side. "What happened to your forehead?"

Okay, stay calm, Carina. You know what to say. She absently fiddled with a thread on her pants beneath the table. "Not a happy story, I'm afraid. I was at Flynn's house the other night and there was a break-in."

Greg's jaw clenched. Whether it was because she'd said she was at Flynn's house or because someone had broken in, she wasn't sure. "Are you okay?"

"A bit shaken, but, yes, I'm okay now."

Greg leaned across the table and closed his hand over hers. She itched to tug her arm away. She just stopped herself.

"I'm sorry." Real concern shone from Greg's eyes. And that right there was why she felt he couldn't be involved in the twins' murders. There was no part of her that thought this man could hurt anyone. He was a doctor. A healer.

"Thank you. I'm glad I came out of it with just a scratch." *Thanks to Flynn.*

"What happened to the guy who broke in?"

"He got away."

"I can protect you," he said quickly. "You know how safe my penthouse apartment in Michigan is. It has great security and a doorman. Nothing like that would ever happen again if you came home with me."

He almost sounded like he was referring to his home as *their* home. Sure, she'd stayed there for a couple of months, but even when she'd been living there, it had never felt like home.

"I have actually been considering leaving Cradle Mountain." Lie. Big. Fat. Lie. "After the break-in…and what happened to the Brown twins. Did you hear about the boys?"

She watched his face closely, knowing Callum would be doing the same.

Greg sighed. "Yes, I heard. Terrible. And I completely agree, this town is too unsafe."

"I can't believe something like that could happen here. Who would do such a thing?"

Greg shook his head. "Those boys were rotten. It could have been anyone. I only met them once and *I* knew that. Imagine how many other people they pissed off."

Dang it. She'd been hoping he'd say he didn't know who did it, or something similar, and the guys would be able to hear and see whether it was the truth or a lie.

"Do you think I could actually know the person?" she asked quietly.

He lifted a shoulder. "It's a small town. And there are a lot of trained killers here."

She tried not to flinch at his words. Flynn and his team. He was talking about Flynn and his team. She shook off his comment. She couldn't allow herself to become distracted.

Greg wasn't getting nervous or sweating at her questions. That meant he was likely innocent, right?

Courtney returned to the table, setting the coffees in front of them. "Here you go."

Carina smiled at her. "Thank you."

Greg thanked her too, but again, only had eyes for Carina. Courtney left the table, and Carina wrapped her hands around the mug. "I, uh...actually shot the guy who broke into Flynn's house." She shook her head, lifting her gaze and watching Greg once again. "It was awful. I've never shot another person before. Have you?"

The second the words left her lips, she regretted them. Was she being too obvious?

This time, he paused. "Have I shot a person before?"

Crap. Definitely too obvious. "Sorry, that was a... I shouldn't have asked that."

Another moment of silence from him. Then his jaw tensed, and he straightened in his chair.

Oh no.

"You think I had something to do with the death of those kids, don't you?"

Her mouth opened and closed a few times before she spoke. "Greg, I—"

"You asked me here, but the only thing you want to talk about are the missing boys, shooting someone, and the break-in at Flynn's house. Do you think I was responsible for that, too?" He looked over her head, scanning the tables beyond her, then stopped on what she was sure was the back of Aidan's head. The veins in his neck stood out.

When he looked over his shoulder, he shook his head and rubbed a hand over his mouth. "I can't believe this."

Yep. She was screwed.

He looked back at her—and his eyes were steely. "I'm leaving, Carina. And I don't just mean this coffee shop. I'm leaving town."

"Greg—"

He stood. "I came here for *you*. Because I care about you. Because I love you, and I honestly thought we could have had a future together. Instead, you want *him*, a man who can't even keep you safe in his own home."

Behind Greg, she could see Flynn was already on his feet and moving toward the table.

Greg's voice lowered. "I hope you don't come to regret your choice."

When he turned, he almost walked straight into Flynn. Everything about the man looked hard and tense. He wasn't happy. Neither was Greg.

"Say it to me," Flynn said quietly. "Tell me you didn't murder those kids or send that man to my house."

Carina hurried out of the booth. Aidan rose behind her. Flynn had told her he wasn't supposed to get involved in the investigation. She was pretty sure asking a guy directly if he killed the twins classified as getting involved.

"I don't have to tell you anything. Get out of my way."

Flynn's muscles bunched. "You don't have to, but it would clear your name. Unless you have something to hide?"

Greg took a small step forward, not looking intimidated by Flynn's size at all. "I don't have to 'clear my name'. *I'm* not a suspect. You, on the other hand, had cause, right? Didn't you threaten those boys?"

"And how would you know that?"

Greg ignored his question. "I'm right. So maybe you coming here isn't so much about keeping Carina safe, but to try to pin a crime *you* committed on another man. What was the plan here? Tell Carina I was lying when I said I didn't do it, just so she'd think I killed them?"

Flynn's hands fisted, his chest moving up and down with his harsh breaths.

Carina took a half step forward, but Aidan touched her arm, halting her. Then Callum was there, stepping beside Flynn and touching his shoulder.

Greg shook his head before moving to the door. He opened it, then glanced back over his shoulder and looked directly at her. "Be careful, Carina. People are rarely who you think they are."

FLYNN STEPPED INTO THE KITCHEN. The scent of Indian spices and sauteed onion permeated the space.

He and Carina hadn't spoken much since returning home from The Grind. In fact, the woman had barely looked at him. Now it was evening, and he was done with the quiet.

He stopped behind her. "Do you believe him?"

The muscles in her back visibly tensed. Then she turned, her eyes guarded. "Which part?"

She knew. But she wanted him to say it. He inched closer. "The part where he said I might have killed the teenagers. I might have somehow instigated the guy hurting you."

The last part, in particular, was ridiculous. But who the hell knew *what* she was thinking? He sure didn't.

Her eyes softened, and this time she stepped forward, running her hands over his chest. "No. I know you would never hurt me or any kids. That's ridiculous."

He watched her eyes as she said it. Listened to her heartbeat. It sounded like the truth. "Then why have you been so quiet?"

"Because *you* were quiet, and I thought you wanted space."

He slid his arms around her before lifting her, turning, and setting her on the counter. Then he stepped between her thighs, holding her hips. "I did. But I've since decided I hate the quiet when I'm with you." He wanted to hear that soft voice of hers. The one that soothed the loud voices in his head. The voices that reminded him of how close she'd been to dying the other night with the intruder. That there were genetically enhanced soldiers out there who meant her or him harm.

Her lips tilted up. "Okay. The next time you get quiet, I'll get loud."

"Thank God." He dipped his head and pressed his mouth into her hair. "I need to ask you something. It's something I've been meaning to ask you for a while."

"Ask me anything."

He straightened. "After the attack, we never spoke about us. I just moved you in here for your safety, and we shifted back together." She remained silent, her expression unchanging. "I want us to be together, and for me to be more than your protector."

When she didn't respond straight away, his gut clenched. Had she not seen them as permanent? Would she say no?

His phone rang but he ignored it. This was too important to miss.

"If you don't want that—"

She touched a finger to his lips, silencing him. "I want you too. I want the kisses and the hand holding and the waking up in each other's arms." She paused. "And I want the love."

This time, his gut didn't just clench, it twisted and tugged. Did she mean—

"I love you," she said quietly. "I know it's fast and our relationship has hardly been smooth sailing, but I can't picture a tomorrow without you in it."

God, those words… they were everything.

His head lowered, and he kissed her, needing to hold her. Feel her.

When he finally stopped, he touched his temple to hers and said in a quiet voice, "I love you too. I've made so many mistakes already, and you've forgiven me every time. I promise you, no more mistakes. I will protect *us* as fiercely as I protect you."

Her smile was watery. "I know you will."

CHAPTER 26

"Flynn, I need to talk to you! I know who killed the twins." Wind blew in the background, muffling Victoria's words. It was the most panicked he'd ever heard her. "I'm not even sure why I'm calling you and not the police. Maybe I'm just in shock—"

A muffled voice sounded in the background. A male voice that sounded far away.

"Shit! He's coming! Call me back as soon as you can."

When the voice message ended, Flynn clicked out of it and pushed his phone back into his pocket before looking around at his team. He'd already played it earlier for Aidan, Tyler, and Callum before they'd left for Idaho Falls. It was now evening, and the entire team was at Blake's house. The women sat in the living room while the men were in the study. They'd assured Paul Simmons that, with his stalker being in Cradle Mountain, he and his wife were safe.

"I called her back but she didn't answer," Flynn said, folding his arms over his chest. "Callum and I went to her house, but there was no sign of her. We also called the hospital. She wasn't working this morning."

"What did Tom say?" Tyler asked.

Flynn frowned. "Apparently, she told some colleagues she was going away for the weekend and may not have reception. There are also rumors she's been trying to get back with me, so Tom thinks this is part of it."

Flynn didn't agree. There had been real fear in Victoria's voice. A fear he didn't think could be faked.

A myriad of frustrated expressions crossed the men's faces.

Logan straightened. "So we find out where she was going and we pay the area a visit."

"Tom reminded me today that we were to stay out of it—"

Liam scoffed. "Yeah, okay. We should stay out of it, when we're by far the best chance of catching this guy."

Exactly.

"At least we know everything we can about the guy who broke into your house," Jason said.

Flynn nodded. The blood sample identified the guy as Ilias Forman. He was exactly who he'd said he was—a former soldier who'd been dishonorably discharged. His dishonorable discharge was only for desertion—failure to return to his military post. He'd spent one year in military prison before disappearing. That must have been when Hylar picked him up to work as a guard for Project Arma.

Liam pushed off the wall. "Everyone knowing what he looks like will also help."

"We'll keep our eyes peeled and stay close to our women." Logan straightened. "Okay. Let's get back out there before they come in here."

Flynn was the first out of the office. He heard her before he saw her. Carina's soft laugh filtered down the hall. The second his gaze fell on her, heat washed over his torso. She sat on the couch, legs folded beneath her, laughing at something Willow said. Her face was the picture of tranquility. It had everything in him screaming *mine*.

"IT'S ALMOST YOUR BEDTIME, HONEY."

Carina just held in a chuckle at the sad pout Mila gave at her mother's words. The kid was beyond adorable. And she had this big Great Dane that was about four times her size. Maybe five. She'd named him Winnie after *Winnie the Pooh*, but honestly, he looked about as far from the cute little bear as possible.

Mila patted Winnie's head. "But, Mama, I'm not tired."

To be fair, it looked like the truth. The kid looked as awake and alert as a person could get.

"How about I make you a hot chocolate before bed?" Willow suggested and rose to her feet.

Mila jumped up, her eyes wide with excitement. "Deal!"

Everyone chuckled this time.

Courtney shook her head as Willow led Mila to the kitchen. "That kid has such a sweet tooth. I'd say she's my best customer at The Grind."

Courtney sat on the floor beside the coffee table, which held about half a dozen half-eaten pizzas, while Grace sat beside Carina on the couch.

"I was the same at five," Grace said. "If my dad got me to eat a vegetable, it was his lucky day."

"Oh my gosh, same." Courtney leaned over the coffee table, picking an olive off a pizza slice and slipping it into her mouth. "So, what do you think they're talking about?"

Carina's gaze flicked to the hall. "I'm not sure. Flynn's been acting strange all day."

Grace tilted her head to the side. "Strange how?"

"He disappeared for a chunk of time with Callum and Tyler, while Aidan stayed with me. I tried asking Aidan where he was going, but all he would say was Flynn was chasing a lead on the twins."

Courtney shook her head. "Something he's not even supposed to be doing."

Winnie rose from his place on his mat and came to Carina before dropping his head onto her legs. She smiled as she stroked the big dog.

"Why would he hide what he's doing from you?" Courtney asked.

That was the question, wasn't it? "Maybe he thinks I can't handle it. I was shaky and had a nightmare after I shot that guy in his house."

"Which is an understandable reaction," Grace said.

"True. Now I'm kind of thinking he's trying to protect me."

Courtney scoffed. "You don't need protecting from information. You know the twins are dead. You shot a man. You're in this. And you deserve to know all the facts. If you want," she continued, "I can force the information out of Jason and pass it on."

Grace scoffed. "And how would you force the information out of Jason?"

Courtney's brows waggled up and down.

Grace shook her head. "Okay. Don't answer that."

Carina laughed right as the guys walked into the room. Flynn was the first man she saw. The only man. His gaze went straight to her, and God, but it was intense. Everything about him was.

She swallowed, only looking away when Logan stepped up to Flynn and said something to him.

Winnie burrowed his head farther into her lap. She looked down, smiling at the big dog. "Do you need to go outside for a second, honey?"

His tail wagged. She chuckled, rising from the seat and heading into the kitchen. "I think Winnie needs a bathroom break."

"Oh." Willow went to step forward, but Carina shook her head. "I'll open the door."

She opened the back door, and Winnie ran straight out. She

took a step outside, but only the one, knowing Flynn wouldn't want her going far.

The night air was refreshing. And having a moment by herself felt good too. She'd never minded time on her own. Time to collect herself and think. These last few days, always having someone watch her...she was grateful, but it was also a bit stifling.

Suddenly, thick, warm arms curved around her waist. She recognized the body immediately. Recognized his scent. She leaned back against him with a little sigh.

"You shouldn't be out here by yourself," Flynn said quietly, pressing a soft kiss to her neck.

Her skin tingled at his touch. And when his breath brushed against the sensitive spot behind her ear, a shudder coursed down her spine. "I'm only a foot out of the house."

Another kiss, this time on her shoulder. "Ilias Forman is like me. He doesn't need much opportunity to take you."

His words were like a bucket of ice water on her head.

She must have tensed, or maybe her ragged breath gave her away, because his head paused before another kiss was pressed to her neck, his arms tightening. "I'm sorry, I shouldn't—"

She turned in his arms. "No. I want to know. I want you to share everything." His face was shadowed, so she touched his cheek, needing that connection. "I don't want you to shield me from anything. I forget sometimes what you can do, and there-fore what...*he* can do." She didn't want to say his name. Carina stroked her thumb across Flynn's cheek. "Tell me what's going on."

When he remained silent, she slid both her hands to his neck and held him.

"I can handle it. I promise. What I *can't* handle is secrets from the man I love. Secrets that involve me or the twins or this town."

He blew out a long breath, eyes skirting above her head for a second before dipping back to her. "Victoria left a voice message on my phone. She said she knows who killed the twins."

She jerked a little in surprise. "That's good, isn't it?"

When he didn't answer right away, her stomach dipped. Why was it not good?

"We can't find her," he finally said.

"You mean she's missing?"

"Not technically. She told colleagues she was going away for the weekend and might not have reception, so Tom won't classify her as missing until Monday."

"Monday? So much could happen in that time."

He nodded. "We're going to look into it."

"Okay." She grazed the warm skin beneath his ear. "I want you to keep me updated." When he was silent, she frowned. "I know the other night was hard for me—"

"You were terrified."

"I know. But it will be worse if you shut me out. I'll *imagine* the worst."

Another moment of silence, then his hands lowered to her butt and tugged her up his body like she weighed nothing. She wrapped her legs around him.

"Okay." His head lowered to hers. "But promise to stay close. No going outside without me or one of the guys."

She nudged her nose against his and shut her eyes. "Thank you."

Then he kissed her, and that tightness in her chest that she'd felt all night finally eased.

CHAPTER 27

Flynn watched Carina from across the room. Something was wrong. Her eyes were pinched, and her back was abnormally rigid.

"Thank you, dear." Patricia took the warm mug of tea from Carina's hands. "I might go have this in the sunroom."

Carina smiled at his mother, but the smile didn't quite reach her eyes. "Good idea. You go. I'll finish these bagels and join you."

Patricia touched her arm before slipping from the room. The sunroom was at the back of the house. The entire place was alarmed today. But even if it wasn't, he would hear if there was someone on the property.

The second the room was empty, he rose from the table, moved up behind Carina, and slipped his arms around her waist. There was a tiny jolt from her small frame. Another sign something wasn't right. "What's wrong, honey?"

Her hands stilled, cream cheese only half covering the bagel in front of her. There was a small pause before she answered. "I don't know."

He applied some pressure on her hips, turning her, but she

didn't immediately look at him. With a finger under her chin, he tilted her head until their eyes met.

"Try to explain it to me."

She blew out a long breath. "I just woke up with this pit in my stomach. Then when we stopped by my place, I looked out the window in my room. I saw Eadie Brown, and she had this look on her face…"

When Carina stopped, he took a half step closer, the hand on her chin slipping into her hair, holding the side of her head. "What kind of look?"

"I don't know how to explain it. When I was staying at my house…every day since the twins went missing, she looked at me like she wanted to beat me over the head with a hammer or something." Flynn's limbs iced at those words. "But this morning, she didn't look so angry. It was strange. And it kind of scared me even more."

"You're safe, Carina."

"It's not me I'm worried about."

God, this woman annihilated him. Her fear made his chest ache. "Nothing is going to happen to you *or* me."

She smiled again. Still, it wasn't as wide as it should be. And he hated that.

He lowered his head and pressed a kiss to her lips. The kiss was gentle. A swipe of mouth against mouth. But almost immediately, he felt some of her tight muscles loosen.

When his head finally lifted, her lips tugged up. That was the expression he wanted from her. "Okay. Your kiss makes me feel a bit better."

"Good. Maybe I should kiss you more, then."

"You need to go check on your mom."

"Mm. I should, shouldn't I?" Another kiss. "Need any help here before I go?"

She shook her head.

"Don't be long."

Finally, he released her. It was so easy to lose himself when he held the woman. She brought him to his knees. Made him weak while also stronger than he'd ever felt in his life. How the hell that was possible, he had no idea.

At the door to the sunroom, he stopped. His mother sat in her armchair, facing the large floor-to-ceiling windows that looked out over the garden. There was an empty armchair beside her. His father's armchair. The two of them used to sit there, side by side, every afternoon with their coffees. She'd never moved his seat. A part of Flynn wondered if she still felt his presence.

He stepped inside the room and settled in his father's recliner. Patricia turned her head, smiling at him.

"How are you doing, son?"

"I should be asking you that."

She reached across and placed her hand on his. "No. You shouldn't. I'm getting old, but I'm still your mother, and I'll always worry about you."

"You don't need to worry about me."

Her eyes softened before turning sad. "I do. Because whether we like it or not, the day will come when I stop remembering altogether. When I forget who I am. Where I am. When I don't recognize my own son's face." Tears glistened in her eyes. He leaned forward, turning their hands so that he was now covering hers.

He swallowed the lump in his throat, hating that any of that would come to fruition but knowing it would. "Mom—"

"I need to know that you'll be okay, Flynny."

"I'll be okay," he said quietly.

She studied his face. And for a moment, he felt like a kid again, looking at the mother who saw too much. "Good. And I want to tell you that I also know the time is coming when I'll need to leave this house."

"Mom—"

"And it's okay, Flynny. You've done so much for me. Given me so much more time here than I would have had. But my episodes are getting worse and more frequent. And I don't want you shouldering that, or worrying about me, any more than you have to."

His voice softened. "I'll always worry."

There was the light sound of footsteps nearing the room.

His mother lifted his hand and pressed a kiss to the back. "I need you to do me a favor."

"Anything."

"I want you to remember me when I'm at my best, not my worst. I want you to remember me as the woman who cooked you apricot pies while you were outside playing in the dirt and wrote you handwritten letters while you were away fighting for this country. I want you to remember me as the wife and mother who held her family close to her heart."

The footsteps outside the door retreated.

"Mom, you've filled my life with so many good memories. I'll never be able to forget a single one of them."

This time, she patted his hand. "Good. And one more thing." She nodded her head toward the door. "Marry that woman. She loves you, and you love her. I can see it as well as you can. Don't let her get away."

There was no way he'd ever be letting Carina slip away from him. She was his, and he was hers. She was it, as far as he was concerned. "I plan on it."

"Good." She returned to watching the garden through the window. They sat there like that for a few long minutes in peaceful silence.

He was moments from getting up and searching for Carina when he heard the sound of motorcycles—several of them—from the street. Flynn frowned, waiting for them to pass.

Only, they didn't. Instead of passing, they slowed.

He jumped to his feet, an uneasy dread filling his gut. "Mom, I need you to come into the linen closet."

The linen closet was the only space in the house with no windows. And it was right off the sunroom.

His mother raised her brows but rose and followed him quickly.

He ushered her inside the small space. "Don't open it or make a sound." He pressed a kiss to her head before pulling the door closed. He'd only taken a single step away when he heard it.

The shattering of glass—followed by an explosion.

CARINA LIFTED the plate of bagels and headed across the room.

God, what was this churning in her gut? It had eased for a second when Flynn kissed her, but the moment he left the room, it returned like a horrible cloud that wouldn't leave her alone.

There was something about the way Eadie had looked at her this morning. Almost anticipatory. Like a promise of something to come. And now it was haunting her.

Carina was about to step into the sunroom but stopped when she saw Patricia lift Flynn's hand and press a kiss to his skin. Then she spoke quiet words to him, and even though Carina couldn't hear what was said, she knew it was personal.

They were having a private moment.

Quietly, she stepped away and moved back into the kitchen. On her way, she glanced out the window, almost expecting Eadie to be there.

Quickly, she shook her head. *Stop it, Carina. You're fine. You're safe.*

Maybe if she repeated those words in her head enough, she'd believe them. She placed the bagels on the kitchen counter and leaned against the sink for a moment. So much had happened in the last few weeks that her emotions were all over the place. That had to be it, right?

She just wanted it all to stop. The danger. The missing people. She tried to take her mind off everything as she cleaned the kitchen.

She was just rinsing the last dish when a light rumble from the street pierced her ears. A motorcycle engine, maybe? The noise got louder.

Frowning, she looked toward the front of the house—just in time to see a brick barrel through the window.

She cried out as glass shattered. She ducked behind the counter, throwing her hands over her head. Her heart pounded hard, even as her breath froze in her chest.

She was moments from rising when an explosion rocked the room, whipping her off her feet and throwing her back.

Pain rippled through her side. Her eyes were still closed as arms wrapped around her back and legs and lifted her off the floor. Then she was moving.

When the sound of gunshots peppered the air, Flynn swore under his breath, tucking her closer and moving faster. Once in his mother's bedroom, he closed the door behind them and locked it before moving quickly into the walk-in closet, pushing hanging clothes aside, and opening a hidden wall safe that Carina had never seen before.

He came out with two guns and pressed one into her hand.

"I need to get out there and kill these bastards," he said quietly. "I'd run us out of here before they could blink, but I can't leave my mom unprotected."

She gave a quick nod, her limbs shaking. "I understand."

He took her face in his hands. "The alarm will have alerted my team. They'll be here in minutes. If someone gets in, shoot first, ask questions later."

His eyes breathed fire. His muscles were bunched and ready

for action. He pressed one kiss to her lips before he moved back to the door, unlocked it, and slipped out.

Carina rushed forward, locking the door behind him. At the sound of more gunshots, she cried out.

Please, God, let him be okay.

She backed away from the door, her gun pointed straight at it when glass shattered in the bedroom window behind her.

She dove behind the bed, terror seizing her chest. Then there was another explosion. The impact threw the bed sideways, toward the wall, shoving her right along with it. She fell to her back, the gun slipping from her fingers and her head clashing with the bedside table.

She scrunched her eyes closed as pain sliced through her skull. Oh, God. When she opened them, it was to see a woman climbing through a hole in the wall, created by the explosion and the shattered window.

Eadie Brown. She wore a black jacket decorated with little skulls and a patch... An MC jacket?

Where had the gun fallen?

Eadie pointed a pistol at her. "I saw him carry you in here. Wanted to be the one to kill you. My guys will take care of your boyfriend. He may be fast and strong, but he's no match for ten guns."

Carina slowly pushed to her feet, hands raised, never taking her gaze from the woman. "It wasn't us, Eadie. We didn't hurt your boys!"

"Stop. Fucking. *Lying to me!* I know your boyfriend murdered them for you! And I'm sure you were there. Watching when they breathed their last breaths!"

She shook her head, ignoring the flickers of pain in her skull. "No."

The woman's smile returned. "I told you I had connections. My boyfriend's a member of the Sun Corpse MC. My boys were going to be initiated into the club. It wasn't hard to convince them to take you out. Then all I had to do was ask the right questions around town, and I found out where you disappear to every day."

"Eadie, please, you need to believe me!"

"What I *believe* is you're gonna die—just like my boys did."

She was going to shoot her.

Carina dove behind the mattress a second before the gun in Eadie's hands went off. Pain ripped through her side as she hit the floor. Her hand found the bullet wound, the sticky wetness of blood seeping through her fingers.

Her vision began to fade. She looked up as Eadie stepped around the bed, gun still drawn, smile still wide.

Carina's breath stalled in her chest. Her vision was blackening.

She was seconds from passing out when another gun went off.

But not Eadie's. It came from the window.

She barely recognized the outline of a big man climbing through the hole in the wall. He blurred before her eyes.

Carina groaned in pain when he lifted her. Then he carried her back through the hole. She was still groaning as he stopped at the side of the house and peeked around the corner to the street beyond.

"We'll just wait for these last two assholes to step inside," the guy whispered. And even though she was fading out of consciousness, she recognized his voice.

The man who'd attacked at Flynn's house.

"Ah, there we go. I knew Flynn would draw them in eventually."

The man jogged across the street and tossed her into the backseat of a car. Pain seared through her side at the rough drop.

Then she heard that familiar voice again, along with the rumble of the engine.

"I've got her. Couldn't kill the guy, but there's an MC doing the job for us. Where am I meeting you to pass her over?"

She tried to hear the voice on the other end, but blood roared between her ears. Her last thought before the world darkened was of Flynn. That she hoped he was okay. That she needed him to survive.

CHAPTER 28

*F*lynn dove behind the couch as more bullets sprayed the house. He'd taken out four guys in seconds. Six remained, four inside the living room and two on the front lawn.

There was a dull ache in his shoulder from where a bullet had struck while he'd carried Carina to the bedroom. He ignored it. Placed his full attention on the bullets going off around him and waited for a chance to return fire.

Suddenly, glass shattered in the master bedroom. Then an explosion.

For a moment, everything else faded. Everything except the noises in that room. The room where he'd put Carina.

He was seconds from rising to his feet and racing to her before the sound of footsteps coming toward him registered. Then a man was there, stepping around the couch. Flynn rolled to miss a bullet, wrapping his legs around the guy's and twisting him to the floor. He stood faster than anyone could track, hauling the man up and using his body as a shield while firing his own weapon and backing toward the bedroom—where he heard a single gunshot.

God, please say the shooter was Carina.

Assholes five and six went down with bullets between the eyes. Flynn got the seventh guy in the chest.

Another gunshot from the bedroom. He was a second from dropping the struggling man in his arms and running when the two guys outside dashed in, and bullets ripped through the space, most of them hitting the man in his hold.

One lucky shot ricocheted off the gun in Flynn's hand, sending the weapon flying.

As the two men continued to draw closer, Flynn cursed under his breath.

After lifting the dead guy in his arms, he threw the body at the remaining men and raced to the bedroom door to smash it open, not caring about the bullets from behind.

His heart stopped in his chest.

Eadie lay on the floor, blood pooling around her. There was also a second pool of blood—but no Carina.

He ran to the half-shattered wall before jumping out, and sprinting to the street. He caught sight of the back of a car just before it sped around the corner. It was too far away to chase.

Goddammit!

He committed the license plate to memory. The make. The model. Everything. And he had to pray that was enough to get her back.

Suddenly, cars showed up on the street. His team, each man armed and ready for action.

CARINA WINCED, keeping her eyes tightly shut. Her breathing was slow, and her body felt heavy, almost numb.

She tried to shift, but exhaustion weighed her down, and then nausea rolled in her stomach. She pressed a hand there and stilled when she felt something beneath her shirt.

Wait…was that…a *bandage?*

Slowly, her eyes fluttered open.

The first thing she saw was a white ceiling with a black pendant light in the center. Slowly, her gaze shifted around the room. It was a bedroom. One she'd never seen before.

Unease slithered in her belly, and when she looked down and tugged the shirt up, a whimper escaped her.

She was right. It was bandages she'd felt under her fingers. And whose shirt was this? It was clearly a man's. Other than a bra and underwear, it was all she wore.

Little bits of her memory began to trickle back to her. Of the men on bikes throwing the brick into Patricia's living room. Of the second brick in the bedroom. Eadie.

And the man…Ilias. He took her in a car.

Fear flashed through her, sweat beading her forehead. Her gaze skittered to an IV attached to her hand and the cord trailing up to a bag of fluids.

Was that the reason for the numbness?

Her hand shook as she touched the IV. She was seconds from removing it when the bedroom door opened.

"You shouldn't do that, sweetheart. It's keeping the pain at bay."

Her breath caught, and a new wave of fear and confusion washed over her.

Greg.

He moved forward slowly. When he reached the bed, he lowered a tray of food to the table beside her. "I also put a mild sedative in there to help you relax," he added.

So that was the exhaustion. The reason she could barely move.

He sat on the mattress beside her, far too close. Then he lifted her wrist, placing his fingers at her pulse and feeling her heart pound. The contact made her skin crawl. But she didn't pull away. Not only because she barely had the energy but because she needed to understand what was going on here. She needed to get as much information as she could to either convince the man to let her go or figure out an escape plan.

"Greg. What am I doing here?"

He lowered her wrist back to the bed, his gaze taking a while to meet hers. "You know the answer to that, Carina."

She shook her head slowly. "I don't."

He lifted his hand and gently pushed some hair behind her ear. Again, all she wanted to do was pull away. She remained where she was. Barely.

"I've loved you since the moment you stepped foot into that hospital. One conversation with you, and I knew—you were mine." His eyes moved over her face. "I'm a patient man, so I was content to be your friend for as long as it took. I waited for you to realize that we were meant to be together."

She swallowed back the nausea crawling up her throat.

His lips stretched in a macabre replica of a smile that curdled in her stomach. "Finally, you agreed to date me. But after only a couple months, I felt you pulling away. I knew it was only a matter of time before you left me. So I did what I had to do to keep you. I reported you for stealing medication."

A gasp slipped from her lips. "That was *you*?"

"You had to realize you needed me. That you couldn't let our relationship just...end." His smile widened. "And for a while it worked. I was your pillar of support, and you leaned on me just like I hoped you would." His expression turned dark. "Then you left. You walked away after everything I did for you."

Everything he did? The man had thrown her life into chaos! She'd lost her job because of him. Her income. Her friends. That wasn't love. That was obsession.

He shook his head. "When you moved here, I couldn't get you out of my head. I needed you back." His hand went to her thigh, and she gritted her teeth against the contact, needing the entire story before she did anything. "I was too subtle at first. Of course the threatening notes weren't enough to drive you back to Michigan."

Carina frowned. "That couldn't have been you. Those notes... they weren't mailed. It had to be someone local."

He nodded. "I've been here. The whole time. Waiting for you."

No. That didn't make sense in her muddled mind. None of this did.

"I was stupid," he continued. "Thinking notes or a simple fall on your porch would drive you back home."

Now she gaped at him. "Fall?"

He lifted a shoulder like it was nothing. "That was just simple olive oil. I poured it on before you stepped outside, and the rain cleared it off before you got home."

What the hell? "Greg. That's crazy!"

"No. What's *crazy* is that after everything, you still wouldn't return to me. I kept checking on you. Calling. Texting. Waiting for you to tell me you were coming home, but you never did!" He took a breath. A moment to calm himself. "Then I saw Victoria glaring at you at that street party. And I saw her looking at Flynn. We got to talking. You know I've always had a way of putting people at ease."

Carina's mouth slid open.

"We met up for coffee the next day. I didn't even need to prod to get her talking about how much she hated you." He shook his head with an amused smile. "Victoria wasn't used to rejection. A few little hints here and there, and the idea of framing you for drugs was planted in her head."

Greg had planted the idea? God, the man was nuts.

"I was watching you that day. I saw you and that asshole leaving the house with his mom. I knew it was the best time. And *everything* went my way. How you left Patricia's so quickly...left the back door unlocked, the house unalarmed...I just snuck in and took her drugs."

The sick feeling in her stomach began to churn and coil. "Where is she?"

The fingers on her leg tightened. "Victoria? She came to see me and, unfortunately, the garage was open that day. She saw the car I took from the boys. The silly woman even opened the trunk and saw the bloodstains. I didn't have a choice."

Finally, she pulled her leg away from him. "You didn't…"

She couldn't say it. Because that would make it true.

"She would have reported me," Greg said, as if what he'd done was completely logical. "They would have locked me up. And I would have lost you."

Murder. The man in front of her had murdered Victoria. "And the twins?"

"I killed the boys for *you*. I could see they were a threat to you. A real threat. I couldn't have them actually hurting you. So I got rid of them."

Her breath whooshed in and out of her chest. She was only hanging on to her sanity by a thin thread. "Greg, you need help."

Like, serious, lock-the-man-up-and-throw-away-the-key help.

Thank goodness he didn't get angry at her comment. He just smiled, almost looking accepting of the level of insanity he possessed. "I don't need help. I need *you*. And I certainly can't have anyone else hurting you or having you."

Having her?

"You hired that man, Ilias, to break into Flynn's house."

The smile wiped clean from Greg's face. "Yes. He was supposed to kill Flynn, not hurt you. I should've had him killed for his mistakes. As it was, I gave him another chance, but only because I know what he's capable of. He's lucky he succeeded the second time."

Greg shifted closer, and she pushed as far away as she could. His hand went to her cheek, and there was nowhere for her to go. Not with the IV in her hand.

"All my life, people have told me how brilliant I am. How I could have the world at my fingertips if I wanted. Then I met you, and I realized *you* were my world. You were all I wanted."

So, this was about Greg never wanting for anything…and the second he didn't get something he wanted, he couldn't handle it.

"I'm telling you all of this so you'll know the lengths I will go to keep you," he said quietly. "This house belonged to a friend of my mother. She had quite a few. No one has come here since she passed. And no one will connect it to me. There's no escaping." He paused. "It's on a large piece of land. You're not bound right now, because I want you to learn to trust me. But if you run, I *will* catch you, and I'll tie you up."

His gaze shot down to her stomach.

"With your bullet wound, you certainly wouldn't get far anyway. For now, your bedroom door will remain locked, and the windows will remain shut."

Oh, sweet Jesus.

He leaned far too close, and his breath brushed her face. "I know you don't love me now, but in time, I promise you will."

When he nestled his head into her neck and lightly touched the bandage around her waist, she screwed her eyes shut. "I'm sorry you got hurt. I never meant for that to happen. Ilias was supposed to kill the asshole and take you from the house. I didn't know anyone else was coming for you."

A kiss pressed to her neck, and she shuddered. Every part of her wanted to push him away. Attack him and run. But her body felt so damn weak. She didn't even know if she had the strength to get off the bed.

He stood. "I'm really excited about our future, Carina."

It wasn't until he was leaving the room that he stopped and looked over his shoulder. "If Flynn survived that motorcycle gang attack, and you behave, I won't send any more hitmen to kill him. I promise."

He waited a moment. Finally, she nodded. Because what else could she do?

Then the door closed, and the click of the lock echoed through the room.

CHAPTER 29

lynn pressed his foot harder on the accelerator. "Tell me you still have eyes on him, Aidan?"

An hour had passed since Carina had been taken. The second his team had shown up at his mom's house, they'd gone inside, killed the last two men, and rescued his mother, while Flynn had taken a car and gone after Forman.

He'd been too late. The asshole had disappeared.

Now, half his team was on the road, searching for the car that took her, while the other half had gone to Blue Halo to search for her using other methods. It was Callum who'd spotted the car in some road surveillance footage in the neighboring town of Ketchum. That was about ten minutes ago.

Aidan had been closest, and he'd found the car almost immediately. Flynn wasn't far behind them. Forman was driving north and moving fast.

The sound of Aidan's engine over the phone rivaled his own. "Still have eyes on him. He's trying to lose me, but I'm not letting that happen. He's headed toward Galena."

"Good. Stay on him. I'm not far behind."

He pushed the car to move faster, ignoring the ache in his

shoulder. He'd wrapped a quick bandage around the wound before resuming the search earlier. That was all he'd had time for. The bullet had only grazed his shoulder.

"Flynn, I need to shoot his tires," Aidan said across the line.

Flynn's heart thumped against his ribs. She could be in the car. Hell, he was hoping and praying she *was* in the car. But if Aidan caused them to crash...

Aidan spoke again, as if he'd heard Flynn's thoughts. "I think it's the only way."

He could be right. And if Aidan didn't stop the car and they lost her...

"Do it."

A few seconds passed, then shots fired.

Fear knotted Flynn's gut, but he pushed it down, knowing this was the best option they had of stopping the vehicle.

"Got his back tires," Aidan shouted. "He's lost control and he's swerving."

The road curved sharply in front of Flynn, and the second he rounded the bend, he spotted them. "I'm coming up behind you."

He cursed under his breath as Forman's car hit a tree—hard. The driver tumbled out, then ran into the wooded area beside the road. Even from here, Flynn recognized Forman. The same guy he'd been chasing in Idaho Falls. The same man who had attacked Carina at his house.

Aidan had already jumped out of his car, disappearing into the forest after him.

As soon as Flynn got close, he slammed his foot on the brake and raced out of the car. He moved toward the crashed vehicle first—and his stomach dropped. No heartbeats.

Scanning the front windows, he noted no one inside. When he forced the trunk open, he held his breath.

It whooshed out. Empty. She wasn't there.

So where the fuck was she?

Fury tightened his chest as he ran into the woods. But instead of forging ahead, he paused to listen.

Leaves rustled in the wind. Birds chirped. But under all of that, he heard the faint sound of footsteps crashing against ground. Fast footsteps. Moving west.

He took off, running faster than he'd ever run before, ignoring the pain to his shoulder and the branches whipping against his face.

It didn't take him long to spot them. Two bodies ahead. When the guy in front changed direction, dodging to the right, so did Flynn, but he ran at an angle, knowing if he moved fast enough, he might just be able to cut Forman off.

He pumped his legs faster, slowly gaining ground. The asshole had just evaded a tree when Flynn took a running leap and pounded into the guy's side.

They slammed into the ground together. The man threw a punch, but Flynn dodged it before returning one of his own right back. The punch caught Forman square in the face, and Flynn swung again.

He was about to throw a third when the guy tossed him to his back. Forman bounced to his feet and pulled a knife from his jeans. Aidan yanked him off his feet and threw him against a tree. The knife fell to the dirt.

While Aidan immobilized the asshole, Flynn stood and lifted the knife before placing it at the man's side. "Where is she?"

"I don't know."

He pushed the knife in, cutting through the shirt and breaking skin. The guy growled and bucked, but Aidan held him firm, making escape impossible.

"Believe me when I tell you, I will slice every inch of skin from your body until you tell me where she is."

Another buck. "I'm telling the fucking truth. I don't know where he took her!"

Footsteps sounded behind them. He already knew it was his team. They would have tracked his and Aidan's phone locations.

"Who's 'he'?"

"Greg."

For a moment, Flynn's entire body iced, rage causing his lungs to constrict.

"All he gave me was a first name, a number, and half the money up front," Forman continued. "I told you, I'm a fucking contractor. I was hired to stalk that family in Idaho Falls to scare them out of town by one of his colleagues. And Greg hired me to murder you—which I obviously fucking failed. He then hired me again to deliver the woman to him on the side of the goddamn road in Ketchum."

"So let's call him," Callum said, stopping beside them. "I'll get my laptop and track his location."

Forman's angry silence and panting breaths were the only reactions they got. Callum and Aidan dragged him back to the car while Flynn followed, ready to chase after him if he tried to get away. When they reached the road, Callum went to the back seat to grab his laptop. Flynn yanked Forman's cell from his pocket and handed it to Callum.

A minute later, and Callum had done whatever he needed to do before handing the phone to Forman. "Call him. Keep him on the line as long as possible."

Flynn stepped forward. "And if you breathe a word about us being here, if you fuck this up in any way at all, I'll make your death so slow that you'll *beg* me to end you."

His eyes flared before narrowing. "Release my fucking arm so I can call. I don't care if the asshole dies."

Aidan released one arm. Flynn moved the knife to the guy's throat this time, pressing just hard enough, so the skin nearly broke.

The phone rang half a dozen times, and Flynn almost thought no one would answer. Then a voice came on.

"What do you want?"

Every part of Flynn tensed at the sound of Greg's voice. Callum's fingers flew across the keyboard.

Forman scowled, but when he spoke, his voice was clear. "When am I getting the other half of my money?"

"Soon."

"Not good enough. I want confirmation that it's been transferred *now*."

"Or what?"

"Or I go to that bitch's boyfriend's house, and I tell him exactly who has her. You know as well as I do, he'll put everything he has into finding you both. It won't take him long."

Greg huffed. "Fine. Hang on a second."

Callum's fingers continued to move.

Footsteps sounded over the line, then the tapping of keys on a laptop.

At almost the exact same time as Greg said, "Done," Callum nodded.

Flynn shot one look at the laptop, committed the location to memory, then raced to his car. Tyler was pulling up behind him as he started the engine. He knew his friends would deal with Forman.

Flynn had to get to Carina, and he had to get there now.

CARINA SWUNG her feet over the side of the bed. For a moment, she closed her eyes as the room spun around her.

Please, God, let my legs hold.

She'd taken the IV out the second Greg had left the room. She didn't know how much time had passed. Not enough. But she had to move.

Slowly, she pushed to her feet. She swayed but didn't collapse. Good. That was good.

With slow, careful steps, she moved to the single window and peeled the curtains back.

Her breath caught in her throat. Wood covered the entire window, stopping her from being able to see anything.

Panic tried to bubble up inside her chest, but she pushed it down. Panic wouldn't help the situation. She needed a clear head so she could think. So she could come up with an escape plan.

She turned, breathing slowly and deeply to keep the pain at bay. For a moment, she grabbed onto the wall, the room once again blurring from the drugs.

When she opened them again, she shot her gaze around the room. It was almost empty. A spare room, maybe? There was a bed, two bedside tables, and a tall chest of drawers. That was it.

Slowly, she moved to the chest and opened the first drawer, leafing through linens. *Come on.* There had to be something she could use to get out.

She gritted her teeth against the ache in her side and gripped the table to steady herself before searching the second drawer.

It wasn't until she reached the third that she spotted the long flashlight. She lifted it out and switched it on. It wasn't a gun, but it was heavy and high-powered.

An idea started forming in her head.

After setting the flashlight on the bedside table, she continued to search the room in case there was anything else she could use. A couple of minutes later, and she knew the flashlight was all she had.

It was fine. That was enough. It would have to be.

At the sound of footsteps on stairs, Carina's stomach dropped.

Now. She had to act *now*.

As quickly as her body allowed, she shoved some of the linens under the blanket, forming a small mound that would hopefully fool Greg into thinking it was a body. Next, she switched off the lights. Because the window was boarded over, the room plunged into complete darkness.

Then, silently, she moved to the wall beside the door. She leaned against the wall to keep herself upright and steady.

Fear gnawed at her stomach, but she shoved it down, inhaling courage.

The door slid open, light slipping into the room.

His steps were quiet thuds as he moved inside. He stopped a foot or so inside the door.

"Carina?"

There was a beat of silence, then he moved forward again.

The second he came into view, Carina slammed the door shut, plunging the room into darkness once again.

"What the hell?"

The words had barely left his lips before she stepped forward and shone the bright flashlight into his eyes.

Greg cried out before bending forward and pressing his hands to his eyes. The second he leaned over, she lifted the flashlight high and, using all her strength, swung it down onto his head.

The hit made a loud cracking noise, and Greg dropped. The moment he hit the floor, she ran, not stopping to check if she'd knocked him out. She ran down the stairs as fast as her legs could take her, stumbling too many times on the way. When she reached the door, she wasn't surprised to find it locked. Greg had warned her.

Exactly why she'd kept the flashlight.

A tall window bordered the door. Leaning against the wall, she took a precious moment to breathe and ward off the dizziness.

You've got this, Carina.

Then she acted, pulling her arm back and swinging the flashlight at the glass. It cracked but didn't shatter. She tried a second time. The stitches in her side tugged and pulled, but she couldn't allow the pain to distract her. She focused on the glass and the way it cracked a bit more. On the third hit, she finally broke through.

A loud alarm blasted through the house.

She didn't pause, instead using the flashlight to break more of the glass and stepping through, ignoring the sharp shards that sliced into her skin.

There were no cars out front, but she hadn't thought there would be, so she beelined for the forest, needing the protection of the trees to shield her. Greg had said it was a large property, that she couldn't escape. But she was hoping and praying that he'd been counting on the fact he'd be uninjured and capable of chasing her if she tried.

Blood began to soak through her top, the dull ache now turning into a throb. Her stitches had definitely pulled open, but she didn't care. She couldn't. Not when freedom was at her fingertips.

When she stumbled and hit the ground, it took every ounce of energy she possessed to push back to her feet. To keep moving. All she cared about was running.

Stones dug into her bare feet, and cold air whipped across her face. The trees and birds quieted, and too soon, she began to slow. Her limbs were heavy, and her wound ached, deeply throbbing throughout her entire body. The temperature was so cold she could barely feel her hands and feet.

She dodged a tree, and fell to her knees with a short scream, then scrambled backward.

A deep hole. A hole she'd almost fallen into.

Piles of dirt surrounded the long pit, and there was a shovel on top of one of the piles. She peeked inside—and the world stopped. Her breath halted in her lungs, and nausea swelled in her gut.

Because there, at the bottom of the hole, half covered in dirt, was Victoria's lifeless body.

CHAPTER 30

lynn found the large farmhouse surrounded by forest and nearly drove through the front door.

His gut clenched when he saw shattered glass covering the porch. He stopped at the droplets of blood on the porch and ground. That meant someone had broken out of the house rather than in. Carina's blood?

But he wanted to clear the house first, just in case she was still inside, so he moved quickly, checking every room. In the upstairs bedroom, his chest seized. There was a small pool of blood on the carpet in the middle of the room. He ran over to the small mound on the bed, ignoring the bag of liquid attached to the IV pole, and pulled back the sheet.

Linens...piled up in a ball.

His brows tugged together. Had Carina done this? To make Greg think it was her? Had she used it to get away?

He moved through the last few rooms. No one here. The house was empty.

The double garage housed the damn car that had driven past his mother's house. A car owned by the twins. And beside it was an empty spot.

He crouched down at the sight of more drops of blood near the empty space. The blood was still wet, not even tacky yet. Either the asshole had taken her somewhere, or Carina had hurt him before running, and he'd gone after her. Either way, it hadn't been too long ago. Maybe Flynn could catch him. The roads nearest the farmhouse had been almost empty. If Greg was on the road, he might just be able to spot him.

Running out of the garage, Flynn was a moment from jumping back into his car when he saw them—small footprints in the dirt leading away from the porch.

Into the forest.

Suddenly, he connected it all. She *did* get away from Greg. Had somehow hurt him. Then she'd run. And he'd gotten in his car to search for her.

The thought had barely entered Flynn's mind before he was running, moving through the trees, and tracking every print in the dirt. It was getting dark, but the dark didn't bother him. He had great night vision. If anything, it was an advantage. He could see what others couldn't.

His heart stuttered at every occasional droplet of blood near the tracks. She was injured. His mind went back to the second pool of blood in the bedroom of his mother's house. Had that been hers? Was it the same injury?

From behind, he could hear the faint sound of cars pulling up. Voices. It was his team.

When he found a hand-dug hole in the forest floor, he paused, cursing viciously under his breath at what was inside. Victoria's body. The asshole had killed her like he'd killed the twins, if the car in the garage was anything to go by. And when Flynn found him—because he *would* find him—Greg was going to pay for all of it.

~

A HOUSE. Carina could just make it out in the distance. It sat tall at two stories, and smoke billowed from the chimney. That meant someone was home, right? *Please, God, let someone be home.*

The air wheezed in and out of her chest. The wound in her side throbbed in time with every heartbeat. Each step was harder than the last. And every time she stopped, every time she paused at all, it took everything inside her to move again. To not fall into a heap on the ground and give in to the pain and dizziness.

She briefly pressed a hand to her side. Blood coated her fingers.

The only thing keeping her going was the house. She'd smelled the smoke before she saw it and used it to push herself to keep moving. She could rest when she was safe. When the psychopath wasn't trying to kidnap her and keep her as an imprisoned guest in his home.

Finally, she cleared the trees. She could have sunk to the ground with relief. She'd made it. And by the look of the lights shining from the downstairs windows, someone was home.

Thank God.

She took a step toward the house, and her legs tried to buckle. But she locked her knees and forced herself to remain upright.

Just a few more steps, Carina. Get to safety, then you can rest. One foot at a time.

With her hand clamped to her side, she almost felt like she was holding herself together. Keeping herself from bleeding out. When she traversed the backyard and reached the front corner of the house, she suddenly clutched it like a lifeline. Like if she let go, she'd fall to the ground and never make it back to her feet.

Her eyes closed. *Deep breath in. Deep breath out. Breathe.*

She repeated those words three times in her head before finally opening her eyes again.

She was moments from stepping forward when the sound of a car reached her ears. The driveway was too long for her to see it yet, but the engine was coming closer. And something inside her, maybe a whispered warning in her head, urged her to move back. Get out of sight. Hide.

Swallowing a gulp of air, she slid backward, pressing against the house, and closed her eyes once more. The car drew closer, causing her heart to speed up in her chest. A chest that suddenly felt heavy.

The car stopped. Then the door opened and closed, followed by footsteps nearing the front of the house. When the doorbell rang, she sucked in a sharp breath.

The door opened, and a man's friendly voice boomed, "Hi there. What can I do for you today?"

"Hi." The dread that had been gnawing at her stomach increased tenfold at the sound of that voice. Oh, God. Greg. "I'm just staying down the road at number forty-two, and I was wondering if you could help me with something."

"You're staying next door? I didn't know anyone had moved in since Margaret died. Nice to meet you, neighbor. How can I help?"

"I have my sister staying with me. She suffers from severe schizophrenia." Sweat beaded Carina's forehead at Greg's blatant lie. "Unfortunately, she went off her meds and had a bit of an episode. Hit me in the head and ran like I was the devil."

A wave of dizziness swept over Carina. She leaned back against the wall and tried to apply more pressure to her wound.

"Jesus, that doesn't sound good. Look, I'd like to help, but I haven't seen any woman around here."

"Mind if I check your property? Being the closest neighbor, and with your fire going, this is likely the first place she'd run."

Dammit. She'd made the obvious choice. And now she might pay the price.

Her gaze darted to the line of trees. If they checked inside the house first or even went the other way around the big place, she might just be able to—

"I'll join you." Heavy footsteps started walking right toward her.

Shit. Shit. Shit.

Ignoring the pain in her side, Carina moved as fast as her injured body would allow toward the back of the house. She'd just turned the corner when she heard the men reach the side.

There was a tool shed right in front of her. It wasn't ideal, but it was all she had. The back door to the house was too far, and even if she made it, there was every chance it would be locked. Then she'd be screwed.

She moved quickly, dropping behind the shed and working hard to quiet her breathing.

The second she was still, the dizziness muddled her brain, and she almost tipped back onto the lawn. She leaned her head against the shed.

"Has she done this before?" the guy asked.

"Unfortunately, yes. It's one of those situations where she doesn't realize what's good for her. It's my fault, really. I should have kept a closer eye on her."

"We live and we learn."

As the footsteps moved behind the house, Carina's breath caught. Her entire body trembled.

When the door to the tool shed opened, she half rose, ready to move around the small shed to avoid them, should they search behind it.

Instead, weak and tired, her knees gave way, sending her thudding to her ass on the ground.

Before she could push herself up, an older man wearing blue overalls stepped around the shed, stopping in front of her.

Their gazes met. For a moment, he was silent as he studied her face. Then his gaze darted down her half-naked body to the large bloodstain on her shirt.

His eyes widened as he turned to Greg. "Hang on—"

The gun went off before the man could finish speaking, the bullet hitting him in the chest and sending him sprawling.

Before she could scream, Greg was moving toward her.

She didn't think, she just acted.

Lifting a leg, she kicked as hard as she could at his knee. He cried out, falling to the ground.

Carina kicked again, this time at his head. He wore a hat, probably to cover his wound, but she was sure she'd kicked him right where the flashlight had hit.

He growled, curling into a ball and grabbing his head. She pushed to her feet and ran around the house. The pain in her side was crippling, but she ignored it and sprinted to his car. She yanked at the driver's door, crying out in anguish when she found it locked.

Footsteps thudded from the backyard. She ran toward the house and moved up the stairs of the porch as fast as possible, almost sobbing in relief when the door opened.

The last thing she saw was Greg leaping up the stairs as she slammed the door closed and turned the lock.

Angry fists hit the wood. "Open the fucking door, Carina!"

She turned to run down the short hall off the foyer, but her legs caved yet again. The second she hit the floor, her mind started to fog. Oh God! She wasn't going to last. She was losing blood, and the pain was weakening her.

Just a bit longer, Carina.

Using every ounce of strength she possessed, Carina pushed to her feet. She wanted to lean on the wall but knew she'd just leave bloody prints, which would lead Greg straight to her.

So instead, she stumbled through the living area to the open kitchen, all the while trying to stem the blood and not leave a trail.

When a gun went off, she jumped, almost falling to her knees again. *Jesus.* He was shooting the door!

She moved faster, grabbing the biggest blade in the knife

block as she went. She'd just stepped away from the counter
when she heard the door opening. Silently, she used the bottom
of her shirt to open the small pantry door and slip inside before
tugging it closed.

Darkness surrounded her. The fear was suffocating. She
closed her eyes and worked hard to simply breathe and
concentrate.

Greg would find her. Probably soon. There was no way
around it. She just had to make sure she stabbed him before he
grabbed her. She didn't think he would shoot her. Not to kill,
anyway. He wanted to keep her as a trophy wife or something,
right?

But maybe that had changed. Maybe her decision to hit him
on the head and run had made him decide to dispose of her, like
he'd done to Victoria and to those kids. The man was unhinged,
so who the hell knew?

"I'm going to find you, Carina." His voice came from the living
area, but his quiet footsteps drew closer. "You shouldn't have
fought me. You should have accepted my love. I would have
treated you well. Now, I'm not so sure you deserve the life I had
planned for us."

He was in the kitchen. Her heart clattered so loud in her chest
she was certain he could hear.

"To be honest, I didn't know I was capable of all this," he said,
almost conversationally. "You've taught me that love makes us do
crazy things. It makes us strong where we were otherwise weak.
It makes us fearless."

Love? He didn't love her. This was a sick obsession. The man
was used to getting what he wanted, and when he couldn't have
her, he'd lost his mind.

She lifted the knife and pointed it toward the door.

"It's why the police never suspected me. Not really. I don't
have a record. I'm educated. Hell, that cop, Tom... He barely
spared me a thought." There was a pause. "The further you

drifted away from me, the further I was willing to go to get you back."

When he drew closer to the pantry, a whimper tried to sneak up her throat, but she swallowed it down.

"Ah, you took a knife. Smart. I wonder if you could actually stab me though? Do you think you're capable of killing a person? It takes a special kind of courage to do that."

He was so close. She steeled her spine. This was the moment. It was him or her.

When the door opened, she lunged.

Greg dodged the knife and grabbed her around the waist. She attempted to wrench away, and they both fell, the clatter of weapons hitting the floor echoing through the room.

The second she hit the hard tiles, pain like nothing else laced through her body. Greg landed on top of her. Her vision tunneled, but she blinked away the darkness, refusing to give in.

She swung a knee up between his legs. He howled, grabbing himself, and she tried to crawl away, but his hand wrapped around her calf, pulling her back beneath him.

Then his hands were around her neck, squeezing.

Her fingers went to his hands, desperately trying and failing to pull them off. Anger distorted his features.

"I would have given you the world!" he shouted, lifting her head before slamming it back to the floor. Another round of pain swamped her. "Anything you wanted, it would have been *yours!*"

Except freedom.

The words were a whisper in her head that had no way of getting out. She couldn't breathe, let alone speak.

The light started to fade to black, the energy to fight seeping from her limbs.

His head lowered. "You should have just loved me back!"

Her legs flailed weakly, and her hands scrabbled at the tiled floor.

That's when she felt something cold by her pinky. Cold and metal.

The knife...

One last fight to live.

She'd barely whispered the words in her head before she grabbed the knife and plunged it into Greg's side.

CHAPTER 31

The blood in the dirt pushed Flynn to move faster. To pump his legs as quickly as they could move. The droplets were few and far between, but there were still too many.

The wind whipped his face, the dirt sinking beneath his feet. He didn't slow. He didn't pause.

Smoke had begun to scent the air. That's where she'd gone.

Did you make it, honey?

His gut told him yes. But his phone hadn't buzzed from his pocket. And he knew the first person she'd have called if she reached safety was him.

So what had gone wrong?

He leaped over a tree root and dodged a bush. Behind him, he heard the faint crunching of leaves. Guys from his team were following. Who, exactly, he wasn't sure. He didn't care. All he cared about was getting to Carina and getting to her quickly. Even a single minute could mean the difference between life and death.

Finally, he spotted the house in a crack between the trees. It was another minute before he cleared the forest. Then, for the first time in a while, he stopped. Paused. Listened.

That's when he heard it. Light thuds from inside the house. Then an angry voice…

"You should have just loved me back!"

Flynn sprinted, barreling through the front door—just in time to see Carina plunge a knife into Greg's side.

Greg cried out in pain, his fingers falling from her neck. But almost immediately, those hands were back, fingers tightening again, his entire focus was on Carina.

Flynn flew across the room—

Snapped Greg's neck before the guy even knew he was there.

He dragged the lifeless body off Carina and dropped to her side. His hands went straight to her wound, pressing down to stem the bleeding. Her eyes were shut.

"Carina! Honey, can you hear me? Talk to me!"

Carina coughed, her chest making a gurgling sound and blood trickling from her mouth. Her lips parted, like she was trying to speak, but then closed again.

Flynn lifted her shirt, cursing under his breath at what he saw. A bandage that was soaked through with blood. She needed medical attention, and she needed it now.

Quickly, he tugged his shirt from his body, tearing it apart and wrapping it around her waist like a bandage.

Footsteps sounded from the front of the house. He looked up, spotting Logan. "We need to get her to a hospital!"

Flynn slid his arms under her back and legs, while Logan moved behind him, searching Greg's pockets until he found keys.

Carina made a whimpering sound as he stood. Fuck, he hated hearing her in pain. "I'm sorry, honey. We'll be at the hospital soon."

There was movement at the back of the house. Footsteps. Then a car sped down the drive. They'd just stepped outside when he recognized Liam driving toward them. He must have tracked their location from the GPS on Flynn's phone.

Blake stepped around from the side of the house, carrying a

man in his arms. "I'm guessing the owner. Bullet wound to the chest, but he has a faint heartbeat."

Logan nodded toward Liam. "Take him to the hospital with Liam. I'll drive Flynn and Carina in this car."

Flynn slid into the backseat, and Logan took off.

"Carina, can you hear me?" He pressed a hand to the wound once again, studying her face. She was so pale. "Honey, please, if you can hear me, talk to me."

Suddenly, one of her hands rose and grazed his chest. "Flynn..."

"Yeah, baby, I'm here. I'm not going anywhere."

"Is he..." She stopped to breathe, and his heart tore in his chest.

"He's dead."

The small line between her brows smoothed. "Good. I'm safe."

Those words... they annihilated him. He lowered his head, touching his forehead to hers. "Yeah, honey. You're safe from danger. But I need you to stay with me."

A STEADY BEEP penetrated the deep fog in Carina's mind. Her brain had been murky all day, pulling her in and out of sleep.

Slowly, her eyes opened, and the first thing she noticed was the darkness outside. The last time she'd woken, it was still daytime. She vaguely remembered Flynn sitting beside her. The doctor telling her about her stitches. About needing to stay in the hospital a little longer.

She looked at the seat next to the bed. The chair Flynn had been in every time she'd woken. It was empty now.

Slowly, she pushed up into a sitting position. Had Flynn gone home to rest? He'd needed sleep and a shower, so it wasn't a huge surprise. She had no doubt someone from his team was posted somewhere in the hospital for her. Probably right outside the room.

Her gaze skittered to the door. She needed to use the bathroom, but she didn't want to ask for help from one of the guys.

Slowly, she swung her legs off the side of the bed and tested out her weight. When it seemed to hold, she rose, gripping her IV pole tightly and taking slow steps toward the bathroom.

She was halfway there when she heard Aidan's curse. Then he was by her side. "What the hell are you doing, Carina?" His arm went around her waist, holding her carefully, shouldering most of her weight.

"Um, I need to pee?" Why was she so embarrassed about that?

"You should have called for me." Disapproval thickened his voice.

"I didn't know you were there." A half-lie.

She took a step, thinking he'd help her limp along, but instead, he gently lifted her off her feet.

"What are you doing?" she cried, grabbing his shoulder with one hand, and keeping hold of the IV pole in the other.

"Helping." He moved across the room and into the connected bathroom before lowering her to her feet beside the toilet. "Do you need help—"

"No!" Her eyes widened. Her cheeks were probably the shade of a tomato. *Heck no.*

He dipped his head, moved back a step, and checked that she was stable. Then he left, closing the door behind him. Even though it was just her in the room, she knew he was right there on the other side, listening in case he needed to rush back in.

Snap out of it, Carina. You almost died. A guy listening to you pee is nothing.

She went quickly then moved slowly to the sink and washed her hands. Then she looked up at the mirror.

Yet again, her eyes almost bugged from her head. Holy hell, she looked like crap. Dark circles shadowed her eyes, and her skin was so pale she resembled a ghost. She touched her cheeks lightly.

The door suddenly opened.

"Hey! I didn't call you."

He lifted a shoulder. "It was quiet in here. I was worried. I take my protective detail seriously."

Clearly!

Then he was stepping inside before lifting her once again and moving back into the room.

She sighed. "Yeah, I think you all have protector genes in your DNA."

"Is that a bad thing?"

"No." Definitely not for the people they protected.

"I just texted Flynn," he said quietly, setting her on the bed so that her legs dangled over the side. "He's downstairs talking to the police. He'll be here in a second."

She swallowed, nodding. She had a faint memory of the police trying to speak to her earlier, but both Flynn and her doctor had insisted she needed more time to recover. At least, that's what she remembered through the fog. That was the only time Greg's name had come up all day. Flynn hadn't asked a single thing about what happened the few times she was briefly awake.

"Hey. You okay?"

Her head shot up at Aidan's question. "Of course."

He looked like he was going to argue but buzzing sounded from his pocket. He tugged out his phone, frowning when he read the screen.

When he didn't say anything, she tilted her head to the side. "Okay, now it's my turn. Everything okay?"

"Just a new job. I'll head to Blue Halo once Flynn arrives."

"At this time?" Her gaze skittered to the window and the darkness beyond. Jeez. She knew they worked in the security business and danger didn't save itself for the hours between nine and five, Monday to Friday, but a new job request could surely wait for daylight, couldn't it?

He lifted a shoulder. "I don't mind."

Before she could reply, the door opened and Flynn walked in. His blue eyes scanned her body from head to toe before his attention shifted to Aidan. "Thanks."

He nodded. "I've got to go to the office. You going to be okay?"

"Yeah. I'll call someone else if that changes."

Aidan smiled at Carina briefly before heading out. Flynn moved in front of her, his hands going to the bed on either side of her hips. "How are you feeling?"

His eyes were so dark and stormy, flicking between hers. Like he was moments from leaping in front of a bullet to save her.

"I'm okay. The drugs are doing a pretty good job of dulling the pain."

There was a small tightening of his eyes. Then, gently, like he was afraid she'd break, he pushed a lock of hair from her face, grazing her skin.

She touched his chest, her voice quieting. "Are you okay? Is Patricia okay?"

There had been so many men with guns at Patricia's house.

He gave a small nod. "A bullet grazed my shoulder, but it's bandaged and already healing. Grace and Logan are taking care of Mom. They said she's a bit shaken up but doing okay. And everyone who attacked us is dead."

A long-relieved breath released from Carina's chest. "I haven't said this yet, but thank you."

"For what?"

"Saving me."

He shook his head. "I didn't. *You* saved you. You fought Greg. You escaped. Hell, you even stabbed him. You are so damn strong, Carina." He lowered his head, his temple touching hers. "And I'm so grateful for that strength."

She wasn't sure she agreed with the part about her saving herself. She'd been a second away from passing out when Flynn had arrived. But she *had* fought. She'd fought with everything in her, for her freedom and the ability to live another day. To return to Flynn.

She shook her head. "I can't believe it was all Greg. The complaint in Michigan. The notes. My fall. The murders." A shudder jumped down her spine at the last part. She would never have suspected the man was capable of any of that. "He always seemed so...normal."

Flynn's hand grasped her hip. "He was good at keeping that side of himself hidden. But I promise you, no one will ever hurt you like that again."

His words had so much conviction that her breathing eased and her eyes closed.

When he cradled her cheek, she looked at him. He stared at her with adoration. With relief. Maybe even a bit of awe. She had a feeling he'd be looking at her like that for a long time.

"I want you to move in with me," he said softly.

She smiled shyly. "But there's no more danger."

He shook his head. "Not because of danger. Although, I don't think I'll be able to take my eyes off you for a while without feeling crippling fear. No. I want you to move in with me because I love you. I want to hold you in my arms every night. I want to wake up and drink coffee with you every morning. I want you, Carina. All of you. As much as I can get."

Wetness filled her eyes. She didn't even need to think about her answer. "Yes."

The hand on her hip tightened. "Yes?"

"I love you so much. And I want to be with you as much as you want to be with me."

Flynn's eyes closed. Just for a second. Then he was kissing her. And the peace she'd almost lost forever returned to her in full force.

CHAPTER 32

*Ai*dan stepped into the Blue Halo building and climbed the stairs. It was late, and they'd spent the day dealing with that damn doctor kidnapping and almost killing Carina. Not to mention the MC attack. So if there was a meeting about a new security job *now*, at this hour, it had to be important.

The one good thing that had come out of the last twenty-four hours was capturing Ilias Forman, the fucking *hired gun*, as he called himself. Aidan and his team had done what was necessary to get as much information as they could from the asshole before handing him over to the FBI. Apparently, he actually lived in Idaho...but there were different guys in a dozen other states. Blue Halo shared that information with the team from Marble Falls, and together, they'd find each and every former guard—and bring them down.

He pushed into the reception area. The text had come from Callum. Over the last few months, Callum had taken over a lot of the administration and technical side of the business. But the entire team helped whenever and wherever they could.

When he stepped into the conference room, he saw Tyler was there too—and both of them looked solemn.

Shit. What was wrong *now?*

Suddenly, his chest seized. "Is it Cassie? Did something happen to her?"

At the thought of anything happening to his ex, everything inside him hurt. No. Not hurt. It tore him to fucking shreds. Cassie might not be his anymore, she may have chosen another man, but that didn't mean his heart just forgot about her. The woman still owned him. And not a day had passed—or would pass—when he didn't love her.

Tyler shook his head. "As far as we're aware, Cassie's fine."

What the hell did that mean? Aidan took another step into the room. "As far as you're aware?"

Callum nodded toward the empty seat. "Sit. The call's about to come through."

"What call?"

"Will you just sit your ass down?" Tyler sighed, shaking his head.

Aidan dropped into the seat at the end of the table. Something was going on. And his team needed to tell him what it was, right the hell now, before he lost his damn mind. He was not a patient man. Never had been.

Callum tapped a few keys on the laptop. "We got an urgent job request. I spoke to the guy briefly, but he said it needed to be *you* who took the job."

"Why me?"

"That was my question too."

When Callum didn't offer anything further, Aidan blew out a frustrated breath. That short patience of his was about to snap. "And what did he say?"

"That's the thing. He wouldn't tell me. All he'd give me was his name. And the name of the woman he wants protected."

Again, his friend stopped before he gave Aidan any information that would be useful. The air tightened in his lungs as he asked, "And what were those names?"

Before Callum could answer, a Skype call came through on the large monitor on the wall, and all three looked up.

The man who appeared on the screen had every muscle in Aidan's body tensing, his hands fisting, and his eyes narrowing.

Damien fucking Webber.

Cassie's husband.

Also, Cassie's childhood best friend. A man Aidan had always liked. A man he'd never suspected would one day take his woman and make her his own.

The craziest part of it all was, Aidan had *approved* of the man's friendship with Cassie. Neither of them had ever given Aidan reason to believe they felt anything more for each other.

"What the hell do you want?" Aidan asked quietly, his voice so low it would be impossible for Damien to miss the anger.

The man's features were shadowed as he stood somewhere outside, in the dark. "Hello, Aidan. It's nice to see you again."

Nice? Aidan could think of a lot of words to describe this moment, but *nice* wasn't even in the vicinity.

Callum leaned forward. "What can we do for you tonight, Mr. Webber?"

Aidan tried not to flinch at the guy's last name. The surname Cassie now used.

"I can't talk long." His gaze skirted somewhere above the camera, then back again. "I also can't give many details. But I have a job I need Aidan to complete."

The last thing Aidan wanted was to work for this guy. "What do you mean, you can't give many details?"

"I don't have the time. They could be watching."

Aidan frowned. "Who?"

"I told you. There's not enough time." He shot a look around again, like he expected someone to join him...or find him. Then he looked back at Aidan. "I need you to kidnap Cassie this Friday at ten p.m."

Aidan's jaw dropped. Callum and Tyler straightened in their seats. Whatever he'd been expecting the guy to say, it wasn't that.

"I'll send you the location to grab her from. I need you to hold her for a week at a safe and hidden location. But you need to make it look like a real kidnapping. No one can know the truth."

It took him a moment to respond. "You can't be serious."

"I assure you, Aidan, I am." For a third time, Damien looked beyond the camera and once more scanned his surroundings.

Aidan leaned forward. "I am not going to *kidnap* Cassie. First of all, that would fucking terrify her. Second, we're not in the business of staging fake abductions."

Damien stared straight into the phone's camera. "It's the only way to save her."

"Save her?"

There was a short beat of silence. "If you don't do this, they'll kill her."

Aidan's insides iced over. When he spoke again, his voice was low and deadly. "You need to give me some fucking details, and you need to give them to me now."

"I've already been on this call too long! I'm going to text you the address from this burner phone, then I'm going to destroy it. You won't hear from me again, and it's important you don't try to contact me."

Burner phone?

"How do we know this isn't some setup?" Callum asked.

Damien's gaze never left Aidan's. And finally, he saw something other than shaky composure in the man's expression. Desperation? "I love Cassie. You know I do. That's why I need *you* to do this for me. You're the only one I trust to do whatever it takes to keep her safe."

His words were like rounds to the chest. Hell, he'd been hit by bullets. This was worse. Hearing the man say he loved Cassie... Hearing that she was in any kind of danger...

"Even if I were to do this, there's no way I'd go alone."

"Then bring a friend. Hell, bring your whole team! Just as long as you shelter her somewhere safe. I need to go." Another flicker of his eyes. "This isn't a setup or a joke or anything else. This is life or death. Whether you believe me or not, I'm going to send the information and then just hope like hell you're in."

The call ended, and the man disappeared.

For a moment, Aidan just sat there, not sure what the hell had just happened. The only thing he *did* know was that he could never let harm come to Cassie. Regardless of whether they were together or apart.

He needed her alive and safe more than he needed anything else on the damn planet.

Order Aidan Today!

ALSO BY NYSSA KATHRYN

Cole

JOIN my newsletter and be the first to find out about sales and new releases!

~https://www.nyssakathryn.com/vip-newsletter~

ABOUT THE AUTHOR

Nyssa Kathryn is a romantic suspense author. She lives in South Australia with her daughter and hubby and takes every chance she can to be plotting and writing. Always an avid reader of romance novels, she considers alpha males and happily-ever-afters to be her jam.

Don't forget to follow Nyssa and never miss another release.

Facebook | Instagram | Amazon | Goodreads

Printed in the USA
CPSIA information can be obtained
at www.ICGtesting.com
LVHW042345300923
759799LV00041B/639